LOVE IN THE STORM

A SMALL TOWN CHRISTIAN ROMANCE

LOVE IN BLACKWATER
BOOK 1

MANDI BLAKE

Love in the Storm
Love in Blackwater Book 1
By Mandi Blake

Published in the United States of America
Cover Designer: Amanda Walker PA & Design Services
Editor: Editing Done Write

CONTENTS

SNACK, FOOD, AND MOOD LIST

I saw @Sweet.CleanReads suggest authors include a snack, food, and mood list to go with their books, so I'm doing it! If you want to eat along with the characters or just set the mood, grab these before diving into the story.

Chapter 1 – You might want to bundle up. It's a snowstorm, so grab your favorite blanket and a cup of coffee or hot tea.

Chapter 3 – Don't forget your gloves like Lyric!

Chapter 5 – It's time for a sandwich. Grab some ham or turkey if you want to have what Asa and Lyric are having.

Chapter 9 – Bacon and eggs (cooked your way). Lyric likes her eggs with ketchup on them, so consider giving that a try.

Chapter 10 – Play a card game! Multi-player games are better. Asa is fond of Texas Hold 'em. Bonus points if you can win with seven two off-suit.

Chapter 11 – Monopoly anyone?

Chapter 12 – Chicken noodle soup! This is my grandmother's recipe, but don't let it get cold while you read chapter 13.

<u>What you'll need:</u>
6-8 chicken strips
3 cups of water
1 can of chicken broth
Chicken bouillon cube
Salt
4 medium potatoes cut into small cubes
(Note: Nanny says don't use canned potato cubes.
Granny says they'd be fine.)
½ an onion chopped and diced
3 carrots peeled and shredded
Flour
Sour cream
1 can of cream of chicken soup
1 pack of egg noodles

Butter

<u>To cook:</u>
Cut up chicken strips and put them in a large pot with the water, broth, bouillon cube, and salt.

Cook for about an hour on medium heat.

Put in onions, potatoes, carrots, and cook until done (I know, that's a very specific time, but it's all I have).

Cook egg noodles in a separate pot with butter and salt.

Mix a can of cream of chicken soup and one large scoop of sour cream in with the noodles.

Add noodle mixture to the chicken and vegetables mixture. It'll be a thin consistency, so scoop out some of the liquid and mix flour into it, adding it back to the soup until you've reached the consistency you want.

Chapter 12 – Doughnuts!

Chapter 14 – S'mores! Asa likes his marshmallows "perfectly toasted" while Lyric (thinks she) likes hers charred.

Air Fryer S'mores

Hershey's Chocolate Bar
Marshmallows
Graham crackers
Crescent rolls

To cook:
Preheat Air Fryer to 350 degrees for about 5 minutes.

Unroll crescent rolls and separate them.

Break graham crackers into smaller pieces and place on the larger side of the crescent roll triangles.

Place a chocolate pieces on top.

Break or cut marshmallows in half and place sticky side down onto the chocolate piece.

Add more graham crackers on top if you'd like.

Fold the crescent roll around the chocolate, marshmallow, and graham cracker. Seal well.

Place them in a single layer in the air fryer and cook for about 5 minutes.

Enjoy them while they're hot!

Chapter 16 – Pancakes, anyone?

Chapter 35 – Get the popcorn ready. It's gonna be a bumpy ride.

Chapter 40 – Bring out the soup leftovers and BREATHE!

Epilogue – Cupcakes for the win!

I hope you enjoy the story with these little additions. Thanks again to Jenn (@sweet.cleanreads on Instagram) for this idea!

1

ASA

Wind pushed against the truck door as Asa stepped out into the swirling snow. Wrapping his arms around the overflowing bags, he shoved the door closed with his elbow and ran through the white night toward Mrs. Grant's house. The freezing air pierced his eyes, causing them to sting as he bounded onto the small, covered porch.

Asa adjusted the bags in his arms to press the doorbell with his knuckle. The chime was barely audible over the gale-force winds. He rubbed one watery eye against his shoulder and then the other.

He hadn't thought this through very well. Mrs. Grant was pushing ninety, and he might be standing there a while before she got up and made her way to the door to let him in.

"I'm coming. Hold your horses," Mrs. Grant chided from inside.

"It's me, Asa Scott."

When she finally opened the door, her short, white hair was flat on one side and puffy on the other, and her glasses sat askew on the bridge of her nose.

"Mom didn't want to be out in the storm tonight, so she sent me to deliver your dinner." He lifted the bags under his arms, indicating the spread of food that would no doubt last this little old woman until next week.

"Come on in," she said, scooting her walker out of the doorway.

Asa stepped into the warm cabin, and a shiver rocked his whole body. He wasn't a stranger to harsh winter weather, but this blizzard was coming fast and strong.

"Just put it over there." Mrs. Grant pointed a skeletal finger toward a round table in the kitchen covered in mail and magazines.

Asa put the bags on the table and started unpacking the food. His gaze drifted to the window every few seconds. The blizzard was only getting worse, and he wasn't looking forward to that narrow mountain road that lay between here and home.

Mrs. Grant waved a withered hand. "You go on home. Tell your mama I said thanks for the food.

She's so good to come all the way out here every week."

So good was an understatement. His mother made meals for quite a few elderly people in town. Betty Scott was in the running for sainthood for sure.

"I'll make sure she knows. Anything I can do for you while I'm here?"

Mrs. Grant was already opening the food containers. "Not that I can think of, but I appreciate the offer."

Asa snuck another glance out the window. "Then I'd better get going." Even as he said the words, a tug-of-war started inside him. He didn't like knowing Mrs. Grant was up on the mountain alone, but the stubborn woman refused to move closer to town.

Her resistance was somewhat understandable when the weather conditions weren't dangerous. Mr. Grant had died over fifteen years ago, but his widow couldn't let go of the memories.

Unfortunately, Asa didn't have any room to talk about moving on. He'd been stuck in the same rut as Mrs. Grant for years with no sign of climbing out.

Mrs. Grant followed him toward the door, holding up her walker so it levitated off the floor instead of using it for stability. "Stop by again some-time. How's that boy of yours doing?"

"He's great. Growing like a weed." Asa laid a hand on the doorknob, eager to get on his way. His mom would rouse the entire police force if he didn't check in with her soon.

"He's a handsome one. I always thought he looked just like you with that dark hair. I know Danielle would be proud of him."

Mrs. Grant's shaky, wistful tone did nothing to quell the stabbing in Asa's chest at the mention of his late wife. The old woman was right, Danielle would have loved watching their son grow up. The injustice never ceased to punch a hole in his gut.

"See you later, Mrs. Grant. Call me if you ever need anything."

"I will. Be careful out there."

Asa gave the old woman a small wave as he jogged out into the cold night. The icy wind pelted his face, and the air stabbed in his lungs. When he closed the truck door, the howling wind in the dark night had chills rushing down his spine.

He started the truck and focused on the little patch of road illuminated by the headlights. The narrow path was almost invisible under the snow. He had chains and four-wheel drive for a reason, but sometimes even the best preparations weren't enough.

The ringing of his phone through the Bluetooth speakers jerked Asa's focus from the road. His son's name lit up on the dash screen, and he pressed the steering wheel button to answer the call.

"Hey, buddy. I can't talk right now."

"Are you okay? Granny is freaking out."

It sounded like Jacob was freaking out a little too.

"I'm fine. Just trying to focus on driving."

"Okay. I wish you were here," Jacob whispered.

Asa sometimes forgot that his son was still a kid. He was smart for a ten-year-old, but things like storms could still be scary, even if Jacob would never admit it out loud.

Asa turned on the steady, sure voice he used to calm frantic victims when he was on the clock. "You're safe. There's no need to worry."

Jacob paused as if still unconvinced. "Okay. I have a lot of homework tonight."

Asa leaned forward, narrowing his eyes at the clash of light and dark ahead of the truck. "You get started, and I'll check it when I get home."

"I need to build a rocket, and I don't know where to start."

Another slash of heartache ripped his chest. Science was Danielle's favorite subject. She should be here building a rocket with their son.

"I'll help you as soon as I get home," Asa promised again.

"You didn't send me any money for the book fair today," Jacob said.

Asa pounded the steering wheel with his fist. The book fair. He'd forgotten all about it. "Sorry. I'll send money tomorrow." Inching around the dark

curve, Asa kept his eyes on the limited road ahead
of him.

"Okay. Will you be home soon?"

"As soon as I can."

"Love you."

"Love you too, buddy. Don't worry about the
storm. You're safe with Granny."

"Okay. Bye."

Asa waited until the call disconnected before
huffing out a nervous breath. Visibility had dimin-
ished to almost nothing. There would be a lot of
emergency calls tonight. It was only a matter of time
before he got the call for backup at the police
department. He'd only been home long enough to
change out of his uniform before his mom asked
him to take dinner to Mrs. Grant.

No wonder Jacob was upset all the time. Asa
hadn't been home much all week. Between school,
work, and errands, there was little time left for just
hanging out together.

His first thought was the injustice. Always. Jacob
should have his mom at home with him tonight, but
cancer hadn't cared about the fairness of it all when
it took Asa's wife and Jacob's mom.

No, he couldn't think about the hurt right now
when he needed all his focus on the winding road. It
was barely after six in the evening, but every inch
that wasn't covered in snow was as black as
midnight.

A loud crack like a gunshot pierced the night. A thick tree fell from the cliff above the road, crashing down as if in slow motion.

Asa gripped the wheel and stomped too hard on the brake. His jaw tensed as he willed the truck to stop, but the vehicle slid smoothly over the icy road, careening toward the tree that thudded to the ground in front of him. Snow and ice shot into the air like a wave. The dark trunk blocked the road from one side to the other.

The seconds before impact were palpable, full of fear and knowing. Nothing but the massive tree would stop the force of the truck.

Head-on or a side impact? Did it matter at this point?

At the last second, Asa turned the wheel, but the tires never gained traction. The impact slammed through the truck, rocking Asa's entire body and plunging everything into darkness.

2

LYRIC

Lyric raced into the living room, trying not to tear apart the cabin she'd just spent six hours cleaning. She'd been over every square foot of the place today—all six thousand of them. Her cell phone could be anywhere.

The howling of the wind was growing stronger. She'd heard they were expecting snow, but it looked like more than a few flurries rushing past the floor-to-ceiling windows in the main room.

Great. Lyric couldn't risk messing up the work she'd just done. The owner, Brenda, would get bad reviews if the place wasn't immaculate when the renters showed up tomorrow afternoon.

"Come on. Where did I leave it?" Lyric lifted one couch pillow, then another. Still no phone.

She stood and looked around the luxury cabin. She could leave without the phone, but what if she ran into trouble on the road? The storm was amping up as if warning her that trouble was waiting just past the door.

Lyric huffed and stomped toward the kitchen where she'd left her purse. She could come back for the phone in the morning before the guests arrived. Preferably after the mountain roads had been treated.

The chime of the phone stopped her in her tracks. She closed her eyes as if shutting out the light would help her listen for the next sound. A few seconds later, the ring chimed to her right.

It was in the kitchen. She jogged into the room and stopped to listen again. After a few more steps, she heard it again.

In the pantry? Really?

She opened the door, picked up the phone from the top shelf, and read the name. Wendy.

Lyric loved her neighbor, and she prayed this was just a friendly call. She didn't have time for any of the bad news that seemed to follow Wendy around.

"Hello."

"Hey, are you okay? I just knocked on your door and realized you weren't home. The weather is getting nasty."

As if summoned by Wendy's words, the wind howled, and something thumped against the side of the cabin.

"I'm finishing up cleaning a rental, and I'm walking out the door now." Lyric braced the phone between her cheek and shoulder as she grabbed her purse from the counter.

"I think you'd better stay put," Wendy said. "There are already headlines on the news about downed trees and cars in ravines."

Nope, not today, Satan. She wasn't getting stuck on this mountain overnight. "Thanks, but I have to work tomorrow morning. I can't afford to be late."

Wendy knew exactly what Lyric was talking about. They'd met at an AA meeting over a year ago, and they'd been looking out for each other ever since. If you could get someone to take a chance and hire a recovering alcoholic, you did *not* step out of line.

When everyone is looking for a reason to write you off, don't let them have it. Kendra's words echoed in Lyric's head as clear as the day she'd heard them.

Wendy's tone was grave now, as if she wanted to press further. "If you say so. I'm sure your boss would understand, considering the crazy weather this evening."

That was probably true. Brenda gave Lyric the job cleaning rentals, and Camille was her boss at Blackwater Restoration. They were both great to work for, and as much as Lyric knew they'd understand if she couldn't show up for a shift, she didn't want to find out.

"I know, but I have to at least try to make it." Lyric paused with a hand on the doorknob. "Wait, why were you knocking on my door?"

There was a slight hesitation on Wendy's end of the call. It was so tiny, Lyric almost thought she'd imagined it at first.

"Oh, don't worry about it now. It can wait," Wendy said.

Lyric peeked out the window beside the front door and sighed. Snow was swirling so hard she couldn't see her car parked fifteen feet away.

Well, there went any chance of leaving here tonight. This snow was coming on much faster than the meteorologists predicted.

A heavy lump of dread settled in her stomach like a boulder. "Looks like I have time to chat right now. This storm is worse than I thought."

"I'm really sorry," Wendy whispered.

"It's okay. Nothing I can do now. Tell me what's up." Lyric settled onto a barstool and propped her elbows on the counter.

"Well, I saw a note on your door, and I didn't think it should stay there, so I was going to knock and let you know about it."

"What kind of note?"

Wendy paused. "An eviction notice."

"What?" Lyric almost fell off the barstool. She grabbed the counter and righted herself. "A what?"

"Have you heard anything about this from Russell?"

Lyric and Wendy's landlord was a nice man, but he was a bit of a recluse. She got a paper bill tucked into her mailbox every month, and she paid them as soon as she could. Unfortunately, she'd been pushing her luck lately. But it wasn't as if she could make money appear out of thin air. She hadn't anticipated how crippling the rent would be after Bethany moved out six months ago.

"No, but I guess I need to talk to him." Not that talking would change anything, but if he was ready to evict her, she'd have to face him at some point. Her breaths grew shallow, and her fingers ached as she held onto the counter for dear life.

"What can I do to help?" Wendy asked.

Lyric let out the biggest breath she could and lowered her forehead to the cool granite countertop. "Nothing. I'll be okay." She was not about to take a penny from another struggling woman.

"I'll do anything I can to help."

Of course she would. Wendy knew what it was like to get her feet knocked out from under her over and over again. "Maybe pray?" The request came out sounding more like a question. Lyric wasn't super comfortable with the idea of prayer yet, but she was learning when to use it. Now seemed like one of those times.

Wendy had only recently started going to

church, and there was a beat of hesitation before she said, "I can do that."

"Thanks so much. Will you take the note down? I'll come by your place and get it as soon as I get home."

"Of course. Be careful out there."

"I will. Thanks for the call."

Lyric lowered the phone and stared at it in her hands. How could she pay the rent when she was still paying full price for all of her mistakes in the past? When was she ever going to get her head above water?

The phone in her hands dinged, and a message lit up the screen.

You have ten minutes remaining. Purchase more minutes to continue service.

The boiling heat welled inside of her, and a scream rolled up her throat and echoed in the large cabin. She let the injustice ring out as she pounded the side of her fist on the counter. Keeping her hand balled up, she breathed through gritted teeth.

Why did bad news seem to pile on top of other bad news? She knew to expect some times to be worse than others, but the realization of the snow-ball effect did little to dampen the heaviness in her chest.

It didn't help that she was stranded in a cabin that probably cost more money than she'd ever earn in her lifetime. Brenda's rental cabins spared no expense. High ceilings, enormous fireplaces, hot tubs, pool tables, and a stocked kitchen. Lyric had bought those groceries this morning, and they'd cost more than she made in a week. Not that she planned to touch them. They were for the renters.

A loud crash echoed through the house, and Lyric jerked, tumbling off the stool. She gripped the counter and quickly pulled herself up. Her heart pounded fast and hard in her chest as she waited to hear anything else.

The noise had been something much bigger than a limb being thrown into the side of the cabin by the wind. She took a deep breath and pushed any horror movie scenes from her mind. No one was waiting to ambush her in this storm, right?

Her heart rate refused to rest as she stayed frozen, listening for more noises. When she didn't hear anything else, she darted for the kitchen. Falling to her knees in front of the sink, she rummaged in the cabinets until she found a flashlight. At least the dark wouldn't get her.

She padded back into the main room, looking over her shoulders continuously as she went. Nothing stirred in the cabin, but the noise had come from outside.

Mustering all her courage, she unlocked the front door. The wind jerked it from her grip as soon as she opened it. She peeked out and up the small hill toward the main road. Headlights beamed at the end of the driveway. Was that a tree across the road? She could barely see through the swirling snow.

"Shoot." Lyric pocketed the flashlight and grabbed the shovel propped beside the door. She tossed snow to the sides as she made her way up the drive to the road.

Her arms ached, and a cold sweat plastered to the back of her neck by the time she reached the truck. The front of the vehicle was mangled, and smoke slowly lifted into the darkness.

Whoever was inside probably needed more help than her limited skills, but unless someone else came down the mountain, she was going to have to face this alone. If this massive tree was blocking the road here, there were bound to be more down the mountain. How long would it take to get help if someone was seriously injured?

The incline of the driveway and the exertion had her panting, drawing the freezing air into her lungs as she reached the truck. Lyric pulled on the door handle, but it didn't open. She'd rushed out so quickly she'd forgotten her gloves, and her hands were freezing against the cold metal.

She pulled again and again, using her body weight to force some movement. "Come on," she begged through gritted teeth. On the sixth pull, the door opened with a metallic creak.

A large man sat in the driver's seat, holding his forehead in his hands.

"Sir? Sir? Are you okay?"

He lifted his head, and dark blood oozed through his fingers and down the side of his face.

No, no, no. She would not pass out. She would not pass out. She'd never been a fan of blood, but she'd just have to block it out. She'd doom herself to an icy grave if she passed out in this storm.

"Sir? Can you hear me?" she said louder.

"Yeah." His answer was gravelly and strained.

"We need to get you to that cabin." She pointed down the hill. "Can you move at all?"

He looked up at her and let his hand fall away from his face, smearing the red down his cheek. "Yeah."

Good. She couldn't drag the much-bigger man down the hill to the cabin on her own. As if being stranded wasn't enough, it looked like she'd be stuck on the mountain with an injured stranger.

3
ASA

Asa rested his head against the headrest. The woman's dark hair was bold against the snow all around them and whipped in the wind, framing her heart-shaped face.

Her face. Between the moments of blurriness, he caught glimpses that he wanted to hang on to.

"Are you hurt anywhere other than your head?" she asked loud enough to be heard over the wind.

His head? What was wrong with his head?

He looked down and frowned at the blood covering his hands before bringing them back to his face. Yep, blood everywhere. He went through vehicular incident procedures enough to dream about them on his off days, but they all involved waiting for the EMTs to clear the victim to move. They wouldn't be seeing any other first responders for a while out here.

The woman bent to put herself in Asa's line of sight. "Listen, I need you to help me get you out of here. We have to get inside. Can you stand?"

The concern in her eyes drew him in, and he focused his attention on her and the questions she asked.

The storm. Right. She was shaking and freezing.

Asa swung his legs out of the truck, and the woman backed up to give him some room. Stars flashed on the edges of his vision. The airbag had done its job for the most part, but it hadn't kept his head from knocking against the window.

When he was on his feet, a wave of dizziness washed over him. The woman was beside him in an instant. She wrapped one arm around his waist and positioned her shoulder beneath his arm.

He sucked in a deep breath of the icy air and steadied himself. "I got it. Thanks."

"You're bleeding. A lot."

"I know." It had been a while since he'd had a big hit like that, but it reminded him of a direct tackle to the helmet he'd taken from a defensive lineman his senior year.

"We need to get you inside." Her dark hair danced in the wind as she pointed down the hill.

Asa gave his truck one last look. He'd just paid it off, and now it was a mangled pile of metal.

The woman tugged on his arm. "Come on!"

Asa slowly followed her down what was probably a snow-covered drive, trudging on the trail in the snow she'd left on her way up to the road. What were the chances he'd wreck near an inhabited cabin on this mountain? Most of the places were vacation rentals. He'd be up a creek without a paddle if he was stuck out in this storm without a place to get warm. He spotted the snow shovel at the end of the drive and grabbed it. They'd need it to get out later.

She jogged up the porch steps ahead of him, and one foot slid across the icy wood. Her arms and legs flailed, sending her flying backward. Asa barely had time to drop the shovel before she slammed into him. He caught her, wrapping his arms around her, but they both went slipping to the ground.

"Sorry!" she shouted above the whipping wind as they pushed to their feet.

Asa offered her another hand. This time, he couldn't feel her grip on his fingers. "You okay?"

"Yeah. Let's just get inside."

They'd been inches from the door when they fell, and now they were both wet and frozen.

The woman rushed inside first, and Asa followed on her heels, slamming the door closed behind him. He held onto the knob for an extra second, hoping the dizziness would subside and he'd be able to stay on his feet.

"Are you okay?" the woman panted.

"My head is pounding, but what about you?"

She nodded. Her face was flushed, but her nose was rosy pink. "Fine. Just frozen."

Asa looked around. The cabin was enormous. Surely, she didn't live here alone. "You have a fireplace?"

She stood and brushed her hands over her hair, trying and failing to smooth the wildness. "It's not my place. It's a rental."

That made more sense. "Are you a guest?"

"No, just the cleaning crew," she said through chattering teeth.

Asa rubbed his hand over his face and remembered the blood.

She pointed to a barstool in the open kitchen and pulled a rag from a drawer. "I need to check you out. Sit right there."

Easing onto the stool, he propped his head in his hands. Closing his eyes only made his shoulders sag with the weight.

The woman appeared at his side, and he slowly raised his head. She stepped right in and started brushing the rag over his face. "Where is your phone?"

"Phone?" He thought for a minute. "In the truck."

She groaned and pressed the rag to his head. "Hold that there. I'll be right back."

"You can't go back out there."

She was already pulling on her gloves. "I have to. My phone isn't working, and I need to call for help."

He opened his mouth to tell her no one was coming to help, but she'd already disappeared. Impulsive woman. Didn't she stop to think before running back outside?

He finished wiping his face with the rag and tossed it into the sink. He'd worry about the biohazard later. She'd rescued him, and he was probably going to have to rescue her.

Asa had just made it to the door when she burst into the room.

"Peas and carrots!" she shouted, bending at the hips and resting her hands on her knees.

"I can't believe you went back out there."

She straightened and shifted her hands to her hips. "Somebody had to. What are you doing up? I said I'd be right back."

"Those are famous last words," Asa said, fighting a grin. She'd really gone back up the hill in the snowstorm to get his phone.

"Not mine." She pulled his phone out of her pocket and held it up. "Can I use your phone to call 911?"

Now she asks. His grin faded quickly. "You can, but you won't get through. Emergency lines are going to be backed up with this storm."

She pecked at his phone. "No reason not to try. I have no idea how to treat a head wound."

"Wait." He laid a hand over hers, stopping her from making the call.

"Why? You're hurt."

Now was a bad time to realize his hand still had blood on it. He pulled it back and wiped it on his shirt, but the red just smeared. "Don't call 911. Call Jameson Ford. He's in my contacts."

She did as he asked and lifted the phone to her ear, pushing her wild hair out of the way.

"Put it on speaker," he said, pointing to the counter.

She did as he said and pointed to the stool. "You need to sit down."

Asa chuckled. She was bossy. This was going to be fun.

Jameson answered on the fourth ring. "Hey, man. You okay?"

Asa rested his head in his hand, and the sharp pain reminded him of the gash. "I've been better. You on duty?"

"Just got called in. Why?"

"I had a wreck way out on North Bend. There's a tree blocking the road, and I doubt anyone is getting out here anytime soon."

"You would be correct. How bad is it?"

"A cut on my head. Some bruises. Not an emergency."

"It looks bad," the woman cut in.

"Who's that?" Jameson asked.

"Lyric Woods," she said. "We're stuck in a cabin on the mountain, and I need someone to walk me through how to help him. He's losing a lot of blood."

"I can do that," Jameson said. "Tell me about the cut."

Lyric stepped closer to study the wound on Asa's head. Her eyes were as dark as her hair, and her nose was thin and straight. She wasn't wearing a lot of makeup, but she had a natural beauty that would make anyone look twice.

Lyric. It was a unique name, but it tugged on the edges of his memory.

A small wrinkle appeared between Lyric's brows. "It's about two inches long and kind of open."

"It'll probably need to be stitched," Jameson said.

Asa turned his attention to the phone. He needed to look at something besides Lyric while she scrutinized him. "That's not happening anytime soon. What can we do right now?"

"I'll ask you some questions. Lyric, can you let me know if the answers are correct?" Jameson asked.

She looked up and nodded confidently. "I can do that."

After dozens of questions and assessments, Asa was beginning to fidget. He needed to call his mom and Jacob and let them know what happened.

A vehicle door slammed on Jameson's end of the line. "I'm at the station, and they're already running calls like crazy. We'll be out there to get you as soon as we can get those roads cleared. Hang tight and call me or one of the other EMTs every so often to check in."

"Thanks, Jameson," Lyric said sweetly. Somehow, she'd befriended him during the short phone call.

"Anytime. Seriously, get in touch with Noah, Lucas, or Travis if you can't get me."

"I'll make sure he checks in with someone," Lyric promised.

Was she his caretaker now? Not that Asa minded much. She was sweet, and he'd have to be blind not to notice she was gorgeous. If he had to wreck on the side of a mountain, this was the best he could have hoped for.

They disconnected the call, and Lyric breathed a sigh of relief. "It sounds like you'll live."

"Thanks. I didn't even catch your name before the call," Asa said. "Apparently, manners are the first thing to go after a head injury."

"Lyric." She extended a slim hand to him.

"Asa." He looked at the dried blood on his palm and lifted it to show her. "Um, I'll take a rain check on the handshake."

Her dark eyes widened. "Oh, you need to get cleaned up. Let me show you to the bathroom."

4

LYRIC

Lyric paced outside the bathroom, listening in case Asa needed help. He hadn't been too steady on his feet, and the last thing they needed was another head injury if he passed out.

She swung her arms around, hoping to generate some heat, but her wet clothes made getting comfortable impossible. She'd been so worried about the gaping hole in Asa's head that she'd ignored her freezing bones.

Of course, they needed to get into dry clothes. She jogged into the master bedroom and retrieved the robe hanging on the closet door.

Back outside the bathroom, she knocked. Asa opened the door, and the words she'd been about to say turned to lead in her throat. He'd washed away the blood, and she could clearly see his face—one she'd seen before and would never forget.

Breathe. Just breathe.

"Um, you need to get out of those wet clothes. If you'll put this on, I'll throw them in the dryer." She shoved the robe at him and kept her gaze on her feet.

"Thanks." He took the robe and disappeared back into the bathroom.

Lyric resumed her pacing, but her steps were quicker now. No, no, no. She was not stranded in a snowstorm with Officer Asa Scott. She should have known that name.

Slamming the palm of her hand into her forehead, she chanted, "Stupid, stupid, stupid."

It didn't seem like he'd recognized her yet, so there was a chance she could get out of this without him realizing they'd met before.

Who was she kidding? With an unusual name like Lyric and a charge of public intoxication and vandalism, she wasn't getting out of this without bringing the past into the present.

To be fair, she hadn't recognized him the second time they'd met. She'd been too drunk to remember the night he arrested her, but she'd never forget the way he'd stood up for her in court. The better parts of that speech he gave the judge were seared into her memory. He'd pleaded with the judge to give her another chance, since it was her first offense.

At the time, his request had seemed like a lucky second chance. She'd since figured out it was the Lord's intervention. There hadn't been a single good reason for him to plead on her behalf the way he did that day.

Lyric cupped her frozen hands around her mouth and tried to calm her breathing. That would have made for a heroic story... *if* it had been her last offense.

Could she make it through just one day without the past coming back to bite her? This time was exceptionally painful, mostly because her shame and embarrassment were about to be on full display. She regretted everything she'd done back when alcohol and drugs ruled her life, but few believed her. Once an addict, always paying for it.

If AA had taught her one thing, it was that she'd better get used to making amends. She'd been sober for five years, but she couldn't shake those old crimes. They hung around like a leech, sucking the life out of her little by little.

The bathroom door opened, and Asa stepped out wearing the robe and holding his wet clothes. "Please tell me this is a nightmare. I feel ridiculous."

"I'll take those." Lyric grabbed them and rushed off to the laundry room. If he didn't recognize her soon, he'd at least get a good look at her blush. Heat was searing through the cold on her neck and face.

By the time she started the load and rushed

back to help Asa, he was already halfway to the living room. Under normal circumstances, she'd be chuckling at the broad-shouldered man in a fuzzy white robe. Today, she couldn't find the humor in it.

She rushed ahead of him. "Here, let me set up a spot for you." She tossed the decorative pillows and scooted the coffee table out of the way. He didn't need anything around that he could easily trip on.

"Thanks. You don't have to do that."

Lyric didn't look up at him as he neared the couch. "Jameson said you need to rest."

Asa lowered himself onto the couch and settled back into a relaxed position. "He was being overly cautious. I don't think I have a concussion, but I'll be feeling a headache for a while."

Lyric tossed a blanket over his legs, itching for more things to keep her occupied. "What can I do for you?"

"Nothing, but you need to get out of those wet clothes. You're shivering."

Wrapping her arms around her middle did little to stop the shaking. "I don't want to leave you, in case you need something. What if you fall asleep?"

"I can sleep. Jameson said there weren't any concussion symptoms that concerned him. Do you have extra clothes?"

She tried to think of anything he might need, but she was so cold her mind was slowing down.

"Lyric, please go get warm. I'm going to call my family and let them know what's going on."

His family. Of course, he had a family. He was a handsome gentleman who stood up for stupid young girls in the courtroom. He'd probably thought he was making a difference in her life back then. That should have been the truth. He probably had one of those perfect TV families, like *The Brady Bunch* or *The Andy Griffith Show*.

Wait, there wasn't a mom in *The Andy Griffith Show*. Maybe not like that one.

Her teeth knocked against each other as she said, "Okay. I'll be right back."

Famous last words? Maybe.

She grabbed the other robe from the master bedroom and locked herself in the bathroom. The reflection in the mirror made her wince. The snow had soaked her hair, leaving it limp and tangled. She'd work on taming the mess later.

Asa, on the other hand, looked like a GQ model after he'd cleaned the blood off his face.

He was definitely out of her league. Married or not.

There was a time when she wouldn't have thought so. She'd been bold, beautiful, and looking for attention when she was younger. But now, she had enough baggage to overshadow any of her good qualities. Everyone could see the toll those years had taken on her.

Stupid. There wasn't another word for it, and she'd thrown away so much of her life and paved the way for an uphill battle. Despite her years of sobriety, nothing about the sober life was getting easier.

Wrapping the robe tightly around her, she avoided glancing at the mirror as she stepped out of the bathroom. In the laundry room, she tossed her clothes into the washer with Asa's and headed back to the living room to check on him.

He was in the same place she'd left him, but now he had another rag pressed against his wound.

She raced to his side. "What happened?"

"I'm fine. It started bleeding again. I think I've got it stopped for now, but I ruined another rag in the process."

"I'll go get the first-aid kit." Jameson had walked her through bandaging earlier, and she hoped she could do it again. Her stomach rolled just thinking about the blood.

When she returned with the kit, her hands were shaking. "Gauze, antiseptic, tape." She named off the items as she pulled them from the box, silently grateful that the antiseptic wasn't an alcohol pad.

"Lyric."

Asa's stern tone pulled her from the task.

He held out a hand as if she might spook and run at any moment. "You don't have to do this. I can handle it."

"How are you going to put it on right? I can help."

"Your hands are shaking."

"I'm still cold," she admitted. "Let me help."

Helping was good. She could do this.

She repeated the assurances one after the other as she bandaged the gash. By the time she finished, the shaking was almost under control.

"There. All patched up." She avoided looking at Asa as she packed up the kit.

"Thanks. Maybe I won't make a mess again."

A mess. Making messes were Lyric's specialty, and Asa seemed far from the mess making type.

She closed the box and set it on the end table nearby. "What do you need now?"

"Nothing. Thanks. Looks like we're just hanging out here for a while."

Lyric groaned. "I'm supposed to work in the morning."

"Better call your boss. I'm sure lots of things will be closed tomorrow, after the mess this storm dumped tonight."

"Yeah, can I borrow your phone?"

"Sure." Asa handed over his sleek smartphone.

She cradled the phone and pulled hers from her pocket. Flipping through the contacts, she found her boss's number and hesitated before making the call.

Asa's hand rested on her shoulder, only reminding her that she was still shaking. "You okay?"

"Yeah. I just don't want her to think I'm a flake. I just started two weeks ago, and I'm already calling in."

Asa frowned. "I think this is an understandable situation. Where do you work?"

"Blackwater Restoration."

"The thrift store downtown?" he asked.

"Yeah." Working at a thrift store was about the most unglamorous job she could imagine, but they'd had a help wanted sign out front, and she'd needed an income.

"Camille Harding is your boss?"

Lyric perked up. "Yes. You know her?"

"I do. She'll understand about the storm."

"I don't know her well, but she seems nice."

"She is. Just call her. If you need my help, I'll explain things to her."

Lyric hated she needed someone to vouch for her. Her word should have as much weight as the next person's, but it didn't.

She called Camille, and her boss was overly understanding, just as Asa said. She also promised to have her husband call to check on Asa as soon as he got in from his shift at the fire station.

Lyric's shoulders relaxed as she ended the call. "She said everything is fine and not to worry about coming in tomorrow. Sounds like things are worse out there than I thought. Apparently, a lot of roads are closed."

Asa rubbed the stubble on his chin. "We should probably turn on the news. I can't believe the power is still on."

Lyric tried not to tense back up, but she wasn't a fan of hanging out in the dark. "Right." She grabbed the remote from the table and extended it to him.

When he didn't take it from her, she glanced up at him. Big mistake because she could see the wheels turning in his head when he looked at her.

Finally, he took the remote and turned on the TV. With the volume low, they watched scene after scene of the ongoing storm damage.

"This is awful," Lyric said. She turned to him and found him looking at her again. His intense stare was heating her up from the inside.

He cleared his throat and focused his attention on the TV. "Thanks for rescuing me. I'm usually the one doing the rescuing."

"Oh?" Everything about the conversation was awkward. She didn't want to flat-out ask what he did for a living, mostly because she already knew.

"I'm a police officer and expecting to get called in any minute now."

Lyric nodded, hoping to think of some wise response. "Cool."

Cool? So not cool.

"Anyway. I really appreciate you getting me out of the storm, but you don't have to wait on me hand and foot."

"I don't mind." She twisted her fingers in her lap and laser-focused her stare at the TV, praying he'd stop looking at her and pay attention to the head-lines instead.

Lyric's stomach growled, and she tightened her arms around her middle.

Asa looked toward the kitchen. "Any food here?"

"I stocked the kitchen today for tomorrow's renters." Lyric stood and brushed a hand down the fluffy robe she wore. "I'll make you something."

"And you," Asa said.

Lyric shook her head. "It's not mine. I don't want the owner thinking I would take anything from her. She trusts me with her cabins, and I like this job. I can't lose it."

"Who's the owner?"

"Brenda Phillips."

"I know her. She won't mind if we eat something."

"Of course you know her," Lyric mumbled. Mr. Do Good knew everyone in town.

He sat up straighter. "Why don't we call her and tell her what's going on?"

Lyric rubbed her hands up and down her arms as she considered. The news would probably be better received coming from him. "Okay."

Asa found the number in his contacts and made the call. Apparently, he knew Brenda well enough to have her number.

"Hey, Brenda. It's Asa." He gave Lyric a thumbs up. "I had a wreck tonight right outside one of your rental cabins. I'm here with Lyric. Actually, she's the one who rescued me."

Lyric groaned and went to check on the clothes. Rescued was a bit of an exaggeration. He wouldn't be singing her praises when he realized who she was.

5

ASA

"Oh, goodness. Are you okay?" Brenda asked, her raspy voice hitting a pitch Asa hadn't heard from her before.

Brenda's personality was bigger than her rental cabin, but Asa had his eyes on the brunette heading out of the room.

"I am. Lyric has taken good care of me."

"Bless that girl. She's a doll."

Asa was beginning to think so too. A bit high-strung but definitely kind. "Listen, since we're stranded here for a little bit, would you mind if we helped ourselves to some of the food?"

"Good gracious, no. Have whatever you like. Lyric knows where everything is."

"Thanks. Any renters trying to come in tomorrow that we need to know about?"

"No, no. I had the place booked through the

weekend, but they emailed earlier to cancel. They can't get a flight into Wyoming in this weather. It's a disaster out there."

"Sorry about the cancellation." He didn't want to wish for Brenda's business to suffer, but he was glad they wouldn't be rushed to get out of here. The storm was still raging outside.

Brenda tsked. "God controls the weather. It's all in His plan."

Lyric walked back into the room, drawing Asa's attention.

"Book the rest of the week under my name. It's the least I can do for letting us stay here."

"You're a sweetheart, Asa. I'll be fine without the rental. You two just stay safe."

"Thanks. I owe you one."

Brenda laughed. "Bye, sugar."

Asa rested his head back as the call ended. The headache was really hanging on.

"Is your head hurting?" Lyric whispered.

When he opened his eyes, she was leaning over him. The light behind her created a halo around her and cast a shadow over her face.

He squeezed his eyes closed. "Yeah. Any chance you have something for it?"

Lyric quickly shook her head. "Sorry. I don't know of any here either."

Asa leaned up. "It's okay. Brenda said we can make ourselves at home."

Lyric clasped her hands in front of her. "What do you want to eat?"

Standing, Asa bit back a grunt. His back was going to be screaming by tomorrow. "Let's see what our options are."

Lyric held out a hand. "Are you okay to walk?"

"I'm fine to walk. Just getting hungry."

Lyric stepped away but kept a watchful eye on him. "Me too."

He followed her to the kitchen where she started naming off the contents of the pantry and fridge.

"That's enough food to feed an army," Asa said when she'd finished her list.

"A family of six was coming in, and they were supposed to stay four days. Guests send Brenda a grocery list before they arrive, and I pick it up. The cabin is a bit out of town, so she likes to have things here for them."

"That's really nice of her. And you."

Lyric moved some things around in the fridge. "I'm sure they pay handsomely for it. Anything sound good to you?"

"A sandwich."

Lyric held up two lunch meat packages. "Ham or turkey?"

The headache was pounding again, and Asa rubbed his forehead. "Either."

She pulled the condiments out of the fridge, and Asa retrieved the loaf of bread from the pantry. Lyric took it from him as soon as he turned around.

"Sit," she demanded.

"You don't have to do that. Let me do something for you for once." He'd been fending for himself for years, and having Lyric do things for him brought back memories of living with Danielle. Things had been so simple when they were married. They were two halves of a whole—a perfect team.

Lyric shook her head, keeping her chin down, and pointed to the barstool. "Sit."

Without protest, Asa relaxed into the seat and propped his head in his hands. Seconds later, his phone rang. About time. Chief must have been busy.

"Hello."

"Can you come in?" Chief Wright asked in greeting.

"Sorry, boss. I just had a wreck in the storm, and I'm stuck out on North Bend Road."

"You okay?"

"Banged up a bit, but I'll be okay."

"Someone on their way to help you?"

"There are other emergencies that need to be taken care of first. A woman in a cabin helped me inside and bandaged me up."

"That's good news. I guess I'll call the next number on the list. You take care and call if you need help."

"I will, sir. Sorry I can't make it in."

"Understood. Talk to you later."

Asa cradled the phone in his hands. Being stuck was one thing, but being unable to help the people who depended on him was another.

"Everything okay?" Lyric asked as she placed the sandwich in front of him. Her dark hair was drying into waves, and color was filling her face. She kept looking away from him, but he was having a hard time tearing his gaze from her. It was almost impossible to ignore the beautiful woman in the room.

Asa put his phone on the counter beside the plate and nodded. "I got called into work."

"And you're upset because you can't make it?"

"Yeah. I know how bad things can get sometimes, and I hate leaving others to deal with it."

Lyric stood across the bar and picked up the sandwich in front of her. "It sounds like you really want to help."

"I do." He picked up his own sandwich and hesitated before biting into it. "Is there anyone you need to call?"

Lyric looked at him. "Like who?"

"Family. Is there someone who's going to be worried about you tonight?" He hadn't even thought to ask before now. He'd been worried about his own check-ins. She might have a husband and kids at home who were worried about her.

She took another bite of her sandwich and kept her chin down. "Nope."

He found it hard to believe she didn't have anyone she needed to check in with.

"You can use my phone whenever you need to."

Lyric shook her head. "You should try to make that battery last as long as possible. It's the only lifeline we have."

"I have a charger in the truck. I'll go get it in the morning if we need it."

She didn't seem convinced. Instead, she avoided looking at him as she ate, and Asa took the chance to study her. Her fingernail tapped a quick beat on the countertop, and her gaze darted from one thing to another.

Was she nervous, or was she scared?

"Lyric?"

She startled at her name. Jerking her chin up to reveal wide eyes. "I think I should check on your clothes." She left the room in a rush, not even giving him a chance to ask his question.

Asa scarfed down the rest of the sandwich and tried not to think too much about what had Lyric so worked up. His phone buzzed with a text message.

Mom: I haven't heard from you in a while. Just checking in.

Instead of texting, he called her. Between the headache, getting bandaged, and eating, he hadn't had a chance to check in.

"Hey." His mother's voice was tired with a hint of concern.

"Hey. Is Jacob in bed yet?"

"Fast asleep. The storm kept him up for a bit, but he finally settled down."

Jacob was a tough kid, but he didn't like too many changes in his life. Asa being gone tonight no doubt threw a wrench in the way Jacob had anticipated the night going.

"It looks like I won't make it home tonight. I had a wreck coming down the mountain. I'm okay, but the truck isn't."

"Oh no. Asa, I'm so sorry. It's my fault you're out in this mess. I should have gotten Mrs. Grant's food to her earlier."

"No one knew this storm was going to be this bad."

"I know. I'm trying to accept the things I can't control, but it's tough."

Asa knew all about that scary lack of control in every part of his life. His wife's death, unpredictable criminals, raising a son–it was a lot to juggle.

"I'm at a rental cabin. A woman helped me inside and bandaged me up."

"Bandaged?"

"I hit my head on the window. Just a scratch, but it bled quite a bit. It's fine now."

"That's good news. No concussion?"

"Probably not. Just a headache."

"Who got you out of the storm?" she asked.

Asa looked around, searching for the woman he was sharing the safe space with. "Her name is Lyric."

"That's good. I'm glad you're not alone. I've been so worried."

"No need to worry."

His mother hummed. "Lyric. That's a pretty name."

"It's different." Asa rolled the name around in his head, but he still couldn't place it to anything else he knew.

"Oh, she's the girl Kendra talks about," his mom said cheerily.

"Kendra Bates that works at Deano's?" Asa asked.

"Yes, I've heard her mention meeting a woman named Lyric for lunch before."

Asa glanced toward the hallway where Lyric had disappeared. "What do you know about her?"

"Kendra says she's a sweetheart. They're pretty close. She helped out when Kendra's daughter and son-in-law had to move back in with them recently."

A helper. That sounded like a solid description of the woman who'd been catering to him all evening. "She seems nice."

Lyric walked in carrying a folded stack of Asa's clothes. As much as he hated putting her out, she was doing a great job of taking care of him.

He sat up and watched her as she moved throughout the space. "I'll call you in the morning, Mom. Thanks for everything."

"Don't worry. We're fine here," his mother assured. "Love you."

"Love you too."

He stood to meet Lyric, and she handed over the clothes, carefully keeping her chin tucked to her chest. "Here you go. Looks like the blood came out too."

"You washed them?" He'd expected her to toss them in the dryer at the most.

"Yes. Was that not okay?" she asked.

"It's fine. Thanks. They would have stayed blood-stained if I'd done it myself." He knew how to get those stains out–perk of the job–but it hadn't been his uniform tonight, and he hadn't been so concerned with preserving his clothes.

"No problem," Lyric said as she turned and started tidying up the kitchen.

Asa left her to it and ducked into the bathroom. Shower was the first thing on his list, and he took advantage of the hot water while they still had it, making sure not to drain the tank in case Lyric wanted a shower too.

When he emerged clean and ten degrees warmer, Lyric was leaned over a paper on the counter.

"What's that?" he asked.

She straightened and looked back to the paper. "A list."

He looked over her shoulder and read the tidy words. "You're writing down all the things we use?"

"I want to pay Brenda back."

Wow, Lyric was really afraid of losing her job over this. He couldn't imagine Brenda was a tough boss. She was well-off and pretty generous when she heard about someone in need.

"Brenda said we could use things here. I told her to book the place under my name while we were here, and she assured me we shouldn't worry about it."

Lyric's eyes widened. "You did? Do you have any idea how much it costs to book this place for even one night?"

"No, but I'd pay it if I had to. Like I said, she told us not to worry about it."

Lyric tapped the pen against the paper, contemplating his words. "Are you sure?"

"I'm sure. Brenda is a friend, and I think you can relax. She won't fire you or make you pay for anything."

Every muscle in Lyric's body was tense, and she wasn't moving, wasn't responding.

"Lyric, breathe," Asa said.

And just like that, she inhaled a deep breath.

He wrapped his hand around hers, giving it a gentle squeeze and ignoring the tingling where her skin touched his. "Are you afraid of the storm?" he whispered.

"No. I mean, yes." She squeezed her eyes closed. "It sounds awful out there."

He leaned in and told himself that the lure he felt toward her was for support or comfort. It was more like a magnetic pull, natural and normal in seemingly irrational ways.

When she opened her eyes, he took in the dark depths and lost track of what they were talking about.

Her gaze lifted an inch, and she took a step back. "You're bleeding again."

6

LYRIC

Lyric reached for the first-aid kit and rummaged through it. Why was she so worked up? She wasn't afraid of storms, just the man from her past she'd rather not face. But when Asa whispered assurances, she was tempted to believe him.

Pulling out the gauze, she looked at the few left in the kit. "Should we call Jameson? We don't have much gauze left. What if we run out?"

"It's fine. We'll use what's left and worry about it later."

"Okay!" The word came out way too chipper, but she was more than happy to go along with Asa's "deal with it later" mentality.

Focusing on bandaging Asa's head wound, she began to relax. He said Brenda was okay with them staying here, and maybe she was. Thankfully, Asa had made that call to her earlier. He was much more trustworthy than an ex-junky.

Would it always be hard for Lyric to trust kindness? It was rare in her world, which made her second-guess it every time. Most everyone who knew about her past was watching and waiting for her to mess up.

Then there were people like her sponsor, Kendra. It had taken months for Lyric to figure out Kendra really wanted to help her. Now, she trusted her friend with everything.

Well, Lyric might not tell her about this little adventure with Asa. Mostly because she wasn't sure how she felt about being here with him yet. He'd recognize her or remember soon enough, and this cozy evening would go up in flames.

She pressed the last edge of the bandage over the gauze and let her fingertips brush down the side of his face, lingering on his skin. What would it be like to be normal? Why couldn't she meet a nice man, date him, fall in love, and live happily ever after? The "meet a nice man" part would always be followed by the revelation of her past and the quick good-bye.

Pulling her hand away, she picked up the wrappers and closed the kit. "What now?"

"You sound like you're waiting for orders from your drill sergeant," Asa said.

She looked up to find him smirking.

"I like staying busy," she said.

"Me too. Sometimes, too much."

Well, that was one thing they had in common. Probably the only thing.

"It won't be long before the power goes out. Is there wood for that fireplace?" Asa asked.

Lyric looked at the monstrous stone fireplace. It was over six feet wide and spanned to the top of the second-floor ceiling. "It's gas."

"Good. We'll at least have some heat."

Something thudded against the window, and Lyric jumped. Pressing her hand to her chest, she willed her heart to slow.

Asa reached out to her, resting his hand on her upper arm. "It's just a limb."

Focusing on calming her breaths, she tried to ignore the warmth of his hand. The storm, the dark night, and the unfortunate person she'd been stranded with were wreaking havoc on her emotions tonight.

His voice was low and calm as he whispered, "Lyric, we're safe. I promise."

"Okay." The word came out with a shudder, making it obvious her central nervous system hadn't gotten the memo yet. "Should we pray or something?"

When he didn't respond, she looked at him. His features had softened, but there was a hint of confusion in his lifted brow. Had she messed up? Was he not the praying kind?

"I can do that." He bowed his head and prayed.

Lyric closed her eyes and bowed her head. She was just getting the hang of praying on her own, and her silent talks with God were often jumbled and disjointed. Not Asa. His words were eloquent pleas and familiar thanks. He talked to God like a friend.

The tension in her shoulders eased as she listened to his words. They could have been pulled from her own mind. Asa prayed for safety and shelter, then he prayed the Lord would calm the storm outside and the storm in her heart.

Lyric bit her lips between her teeth. She knew Kendra prayed for her, but hearing a stranger's prayer with her name in it was comforting in a way she hadn't expected. He didn't know half of the unease in her heart, and he didn't ask. He saw her struggle and took it to the Lord.

She hadn't been following Christ for long, and she often hesitated and questioned how to do any of it. Anyone with eyes could see Asa had a strong faith, and she wanted that more than anything right now. She felt the peace in his prayer and remembered she wasn't alone.

With his "Amen," Asa looked up at her with an assuring smile and asked, "Better?"

She was going to cry. The tears were close, and they pricked behind her eyes. She sucked a breath through her nose, but the onslaught was too strong. Her voice trembled at the word, "Yeah."

Asa opened his arms, and she didn't fight the urge to lean into him. She needed a hug right now, and he was the only person around.

Burying her face in his chest, Lyric let her tears soak his clean shirt. His arms wrapped around her, holding her tight, and she relaxed into the safest place she'd ever known.

His hand stroked her tangled hair. "Let it out. It's been a stressful night."

Lyric chuckled. "You can say that again."

"Everything will be okay, and we'll get out of here."

The cabin was quiet, except for the wind thrashing outside, and she was able to slow her trembling breaths. Asa held her until she lifted her head.

"Thanks." She stepped back to wipe her cheeks.

He casually leaned back against the kitchen counter. "Do you go to church around here?"

"I've been going to a church in Silver Falls."

"You live there?"

"No, I live here in Blackwater."

"You have any other business out there?" he asked with a lifted brow—the one on the opposite side of the gash near his hairline.

Lyric fidgeted with her fingers. He didn't know how hard it was to show up in a small-town church when everyone knew your face and name from mugshots printed in the local newspapers. "No."

Asa paused for her to continue, but he would have to keep waiting. She wasn't ready to tell him she couldn't sit in a church in Blackwater with the same people she'd hurt. They'd never let her in.

"Sorry, we don't have to talk about it if you don't want to," he whispered.

"It's okay. I'm just getting used to this faith, and I'm afraid to mess up."

Asa's eyes widened. "You think you're not allowed to mess up? Who told you that?"

"No one, I guess. I want to be a good Christian and do all the things right, but I'm scared of not being good enough."

Asa shook his head and kept his gaze on her. "Everyone messes up, even Christians. It's how we fix it that matters."

Lyric hadn't thought of it that way before, and she didn't know what to think of being expected to mess up. She'd spent the last few years walking on eggshells. Don't relapse. Don't be late. Don't get fired. Don't miss a bill. It was exhausting, and her soul was tired.

"And it never ends," Asa continued. "You'll never be perfect. You're going to have to ask for forgiveness for the rest of your life. We should always try to be like Christ, but it's impossible. God gives you grace. Give some to yourself."

She wanted to believe him. She wanted to trust him. But just like the salvation she'd heard about in church, it sounded too good to be true. "That's easier said than done. I did a lot of bad things. I don't think I can come back from all that."

Asa stood taller and took a step toward her. Now she'd done it. She'd confessed, and he'd put the pieces together. She was a criminal, and he was the law keeper. They were on opposite ends of the moral spectrum.

Instead of telling her she was right, he stood before her and said, "You can. No one is too far gone to be forgiven."

She narrowed her eyes. "How can you say that? You deal with the worst people in the world every day."

"But I also see the best people, and sometimes, those are the same. I've been working long enough to see people be punished and learn their lesson. It doesn't always happen, but sometimes it does, and that makes what I do worth it."

A smile lifted Lyric's lips. "You're a good man. You don't have an easy job." She'd had her fair share of run-ins with the police, and none of them had been pretty, whether it was herself or someone else receiving the reprimand.

"It's what I was called to do."

"Called?" she questioned.

"I think the Lord gave me the skills and determination to handle what I do. I'm not going to say I always enjoy it, but I see the need for it, and I think it's what I'm meant to do."

He felt called by the Lord? To be a police officer? Why would the Lord call one of His children to do something so difficult day in and day out?

"I guess I haven't ever been called to do anything," she said.

"You'll know what it is when the time is right. Be patient."

Lyric laughed. "I don't have a patient bone in my body. I think something and I say it, or I have an idea and I do it."

Asa scoffed. "I've noticed. Who runs back out into a storm?"

"We needed your phone!"

Holding up his hands in surrender, Asa smiled. "Fair enough, but I still think you should have layered up a little more first."

Lyric scrunched her mouth to one side. "That's a valid point."

"Thinking things through never gets anyone in trouble," he said.

She held up a finger. "What if it's a time-sensitive situation?"

"You still need to think. That part is important."

She crossed her arms in front of her chest. "I'll take that into consideration before I run out in the storm again."

Asa looked at the windows. Nothing was visible in the darkness outside. "It sounds like it's dying down."

"We should check the weather forecast."

"Good idea." He covered his mouth while he yawned. "If the danger has passed, I'd like to hit the hay."

Lyric tucked the robe tighter around her and headed for the living room where the TV was still muted on the weather radar.

"Are your clothes almost dry?" Asa asked.

"Well, I really don't want to dry my sweater unless I have to. It'll shrink. I figure I'll let it hang overnight, and then maybe it'll be close to dry, and I can tumble it for a few minutes."

"Sorry. You should have put yours in first."

She shrugged and fell back onto the fluffy couch. "It's no big deal, as long as you're not bothered too much by my robed state."

Asa rubbed his forehead. "Not too much."

The strain in his words made her pull the collar of the robe high on her neck. There, no peeks allowed.

He pointed at the TV. "Looks like this round is over, but another band is close behind."

"Great. More snow on top of the snow we already have. I bet my car is buried."

"You're probably right. It might be a while before you can get down the mountain."

"How long do you think we'll be here?" she asked.

"Maybe a couple of days." He sat up straighter and looked around. "Where is my phone? I just thought of something."

Lyric spotted it on the end table and handed it to him.

"I was on my way home from taking food to Mrs. Grant when I wrecked, so I want to make sure she's okay. If we can't get down the mountain, she can't either."

"Oh, good point."

Asa scrolled through his contacts. "Yeah, and she's old, so if the power goes out and she doesn't have a generator or gas heat, that might escalate our chances of getting rescued sooner. She'll be a priority."

Lyric liked the sound of that, and she was beginning to like this new comfortable state she'd fallen into with Asa. She watched the forecast while he talked to Mrs. Grant. Photos and videos of the devastation flashed one after the other, and Lyric's stomach began to roll at the scenes.

By the time Asa was telling the woman to call him if she needed anything, Lyric's eyelids were heavy.

"What did I miss?" he asked.

"Snow, wreckage, fallen trees, more snow."

Asa rubbed his jaw and watched the radar.

Exhaustion weighed heavy on her shoulders, but she wasn't ready to leave Asa's side. Knowing he was near was comforting.

He looked at her and grinned. "Get some sleep. I'll keep an eye on things."

"You need sleep too," she said.

"I'll sleep a little, but I need to check the forecast every few hours."

She glanced over the back of the couch toward the hallway leading to the bedrooms. "You have a bedroom preference?"

"Take the one you want. I'll have what's left."

She let out a big yawn that refused to be contained. "Then I'll try to get some sleep in a comfy bed until the storm wakes me up."

"Good night, Lyric."

She paused and looked back at him. "Good night. Please don't hesitate to wake me up if you need anything."

Asa smirked playfully. "I'm not waking you up."

She fidgeted for a moment before taking a few steps backward. "Okay. See you in the morning."

"Sweet dreams."

She turned and walked faster, needing to put distance between herself and the handsome man who'd be sleeping in the next room tonight. Closing herself in the first room she came to, Lyric flopped face-first onto the bed and groaned.

"This isn't real," she mumbled into the soft

comforter. "I am not stranded in a luxury mountain cabin with Officer Handsome."

She rolled onto her back and stared at the ceiling. He wouldn't be so nice to her if he remembered her or knew about the things she'd done.

7

ASA

At four in the morning, Asa poured a cup of warm coffee from the carafe. He'd only turned on one small kitchen light, and he was focused on preventing a spill when movement to his right caught his attention.

Lyric walked into the kitchen with her arms wrapped around her middle. Her steps were silent as she padded toward him. The TV was still on the news channel, casting a dim glow over the open room.

He took the first sip and leaned against the counter, watching her move in the dark. It was the exact opposite of the way she'd come barreling into his life. There hadn't been anything quiet in his heart about Lyric last night.

Maybe he'd learn in time, but he hadn't figured her out yet. She was independent but not confident.

She was helpful but impulsive. She was kind but still doubting herself.

"What are you doing up?" she asked. Her voice was sleepy and sultry, and it did nothing to quell his attraction to her. The robe didn't do him any favors either.

"The storm is starting up again. I got up to check the weather."

She pointed to his cup. "And you needed coffee for that?"

"I wasn't planning to go back to sleep." Not that he'd slept much anyway. Worrying about Jacob, the storm, and Lyric had kept his mind busy.

She tucked her arms closer around her. "Did you sleep at all?"

"A little. You?"

Her smirk was barely visible. "A little."

"Want to watch something besides the weather?" he asked.

"Yes, please. I can't look at the photos anymore."

Asa followed her into the living room, and he muted the TV as they sat down. "Want to talk instead?"

Lyric curled her legs under her on the couch. "You talk. I'll listen."

He chuckled. "I was thinking you could do the talking."

"I'm not awake enough yet." She hummed as she

thought. "Did I hear you talking about your son earlier?"

"Jacob. He's ten." A surge of pride filled Asa's chest. "He's awesome."

"I'm sure he is."

"I talked to him right before I wrecked. He wasn't too happy with me."

Lyric straightened. "Why?"

Asa scratched the stubble on his chin. He was in dire need of a shave. "I'm not the best at remembering all the school activities. It's a lot."

"You mean like dress-up days?"

He chuckled. "Yeah, those."

"That's not that big of a deal, is it? Doesn't his mom help out with that?"

An image of Danielle flashed in Asa's memory. She would have done all those things and loved them.

"It's just me. Well, my mom helps, but Jacob's mom passed away four years ago."

Lyric gasped and covered her mouth. "I'm so sorry."

It was the expected reaction—one he'd become immune to in the last few years. He still hadn't figured out what to say in response. He couldn't say, "It's okay," because it wasn't.

"Asa, I'm sorry."

"It's been a rough few years."

"I can't imagine. Is Jacob with your mom tonight?"

"Yeah, and she takes good care of him. She takes him to school and picks him up on days when I work over, so they spend a lot of time together."

Lyric watched the muted TV for a moment before turning back to him. "I bet being a single parent is tough. No wonder you're forgetting dress-up days."

"Actually, this time I forgot to send money for the book fair, but Danielle wouldn't have missed any school activity. She was a middle school science teacher, and she loved everything about the school experience. Field trips, experiments, pep rallies, ball games–she was in the middle of everything."

"And you're feeling like a failure because you're not as good as the MVP?"

Asa lifted his head. "What do you mean?"

"I mean, don't be so hard on yourself."

Asa let out a single laugh. "Look who's talking."

She chuckled. "Fair enough."

A zap followed by a loud, electric sizzling had both of them sitting up and alert. Lyric covered her ears as the roar of the wind grew louder. Seconds later, the TV went off.

"It's okay," Asa said quickly. "It sounded like a transformer blew."

Lyric tucked her arms around her middle. "Is that dangerous?"

"It just means we don't have power anymore, and I don't think there's much chance of it coming back anytime soon."

Lyric breathed loudly. "We still have a while before sunrise."

"Not long. Maybe an hour." The sky wasn't getting lighter yet, but the storm might be blocking the sunrise.

"Okay, what do we do now?" she asked.

Pulling his phone out, Asa turned on the flashlight and looked through his recent contacts. "I'll text my mom and ask her to call if there's any danger headed our way."

"Then what?"

"Then we wait."

Lyric's pitch rose. "Wait? I'm not good at waiting."

"You don't say."

She playfully swatted his arm.

"Are you assaulting an officer?" he asked.

That earned him a smile he could barely make out in the light from his phone. "Guilty."

He tossed her a pillow and blanket from the love seat. "Get some rest."

"What are you going to do?"

"The same. Right here." He settled into the recliner and flipped the footrest out.

Lyric cuddled with the blanket on the couch and

flopped from one side to the other. "It's still so loud outside."

He checked his phone, and a message from his mother was waiting. "Mom said she'd let us know if things get bad. You can relax."

"Okay. Thank you," she whispered.

"No problem. Sweet dreams."

Asa rested his head back and stared at the ceiling. What was happening? Knowing his mom and Jacob were safe left him free to focus on the here and now, and Lyric was very much in the forefront of his mind.

Turning his attention back to her, he watched her shoulders rise and fall with her breaths. He liked helping people, even if it was only assuring Lyric that they'd make it through the storm. However, she seemed intent on taking care of him too. That was a dynamic he hadn't experienced with a woman since Danielle passed.

Moving on had always been a blur in the future, but working through a tough situation with Lyric by his side felt nice in uncomfortable ways. Danielle had been his high school sweetheart before she'd become his wife and the mother of his child. They'd lived as one for half their lives. Working alongside another woman wasn't something he'd planned to do.

But Danielle had asked him to keep his heart open before she died. He'd promised her he would, but it was a promise he hadn't kept. He didn't know how. His heart had stayed closed to everyone except his family and friends, and he liked it that way.

Now, he was being forced to spend time with a woman, and it was all new. Was this part of the Lord's plan, or was it only the different dynamic that had Asa questioning everything?

Lyric wasn't like any woman he'd met before, and she'd surprised him in countless ways in the last ten hours.

When her breathing evened to a deep, steady rhythm, he closed his eyes and drifted off to sleep.

The ringing of his phone startled him from a deep slumber, and he patted around for the device. Where had he left it?

"Here." Lyric handed it to him.

He answered without checking the caller ID. "Hello."

"Hey. Did I wake you?" Brenda asked.

Asa rubbed his eyes and sat up straighter. "Yeah, but it's fine. What can I do for you?"

"Is the power out at the cabin?" she asked.

"Yeah. Just for a few hours."

"There's a generator on the concrete pad out back if you need it. It should have gas."

Asa stood and began pacing, trying to force his body to wake up from the peaceful sleep that wanted to pull him back in. "Thanks. I'll go get it soon."

"Sorry I woke you. Is Lyric okay too?" Brenda asked.

Lyric sat up on the couch, watching him like a hawk. The dim morning light cast an ethereal glow around her.

"She's fine."

"Good. You take care of her."

Of all the things that had happened last night, taking care of Lyric was the least expected. "I will."

"Good. Call me if you need me."

"Thanks. Talk to you later." Asa disconnected the call and looked at Lyric.

"Well?" she asked.

"Brenda said there's a generator out back."

"Do you know how to use it? Because I don't."

Asa stretched his arms above his head. "I got it covered."

Lyric jumped up from her seat. "I'll go get it."

"Wait. We don't need it right this second. We have the gas fireplace. We can turn it on later to make sure the food in the fridge and freezer don't ruin."

"Okay, I'll be right back."

When she disappeared down the hallway, Asa dumped the cold coffee out of his cup and rinsed it in the sink. There wouldn't be any more unless he hooked the generator to the coffee maker.

Less than a minute later, Lyric jogged out of the hallway and to the back door. She was wearing jeans and a sweater now, and when she grabbed her coat and started putting it on, Asa put the carafe in the sink.

"Where are you going?"

"To get the generator," she said as she slipped on a boot.

Asa sprinted for the door and put a hand on the knob. "Lyric, stop and listen. We don't need it yet."

"But we will," she said as she slipped her other foot into a boot.

Asa sighed. "If you're determined to go right now, let me get my coat and shoes on."

Lyric opened the door. "You don't have to."

"Wait," Asa said, but she was already out the door. He sighed and slipped on his boots. "Crazy woman."

8

LYRIC

The wind was stronger than before, and the blast of cold threatened to knock Lyric off her feet. She hunched her shoulders and tucked her arms around her as she trudged through the snow to the stairs leading down.

The wetness had soaked through her pants by the time she made it to the ground level. The covered area was sheltered from the bulk of the snow, but the layer of white still coated everything. In the farthest corner, she spotted the red-and-black top of what must be the generator.

Standing over it, she brushed the snow away until the metal handles were visible. Okay, she knew how she'd be moving it, but where to? When she turned around, Asa was trudging through the snow toward her.

"What are you doing?" he shouted above the wind.

"Getting the generator." She pointed to it. She'd seen one before, but she'd never had to use one herself. Someone else had always been around to make the magic happen.

"You can't just run out into a blizzard," he said.

Ignoring his sharp tone, she looked around. "Where do we need to move it?"

He pointed to the door and stepped up to the generator. "Can you clear a path?"

Jumping into action, she spotted a shovel propped against the house and began pushing snow out of the way. When Asa lifted one side of the generator to roll it on the back wheels, he leaned as he pulled it. Maybe she'd been a little hasty running out here. From the looks of it, that thing was heavier than she'd expected.

Lyric ran to the door of the cabin and turned the knob. It was locked.

"I have to unlock the door!" she shouted. The icy air seared her lungs as she jogged up the stairs, careful to keep her footing on the built-up snow.

The heat inside the cabin did little to knock off the cold as she stepped inside. Keeping her momentum, she ran down the stairs and quickly unlocked the basement door. The storm pushed its way into the peaceful warmth of the cabin, but she held the entryway open, making room for Asa to enter. He left the generator outside and headed for the refrigerator.

"That one doesn't have anything in it." Her teeth chattered as she spoke.

"I know, but it's the only one we'll be able to hook the generator to. We can move the food down here."

When he started pulling the refrigerator out of its custom cut nook, Lyric stood behind him. He pulled the heavy appliance slowly toward him. What could she do to help?

Looking back at the door, an idea crossed her mind. She jogged back outside and ignored the freezing wind as she gripped the generator handle with both hands. It was much heavier than she'd expected. Maybe if she used all of her body weight, she could get it inside.

"What are you doing?" Asa asked behind her.

"Bringing the generator in," she said with a grunt as she pulled on the heavy appliance, failing to move it even an inch.

Asa put his hands on top of hers. "You can't bring it inside. It emits carbon monoxide. We have to run extension cords."

"Really?"

"Really. Get back inside, please."

This time, Lyric was glad to do as she was ordered. Once they were both inside, Asa closed the door behind them.

"What are you doing?" he asked again.

"Trying to help!" The words came out louder than she'd intended, but her frustration was pressing on the walls of her chest. Couldn't he see she was trying?

Asa took a calming breath and leveled his gaze on her. "I'm glad you want to help, but can you please stop doing stuff?"

If his words hadn't been laced with a gentle plea, she might have smarted off to him. Instead, she was compelled to obey. All her good intentions had been useless and messy so far.

"Okay. Will you at least tell me what I should be doing to help?" She tried to hide the defeat in her voice, but even she could hear it.

"Can you bring the food down here to the basement kitchen?"

"Yes. I'm on it." She sprinted for the stairs, taking them two at a time.

Asa called out from behind her. "Just the fridge. Not the freezer."

"Got it!" She shouted over her shoulder.

Minutes later, she carefully made her way back down the stairs with arms overflowing with cold fridge items. She might never warm up after this.

Asa had an orange extension cord trailing through the room, and he was hidden behind the fridge. She stuffed the items in and ran back upstairs for more.

After a few trips, the fridge was stocked, and Asa was finished hooking up the generator.

Lyric rested her hands on her hips. "Are we finished?"

"I think we're finished. The fridge, hot water heater, and fireplace fan are hooked up."

"So are we moving our home base down here?" The smaller living room was cozy and had large windows like the upper floor. The couch was a leather sectional, and a separate love seat looked like it had two reclining seats.

"I think we need to. The upstairs fireplace will keep the area right in front of it warm, but it won't heat the room without a fan."

"Okay, sounds good." She tucked her arms around her wet body and tried to calm the shaking.

"The water heater is good to go if you need a bath."

"A bath?" Soaking in a tub of hot water sounded like the stuff of dreams right now.

Lyric's stomach growled loud enough to be heard over the ruckus outside.

Asa grinned and tilted his head toward the downstairs bedrooms. "Why don't you get warm and dry, and I'll find us some breakfast."

She tightened her jaw as she tried to stop the chattering of her teeth. "You want me to dry your clothes again?"

He looked down at his wet pants. "I'll get those started while you get warm. We can dry yours too."

She'd thrown on her pants straight from the dryer before rushing outside, and she was lamenting the loss of their warmth. "Looks like we're back in the robes."

Asa scrunched up his nose, making an adorable face at odds with his masculine features.

"You like the robes," she teased.

"They have their perks," Asa said, shrugging one shoulder.

Lyric narrowed her eyes. "There's more than one?"

"Nope. Just the fluffy softness," Asa answered quickly.

Smirking, Lyric let her gaze linger on him. Flirting with the hot cop and lounging around in robes together was dangerous. Now he'd offered to make her breakfast while she relaxed in a hot bath, made possible by his fantastic knowledge of generator operations.

"A candle-lit bath sounds perfect," she said as she turned to go.

Just before she rounded the corner, she snuck a peek at Asa. He was leaned back against the kitchen counter with his arms crossed over his chest, and his stare was locked on her.

She might not need a bath to warm up if Asa kept looking at her like that.

9

ASA

Asa stepped out into the icy morning, grateful he'd taken the time to layer up first. Everything was covered in a thick sheet of white, and the sting hit his lungs like a punch.

Seriously, why had Lyric rushed outside to get the generator? A few minutes to put on gloves wouldn't have hurt. Impulsivity didn't make much sense. He took his time and prepared for everything, and he still forgot things, like Jacob's field trips.

Well, maybe his way wasn't working either, but at least he wasn't in danger of getting frostbite on the way to his truck.

With Lyric out of sight, he could focus on things that needed to be done, like getting his phone charger from his wrecked vehicle at the end of the drive.

After shoveling a path in the snow, he made it to the truck. Snow covered the wreckage, masking the damage. It had been too dark to see much the night before, but Asa's bet was it would be totaled. He'd been driving the same truck for years, and it had served him well.

He'd taken Jacob on their first hunting trip together in that truck. It held some of the best memories of his life.

It was just a truck–a material possession. He'd come out of it with a scratch, and he'd walked away from the incident thanks to Lyric.

Asa might not agree with her spontaneity, but her quick action had certainly done him some good.

He shoveled snow away from the door and pried it open. The inside was trashed. Nothing had stayed in its place during the wreck. Rummaging through the scattered things, he spotted the charger and shoved it in his pocket along with his wallet, gun, and an extra jacket. He'd grab the other things when the wrecker came.

On his way back to the cabin, he stopped next to the mound of snow that covered Lyric's car. He didn't have the keys now, but if they ended up stuck here much longer, he'd make another trip out to get her things if she wanted.

Lyric hadn't asked for much of anything really. There were a million things she could have complained about, but she'd taken it all in stride, trying her best to make their situation better. Asa hadn't expected to feel like part of a team when they were first snowed in together, but now the dynamic they'd settled into was working.

He stepped back inside and pulled off the layers. They'd need to be dried again. Quickly closing himself in the bedroom, he located the dreaded robe and changed out of his wet clothes. Asa hadn't worn a robe in his life before yesterday, and he was making up for lost time. He looked down at the lower halves of his legs and frowned. He wore shorts in summer. This wasn't any different, right? The fluffy material was great and all, but the possibility of exposure kept him on guard.

He padded downstairs in his bare feet, hooked the dryer to the generator, and threw his clothes in. The fan in the fireplace was circulating the warm air now, and this level of the cabin was toasty. Too bad he couldn't shed a layer to find a comfortable medium.

His stomach rumbled, and he checked the fridge. The bacon and eggs were calling his name, and he eyed the stove. There were few things he wouldn't do for bacon and eggs.

He grabbed the pack of bacon and the carton of eggs and halted. How did Lyric like hers cooked? He opened and scanned all the cabinets, making sure he had the things he'd need.

Asa was pulling the bacon out of the pan when Lyric walked into the kitchen. She stretched her arms above her head, and he stared long enough that the flimsy meat flopped off the fork.

Lyric grinned in a contented way that had Asa's central nervous system jamming up. Her dark hair was pulled up in a bun, and she was back in that stupid robe again.

It was a stupid robe because it made *him* stupid.

She closed her eyes and inhaled a deep breath. "It smells amazing in here."

"Um, I didn't know how you liked your bacon. Or eggs. Or if you liked bacon and eggs."

"Love them. However you cook them. As long as you're doing the cooking and not me, I have no complaints."

"You don't like to cook?" Asa asked.

Lyric leaned back against the counter. "I do, but I want to curl up in a sleepy puddle right now. I slept so restlessly last night."

"Eat breakfast, then take a nap," he offered.

She yawned and shook her head. "I'll try to tough it out."

Asa opened the egg carton and pulled out four. "So, what's the verdict on your eggs?"

"Scrambled or fried."

"Noted. Why don't you sit down, and I'll bring it to you when it's ready?"

"I'll set the table," she said as she reached for the cabinet beside the microwave. Next, she pulled a bottle of ketchup from the fridge.

Asa eyed the bottle. "Why do you need ketchup?"

"I like ketchup on my eggs."

"On eggs? Are you sure?" That sounded disgusting.

That earned him a mischievous grin. "Yes, I'm sure. Are you picking on me?"

"Not at all." He gave her a quick wink before turning back to the griddle.

If Lyric's low tone and Asa's instinct to wink were any indication, they'd now moved to the flirting stage. He had no idea how to flirt. It had been over a decade since he'd dated, and those dates had always been leading to a lifetime together. His relationship history consisted solely of Danielle.

He should stop whatever was getting started with Lyric. Their protected and imagined life inside this cabin wasn't real, and it was dangerous to fall into that comfortable trap.

"I've got the napkins," Lyric said behind him before rushing back to the table.

But they made such a good team. Why did it affect him so much that they moved easily in the same spaces together?

Lyric was hardworking. He could appreciate that about her.

And she was beautiful. He couldn't forget that after he'd memorized her features while she bandaged his head last night.

He'd have to be dead to miss her selflessness. She'd run out into the storm to help him–a stranger.

Asa plated the scrambled eggs and brought them to the table. "Breakfast is served."

Lyric's lighthearted happiness was a complete change from her nervousness last night. The storm was gone, for now, and so were her concerns.

"Thanks so much. This looks great." She eyed the food but didn't reach for any of it.

"What's wrong?" Asa asked.

A glimmer of that uncertainty was back. "I was waiting on the blessing. I was hoping you would say it."

Asa relaxed. It felt good to share a meal with someone who wanted to thank the Lord first, even if she wasn't comfortable enough to say it out loud herself.

"Sure." Asa bowed his head and blessed the food.

Lyric reached for the bacon as soon as her eyes opened. "Where'd you learn to cook like this?"

"Mom made me learn. She said I didn't need a wife if I needed her to cook for me."

Lyric covered her mouth as she choked on a bite of eggs. "She did not."

"She definitely did. It came in handy when Danielle got sick."

"I'm sorry." Lyric pushed her scrambled eggs around her plate. "What happened?"

"Cancer. It took her quickly, but we still had to witness those awful days when she was in pain." The memories still stabbed him in the gut from time to time. Watching the person you love suffer got a hard zero out of ten.

"How did Jacob take it?"

"Horribly."

Lyric tilted her head, clearly upset over the loss of someone she'd never met. "I can't imagine. It's great that he has you though."

"Actually, having each other got us through some hard times."

"That's good." Lyric looked at her plate. "My sister has kids."

The question bubbled up his throat, but he swallowed it back down. Asking Lyric if she wanted kids felt too much like a conversation a man and woman would have if they were dating.

But he wanted to ask. So what if they'd known each other for half a day? They only had each other now, and every minute here had the feel of time condensed by pressure. The end was in sight, and it gave him the urge to cram everything into these dense moments.

Lyric raised her head and sighed. "I'd love to have kids someday, but I don't know if it's in the cards for me."

Asa chuckled at Lyric's serendipitous comment. "Speaking of cards, you up for a game?"

10

ASA

Asa dealt the flop and picked up his cards. "What do you have?"

They'd been sitting on the floor by the fireplace while he taught Lyric the basics of Texas Hold 'em, and a sheen of sweat formed on his temples. Was it the fire or sitting so close to Lyric that had his blood heating?

Lyric leaned closer so he could see her cards. "Seven and two."

Asa chuckled. "Of course you'd get the worst possible hand."

She looked up at him and frowned. "Hey!"

"It's a real thing. Seven two off suit is almost impossible to win with."

Lyric threw her head back and grunted. "I'm terrible at this game."

"Hold 'em is really all about the bluff. When I

was in high school, my friends and I used to have a side bet. Anyone who could win with seven two off suit got the side pot."

"You just said it's the worst hand."

"But if everyone *thinks* you have a better hand than the one they're holding, they might fold."

Lyric narrowed her eyes at him. "You're lying."

"I'm not! At least not right now." He tried to keep a straight face, but his mouth was stretching into a smile, despite his best efforts.

"Did you ever win with this hand?" she asked.

"Never. I'm a terrible liar."

Lyric bumped his shoulder with hers. "That makes sense. You definitely have a good cop vibe going on."

Asa folded his hand and stacked the cards. "You're not the first one to say that."

Lyric nudged him with her elbow. "I didn't mean anything bad by it."

"I know. The phrase always reminds me there are bad cops." Blackwater had a decent force, and he was proud to be a part of it. Unfortunately, he still ran into troublesome officers in his line of work.

Lyric tossed her cards onto the stack. "I'm getting the sense you try to save the world on a regular basis."

"No." His response was quick.

Lyric cleared her throat. "Or yes. Police officers are people, and people aren't always good."

"Yeah, but we're supposed to be better."

Lyric laughed. "Better people? You don't really believe that being a police officer makes you a better person."

"No, it doesn't. But it would be great if the people who took on this responsibility cared about their mission–to serve and protect."

Lyric leaned back against the couch and tucked her legs to the side. "You're a better man than most, police officer or not. Be prepared to be disappointed if you keep those high expectations."

Asa leaned on the couch beside her. "Someone's cynical."

She looked away. "Just realistic. Not everyone has a perfect life."

Asa watched her, noting her tells–averting her gaze, fidgeting her fingers in her lap, and the way she chewed the inside of her cheek.

"Hey," he whispered.

She reluctantly turned to him.

When he had her attention, he held her gaze, daring her to open up to him. "What's your life like?"

She slowly shook her head. The motion was almost indiscernible, but it told him more than her words. "Nothing like yours."

He couldn't imagine it was so different. She didn't have a family, but she had jobs, and they lived in the same town. They both went to church and had friends. That didn't sound so different.

Without warning, she stood. "Let's play a different game. I saw Clue in one of the upstairs closets."

Asa stood, unsure if the quick change in subject was a gift or not. "I don't know how to play that one."

Lyric shouted over her shoulder as she started up the stairs. "Well, I've never played poker, so it's your turn to be at a disadvantage."

Asa rubbed his fingertips over the bandage on his head. He'd been at a disadvantage since yesterday. What was it going to take to get Lyric to trust him? One minute they were talking, and the next minute she was running.

Asa stared at the page in front of him. He'd checked off the cards he'd been dealt, but he hadn't been able to eliminate many others. This game was going to take forever.

Lyric hid her clue sheet behind her hand and scribbled.

"Wait, what are you doing?"

She looked up, and her feigned innocence wasn't convincing. "Nothing."

"Did you just mark something off? How could you have eliminated anything?" he asked.

She laid her sheet face-down on the rug. "It's a secret."

"You're cheating."

"I am not!" She picked up the dice and rolled a combined nine. She hopped her character piece on the Clue board, headed for the pool in the center.

Asa sat up straighter. "What are you doing?"

Lyric tapped her red piece in the middle of the board and looked up at him. Narrowing her eyes, she whispered, "I'm not doing anything, Mr. Green. Just making an accusation."

"There is no way you could already know the answer."

"Oh, but I do. It was me, in the observatory, with the candlestick."

Asa stared her down. "There's no way."

Lyric smiled. "But there is." She reached for the folder that held the answer, and Asa lunged for it at the same time. They wrestled over the folder, until Asa fell over on the board and Lyric toppled beside him. She was laughing, but Asa was determined to get to the bottom of this.

He stretched out on the floor, holding the folder out away from her as he opened it. She fell into another fit of laughter as he pulled out the cards–Miss Scarlet, the observatory, and the candlestick.

Sitting up, he stared at the cards. "How? How did you know?"

Lyric rested her chin on his shoulder. "You're too easy to read."

He turned his head, realizing too late that she

was so close. Less than two inches separated them, and her smile was even more powerful this close.

"What does that mean?" His words were low, born of the half-breath he'd been struggling to take.

"It means I could tell what you had and didn't have based on the suggestions you made and the way you reacted to mine."

"I'm not that easy to read," Asa said. He glanced at her mouth that was perilously close to his.

If he leaned in just one more inch...

"But you are," she whispered.

Her words jerked him out of the trance, and he snapped his gaze back to her eyes. The coy look she gave him said she knew exactly how much he wanted to kiss her.

Maybe Lyric was right. He wasn't being too subtle about the way she affected him, especially when she was so close. It was impossible to drag his thoughts away from her.

She looked down at the cards he held, and he did the same, thankful to be free of her hypnosis.

"You really didn't cheat?" he asked.

"I really didn't cheat. I just narrowed things down until only the correct answer was left."

"You'd make an awesome poker player," he said.

She stood, and Asa tossed the cards onto the board. He'd have to get this game for Jacob. He loved solving riddles and mysteries.

Lyric padded off toward the laundry room. "I'm going to check on the clothes."

Asa picked up the cards and pieces and put them back into the box. Even with Lyric out of sight, he made sure to keep the fluffy robe tied securely around him and covering all important parts.

Yeah, he was putting his clothes back on, wet or dry. Wrestling on the floor was a gamble he wasn't about to attempt again without pants on.

He studied Lyric's check-off card. No wonder she'd won. There were tiny notes in the margins about his facial expressions as well as scattered question marks, circles, and stars. She was using some special Clue code she'd failed to tell him about.

"I have clothes!" Lyric shouted as she ran back into the room. She'd changed back into her jeans and sweater, and her hair was down, hanging in loose waves past her shoulders.

"What is this?" Asa asked, waving the paper in the air.

Lyric laughed and tossed his dry clothes on the couch. "It's a mess up here." She tapped her fingertip against her temple.

"How did you know all this stuff?" Asa asked, waving the clue card in the air.

She laughed again, and the joyful sound wrapped around him, filling his chest with a fire that sparked and grew.

"I want a rematch!" Asa got to his feet, keeping the robe in a good position.

"After lunch. I'm starving."

Asa looked at his phone. They'd been playing games for hours. "Let me get dressed, and I'll hook the generator to whatever we need."

Lyric waved a hand over her head as she headed up the stairs. "I'll figure it out."

Of course she would figure it out. She'd also probably get frostbite or third-degree burns in the process, but he was learning to step back and let Lyric make her own way.

He grabbed his clothes and headed for the nearest bedroom to change.

Back in his clothes, he went looking for Lyric. She'd made two plates with sandwiches and chips.

She was in the middle of a huge yawn when he walked up, and she covered her mouth with one hand and gestured to the bar with the other. "Have a seat."

Asa sat on a barstool, and Lyric slid the plate in front of him.

"What can I get you to drink?"

He rolled his eyes at her impulse to serve but played along. "Water, please."

She turned and grabbed a glass from the cabinet and filled it with tap water. "I promise these dishes are clean."

When she slid the glass onto the bar beside him, she smiled. "Can I get you anything else, sir?"

He rested his elbows on the bar and locked his gaze with hers. "Have you ever been a waitress?" She played the part too well to be someone who didn't know the ins and outs of the service industry.

But a shadow immediately darkened the light in her eyes at his question. "Yeah, once upon a time." She turned her back to him and closed the mayonnaise jar and deli meat container.

Teetering on the edge of caution, Asa let the failed conversation go. Why didn't Lyric want to talk about herself? He knew she had a sister, and he knew where she worked and went to church, but everything else about her was shrouded in mystery. Was she a private person, or was she just not comfortable talking with him?

They were still strangers. They'd met less than a day ago. Why did it feel like longer? Was it the forced proximity? The helpfulness on both sides? The instinctual team mentality they'd slipped into?

Whatever it was, he didn't like the walls she was putting up. The rational and careful thing to do would be to keep his own distance, but logic and reasoning didn't live here.

Lyric grabbed her plate and slid onto the stool beside him. "I tried, but I don't think I'm going to be able to keep my eyes open much longer."

"Take a nap," Asa said before filling his mouth with the sandwich.

"What are you going to do?" she asked.

Watch you sleep wasn't a good answer. "Probably read. I saw a Louis L'Amour book on the shelf upstairs."

"Sounds incredibly entertaining."

Asa chuckled and nudged her shoulder with his. "When was the last time you read a book?"

Lyric tapped a fingertip against her cheek. "High school."

He pinched his lips between his teeth to hide his smile.

"Are you judging me? When was the last time *you* read a book?"

"You got me there. Probably in the academy."

"When was that?" she asked.

Asa squinted up at the fancy light fixture that hung above the bar. "About fifteen years ago."

"Ha! I graduated from high school eleven years ago, and I know I read *Dracula* in my last semester."

"You win, but I'm going to change that while you nap."

Lyric yawned again, and Asa did the same.

She stood, taking her plate with still half a sandwich left to the garbage can. "I'm not worried. I saw that book you're talking about, and it'll take you a month to read it. Plus, I bet you fall asleep too."

"Want to make that an official bet? I bet I can

stay awake and read a hundred pages while you sleep."

She folded her arms across her chest and gave him a confident smirk. "Loser makes dinner?"

"And dessert."

Lyric's eyes widened, clearly intrigued by the mention of treats. "You're on."

They shook on it, and Lyric waved a hand over her head as she sauntered toward one of the bedrooms. "Good night!"

As soon as he heard the bedroom door close, Asa left the remaining chips on his plate and rushed up the stairs, suddenly realizing one hundred pages might be impossible if Lyric decided to only take a twenty-minute nap.

11

LYRIC

"You did not win!" Lyric shouted.

"But I didn't fall asleep."

Asa was cute when he was trying to dig himself out of a hole. Who was she kidding? He was more than cute. Ridiculously handsome? Charming? Too hot for his own good?

"You didn't read one hundred pages. You read thirty!" She picked up the book and flipped to the page he'd marked. She held the measly thirty pages between her fingers and let the rest of the book dangle. "This is pitiful."

Asa pointed a stern finger at her. "Hey, I worked hard on those thirty pages."

"I could *write* thirty pages in an hour and a half. Are you sure you didn't fall asleep?"

Asa jerked back as if she'd slapped him. "Are you insinuating that I'm lying?"

Lyric took a step closer, bracing her hands on her hips. "You don't even know what insinuating means."

"That's it. You've insulted my intelligence." He threw his hands in the air and stalked off. "Bring out Monopoly. I'm taking you to the bank!"

Covering her mouth, she held her breath to dispel the giggle in her throat. Asa could somehow be the determined provider and a lighthearted jokester, and the way he read her like a book only served to stir the warmth in her chest whenever he was around.

"And I'll tell you what insinuate means when I get back!" he shouted from the stairs behind her.

"No cheating!"

"I don't cheat!"

With Asa out of sight, she let the laughter free. Her chest felt lighter than ever. Bubbles of joy burst in her middle, and she might as well have been floating on air.

Maybe it was the nap. She'd been exhausted after the constant storms, and knowing Asa was in the next room calmed her into the deepest sleep she'd had in ages.

She laid the book on the end table, careful to mark his page with the leather coaster. Seconds later, Asa's quick steps thudded on the stairs.

He rounded the corner with the rectangular Monopoly box in his hands and a determined look on his face. "Insinuating is like implying something indirectly."

Lyric tilted her head and tapped a finger against her chin. "Is that what I did? I thought I was pretty direct."

Asa huffed and tossed the box onto the area rug in front of the fireplace. "Stop messing with me and choose your game piece."

Lyric sat on the floor with her knees pulled up to her chest and her back resting against the couch. Thankfully, she was in dry clothes again. The robes were a wardrobe malfunction waiting to happen. "Should I be the banker?"

Asa pointed at her with wide eyes. "Insinuating."

She hid her face in the gap between her chest and knees and giggled softly. She was having too much fun messing with him.

"What's your piece?" Asa asked.

Lyric leaned over the board to study the pieces he'd placed in the middle. "I'll take the car." She reached for it and rubbed the worn metal between her fingers. The classic car sparked a memory that was comforting and dangerous at the same time.

"Really? I had you pegged for a thimble."

"Why the thimble?"

Asa shrugged and picked up the ship. "I don't know. You seem like the type who knows how to sew and do all those classic homemaking things."

"You're joking. I know nothing about sewing."

He counted off a few five-dollar bills and handed them to her. "You seem like you'd know how to do anything. I just took you as the resourceful type."

Resourceful? Yes. Resourcefulness related to homemaking? No. Necessity was just the mother of invention. She'd manipulated her way out of debts and binds, but she'd never been mistaken for the wifely type. Well, she'd been known to messily sew a button back on when she hadn't been able to afford to throw out a shirt, but desperate times called for desperate measures.

She carefully placed the car on the starting square on the corner of the board. "No. Never learned how to sew."

"Why the car?"

Lyric risked a glance at Asa. He'd paused his counting with the bills still in his hands. There was a silent plea in his eyes, waiting with bated breath for some little piece of information about her. So much of her life was covered in the darkness of her addiction, but she could give him a glimpse of one of her favorite memories.

"My dad loved classic cars." She tapped the car piece and leaned back against the couch.

"Loved?"

"He's not dead," Lyric whispered. It was as much as she was going to say about her dad. Asa must have picked up on her unwillingness to say anything else.

"I never get to be the car," Asa admitted. "Jacob is obsessed with anything with wheels and a motor."

"Let me guess. You're always the ship."

"Why do you think that?"

Lyric shrugged. "I've pegged you for the loyal and dependable type."

Asa laid the fake money on the board, rested his arm on his bent knee, and gave her his full attention.

"Is that a bad thing?"

Had she said something wrong? She hadn't meant to upset him.

Lyric shook her head slowly, keeping her gaze locked on Asa. "Not at all."

It was just that those were qualities she'd thrown out the window in her early adult years. Instant gratification, manipulation, and disregard for others were her prevalent traits, and her morals had ceased to exist. Setting her sins up against Asa's clean slate was like trying to mix oil and water. It might look like it was working for a moment, but it would never happen in the end.

Asa picked up a small stack of Monopoly money. "It says we each start with $1,500. You want to count yours to make sure I got it right?"

Fifteen hundred dollars. The amount she was behind on her rent. The colorful papers of the fake money taunted her, and she laid them out on her side of the board. "No, I trust you."

She hadn't meant to sound defeated. It was true

that she trusted him. It was also unfortunate that she had plenty of money to spend on property in a board game but not in real life where she needed it most.

Asa held out the dice. "Ladies first."

Taking the dice into her hand, she felt her good mood slipping away. This was her chance to forget about the worries that waited in the real world. Why couldn't she take advantage of this sheltered care-free time while it lasted?

After five trips around the board, even her pretend wealth was dwindling. Her mood was sinking too, and Asa was clearly easing up on all the buying and building to narrow the gap between them.

"Lyric."

She looked up but stayed quiet.

"Are you okay?" His words were soft and concerned, brushing over her like a comforting touch.

"Yeah." In truth, she was fine. The buying and taking aspect of the game just hit a little too close to home.

"Lie," Asa said.

Lyric tossed the dice onto the board. "Not a lie. I just don't understand how to win this game."

"You buy property and other players pay you when they land on it. It's a race to see who can build up their fortune."

"I've never been good at that." Lyric rubbed her

palms on her thighs, itching to get away from Asa and the game that had her lungs tied in knots.

"We don't have to play. Or we don't have to declare a winner. If you're not having fun, let's do something else."

She rubbed her hands over her face. "I'm sorry. I'm not trying to be a sore loser."

"You mean like I was when you kicked my tail at Clue?"

That eased the tension between them a little. So what if she had some weird hang-up with Monopoly? They could do something else.

But that was quitting–something she hadn't been allowed or able to do since she started the uphill battle to sobriety.

Asa started picking up pieces and cards and stacking them back in the Monopoly box. "You hungry?"

She wasn't really, but figuring out what they would eat and preparing it would take her mind off other things. "I think one of us owes the other dinner."

Asa closed the box and laid it to the side before standing and offering her a hand.

Taking his offered hand wasn't something that should make her think twice. In fact, she should welcome it. He was being a gentleman and helping her off the floor.

Still, taking it felt like a risk because she wanted

so much more than a helping hand. Why did he have to be so good, handsome, kind, and all the things she desperately wanted but had no right to hope for in life?

And now she was being a vapid woman with mercurial feelings. Asa seemed to bring out the insecurities in her along with unfiltered joy.

She was a broken-down car. He was a steadfast ship.

As soon as she placed her hand in his, she felt it–the strength and warmth she craved down to her bones. It swallowed her up, and she was its willing prey.

With one solid movement, Asa pulled her to her feet, but she didn't stop there. Momentum sent her toppling into his chest. Her hand splayed over the hard muscle beneath his shirt, and the rest of her body stopped flush against his.

If being this close bothered him, Asa didn't show it. Her heart was pounding like hooves at the Kentucky Derby, but Asa didn't step away from her. In fact, he leaned down and brushed his lips against her ear. His words were deep, but the wisp of his breath on her ear sent a chill down her spine.

"I fell asleep."

This was a first. Her mind was short-circuiting, and she had no clue what those three words meant. Her skin was alive and humming at his proximity. If she turned her head half an inch, her cheek would brush against his.

Still reeling, she couldn't figure out what he was trying to say. "What?"

"I fell asleep. I lost the bet."

Oh, the bet. She'd just brought it up herself, but the bet was the last thing on her mind when her body was pressed up against Asa's.

When he pulled away from her, his movements were slow, like a magnet pushing against its opposite pole. "I'm going to check in at work and home. Take a look at our dinner options and let me know what you want."

Before she could gather her wits to respond, he was walking away.

12

ASA

Every muscle in Asa's body was coiled tight, strained to the breaking point with tension, as he walked away from Lyric. He wanted to turn back around, but if he did, he wouldn't be able to fight the instinct to pull her in close and press his mouth to hers.

Watching her slowly pull away from him throughout the last few hours had been an eye-opener, and not in any of the ways he'd expected. He wanted her happy and playful the way she'd been when they'd played Clue. When her walls went up, Asa didn't like it.

The realization? Lyric was going to bring him to his knees, whether he was ready or not.

Closing himself in the bathroom, he leaned against the door and pulled out his phone. There were a few emails from Jacob's school monitoring the closure, winter weather alerts, and breaking news headlines. Three texts waited.

Mom: You still okay?

Dawson: Dude, call me.

Chief: Should make it your way tomorrow morning.

Good updates. Asa sent a quick thanks to his boss before calling his mom. When the call went to voicemail, he tried Dawson, who answered on the first ring.

"You're alive!" Dawson shouted.

"I'm snowed in, not on my deathbed."

Dawson exhaled dramatically. "I know, but I was worried. When Chief said you weren't coming in, I just knew it was because you were unalive."

Asa chuckled. "Special circumstances this time, but I'm still breathing."

"I wasn't going to believe it until I heard it from you. Chief said you had a wreck though. You still in one piece?"

"Oh, yeah. Just a scratch." Asa rubbed his fingers over the bandage on his head. It would be sore for a while, but it could have been much worse.

"I also heard you're shacking up with a *woman*." Dawson drawled the last word like a kid in grade school talking about cooties.

Asa pinched the bridge of his nose. Dawson was a good friend because he was honest, loyal, and dependable. Mature, he was not, but he balanced out Asa's stern demeanor. Thanks to

Dawson, Asa had been able to laugh again after Danielle died.

"There's a woman here, but–"

"I heard she's taking good care of you."

Asa jerked his head up. "How'd you hear that?"

"Your mom." Dawson's humor disappeared, replaced by the no-nonsense tone he reserved for sharing information in the line of duty.

That was another reason Asa liked Dawson: He took their responsibilities seriously.

"I stopped by to check on her and Jacob after Chief said you were stuck on the mountain."

"Appreciate it. I talked to her earlier, and she said they were doing okay."

"Yep. Jacob showed me his latest model. A '66 Chevy Nova." Dawson whistled high. "That thing is sharp."

"He's ten. When can I expect the obsession with super rare and expensive cars to subside?" Asa asked.

"Beau never got over it, but look at him now! He's living the dream."

Their friend, Beau Lawrence, was raised on a farm, but he was born to be a mechanic.

"I'm not sure spending eight hours a day covered in grease is considered living the dream," Asa quipped.

"Says you. Beau would think differently. If Jacob

wants a classic car when he turns sixteen, tell him he'll have to build it."

"That's the only way he'd get a car like that." While Asa was happy to spend the time in Beau's garage fixing up cars with Jacob, affording one was a different story.

"Stop that. I can hear you worrying from the other side of town. Jacob is cool. He'll be fine if you don't buy him an expensive car."

"I know." Maybe building a car together was the better option anyway. They already spent a lot of time at Beau's garage.

"You dodged my question about the woman," Dawson said.

Asa had almost believed he could end the call without having to circle back to the topic. "You didn't ask a question, and you already heard all there is to know."

"Is she hot?" Dawson asked.

Asa chuckled once before curbing the reaction. Dawson didn't have a shallow bone in his body, and he only ever talked about one woman.

"I plead the fifth."

"Is she old?"

"Not answering that either."

"Come on! Give me something. Is she standing right there? Is that why you can't talk about her? Say one for yes and two for no."

"No."

"You are terrible at following directions."

"Why did you want me to call you?" Asa asked.

"So I could ask about the woman. Is she single? Will you tell her I'm single?"

A twinge of guilt stabbed through Asa's insides. Was it jealousy? Lyric was single. He was positive of it. She would have put a stop to the flirting by now if she had a guy at home worried about her. Plus, she hadn't asked to use his phone to call anyone but her employers.

But that's not what caught Asa's attention. It was the thought of Dawson with Lyric. It didn't sit right with him.

"What about Olivia?" Asa asked.

Dawson's tone was lower and void of any of the playfulness from the moment before. "What about her?"

Olivia was a sore spot, but it was his first thought after picturing Dawson hitting it off with Lyric.

"Sorry, man. Maybe one day–"

"It's cool. I'll let you know when we get a chance to head up your way. What do you need us to bring?"

He shouldn't have brought up Olivia. Dawson had been holding a torch for Beau's younger sister since they were ten, but Olivia was convinced she and Dawson were better off as friends. That kind of rejection had to sting a man's pride.

"I don't need a paramedic, but I will need a tow," Asa said, happy to change the subject.

"Wrecker it is. See ya."

Asa pocketed his phone and went looking for Lyric. He'd only needed a few minutes away from her to get his head on straight. At least, that's what he kept telling himself.

In the upstairs kitchen, he found her standing in front of the open pantry. Her dark hair fell in a wall down the side of her face and flowed over her shoulder. The instinct to touch it had his fingertips tingling.

"Any luck?" he asked.

She narrowed her eyes, staring intently into the pantry. "I'm trying to think of something to cook on the stovetop or the griddle."

"I'll hook the generator to whatever we need." He reached for a can on the shelf, careful to hold his breath when he was this close to her. The last time he'd been this close, her scent had tingled in his nose, sending sparks into his brain. "Soup?"

Lyric took it from him. "Chicken noodle. Yum."

"Crackers?" he asked, scanning the shelves.

"Right here." Lyric held them above her head as if she'd just completed a challenge.

"Perfect." Asa grabbed three more cans of soup and gestured for Lyric to lead the way back downstairs.

"Do we need all of those?" Lyric asked, eyeing the load of cans.

"I'm a grown man. I'm eating at least three cans of soup."

Lyric laughed and headed for the stairs. "Wouldn't want you to get hangry. Do you keep a stash of doughnuts in your patrol car?"

"You think you're funny, but I happen to like doughnuts. Not because I'm a police officer. They're just good."

Lyric laughed. "Agreed."

The cheerful sound made him forget all about his hunger. They set the soup and crackers on the counter and got to work.

As soon as he finished, his phone rang in his pocket, and he answered the call from his mom.

"Hey, how's it going?"

"Good," his mother crooned. "We're making cookies and goodie bags for the class reading party. It was supposed to be tomorrow, but the teacher called and said they were postponing it to Monday because of the weather."

Asa leaned against the counter and watched Lyric pour the soups into the pot. He was supposed to be cooking, but she'd taken over as if they were two players on the same team. "Jacob going stir-crazy?"

"Not at all. He put together the model car we bought at the hardware store last week."

"Good." Asking a ten-year-old to stay inside all day was tough. If the snow wasn't covering the bottom five feet of everything, he could play with his friends in the neighborhood.

Asa was the kind to get bored inside easily too, but Lyric had kept his attention for hours.

"Everything okay where you are?" his mom asked.

"Great. Lyric is making soup right now."

"Tell her I appreciate her taking care of you," his mother said.

"I could take care of myself if I had to."

"But I'm glad you don't have to. Life is better with someone beside you."

Asa glanced at Lyric. He was a father, and Jacob was his top priority. Staying out of the dating scene had always been the safe option. If he dated, the woman would have to understand Asa and Jacob were a package deal. He wasn't looking for a fling, and he wasn't the type to give up when things got tough.

Indecision warred within him. He wanted to listen to what his mom was saying, but he also didn't want to forget the love he'd had with Danielle. How could he put himself out there again?

Despite all those things, he couldn't ignore the pull he felt toward Lyric. Meeting her had opened his eyes to all the things he'd been missing.

"You're right about that. She's been a big help. Is Jacob around?"

"He just put on those headphone things to play a

game," Asa's mom said, clearly stumped by anything to do with the Xbox.

"I'll call him later. Thanks for everything."

"We've got it covered here. Love you."

"Love you too."

Asa laid the phone on the counter beside him and crossed his arms over his chest. He missed his family, but knowing they were taken care of eased his worries. Was it enough to let him relax and enjoy his time with Lyric?

13

LYRIC

Lyric stirred the soup more than necessary. She'd overheard Asa's conversation with his mother, and the love in his tone both warmed her heart and made her long for that bond she missed with her own parents. As far as she knew, they still lived in a suburb outside of Casper.

She hadn't meant to listen in, but Asa hadn't gone into another room or tried to hide his conversation. She wasn't the sneaky, spying type, but her track record made most people wary of the information they shared around her. Addicts never trusted each other, and with good reason. Her "friends" had been overly cautious, and it hadn't taken her long to build high walls around her life in that environment.

Being around Asa was different, only because he didn't know any better. If he knew the truth, he would have kept her at a distance, shielding himself and the people he loved from the wreckage addicts were known to inflict on anyone who dared get too close.

Asa stepped up behind Lyric, and she bit her lips between her teeth to stifle her smile. It was impossible to ignore her body's reaction when he was so close.

He didn't treat her like a criminal. Well, he had once, but even then, he'd believed she deserved a second chance.

Asa inhaled, and a content hum rumbled in his chest. "Smells great."

"Good. I've been slaving over this meal for hours," she joked.

Asa's soft chuckle sent a thrilling chill up her spine.

He leaned back against the counter beside the stove and crossed his arms over his chest, accentuating his muscles. "Mom said to tell you she's glad you're taking care of me."

"I think it's been the other way around," Lyric admitted.

"Nah. If you hadn't been here, I wouldn't have had a place to go after the wreck."

"But I didn't actually *do* anything," Lyric said.

"You did. You went out in the storm to help. You bandaged my head. You washed and dried my clothes. You ran back into the storm to get the generator."

"That wasn't my most heroic moment."

"It was still appreciated. Of all the people I could have gotten stuck with, I'm glad it was you."

His sincerity was heartbreaking. He was blindly trusting her, and she selfishly wanted to hang onto the hope that he could see the person she was working on instead of the screwup she'd been.

"I'm glad you're the one I got stuck with too, although I hate you're stranded out here away from your family."

"It helps to know they're safe at home."

She risked a glance at Asa, and he was looking back at her. Knowing his family was taken care of left him without anything to focus on except her, and she selfishly wanted all his attention. Asa had a way of making her feel special, wanted even. His gaze was adoring and held none of the scrutiny and glares she usually got from people who knew her past.

"They're lucky to have you," Lyric said.

Asa shifted his stance, which brought them closer together. "Who do you have?"

Lyric's eyes widened. "What do you mean?"

"I mean, your family, friends, anyone. Who's important in your life? I have Jacob, my mom, and my friends. Who do you have?"

Lyric felt her heart rate rise and her breaths strain. She used to have people–ones she could count on–but she'd chased them away with a series of bad decisions.

She tore her gaze from Asa and flipped off the stove burner. "I think this is ready."

Asa caught her arm as she turned to get the bowls. His grip was gentle, asking instead of demanding she acknowledge his question.

"I'm sorry. You don't have to tell me anything," Asa said. "I'm just curious about you. All of this feels like a big step for me, but it also doesn't. Does that make sense? For the first time in years, I want something. I want to know more about you, but only if that's something you want to share with me."

The hurt in his tone made her chest ache. It wasn't his fault she was afraid. He was the last person she should fear. He was the dictionary definition of "good guy," and he didn't deserve the caution that was a part of her everyday life.

"My family isn't like yours. I do have one friend, and she's good to me, but that's all."

Asa's hand slid down her arm. He threaded his fingers with hers and tightened his grip, as if firmly planting himself beside her. "What if I said you can have me?"

That did it. Those words and the sincerity behind them had Lyric's eyes filling with moisture, and she didn't want to break down in front of him.

Before the waterworks started, Asa tugged on her hand. When she let her body sway toward him, he cradled their joined hands to his chest and wrapped his other arm around her. With her cheek resting against his chest, she let a tear silently fall onto his shirt. It was gone in an instant, soaked up by the fabric.

He was pulling the sad and broken parts away from her. Letting the hurt leave and breathing in his comfort freed her in a way she didn't deserve.

"I'm just scared," she whispered.

"Of what? I thought you'd gotten the memo I'm not an ax murderer."

Lyric chuckled and buried her face deeper into his chest. His grip tightened around her, and she inhaled. Asa's embrace was the perfect combination of strength and gentleness as he offered her something that wasn't intended for her. A woman with a rap sheet didn't get to find happiness with a man like Asa.

She sighed and lifted her head. "I don't know. It's stupid."

"Nothing you're scared of is stupid. Well, if you told me you're scared of bunnies or something, I might think that was stupid."

A giggle bubbled out of Lyric's chest. There was a time in her life when she had been fearless to a fault. *She* was reckless, and she hadn't been afraid of anything.

Now, she knew what it was like to lose everything.

When Asa said she could have him, she'd been instantly afraid of losing him. But looking up at him erased some of her worry. The look in his eyes promised honesty, and she clung to it like a lifeline. If she wanted Asa, she'd have to be brave enough to fight for something out of her reach.

"I'm scared of this. You. I'm scared because what I feel is big and fast. I know things wouldn't be the same if we'd met under different circumstances, and–"

"But we didn't," Asa interrupted. "We met this way, and maybe that was what we both needed." His gaze lowered to where his hands rubbed up and down her arms. "I haven't taken the time to meet someone or date. I'm not sure I would have ever stepped out of my comfort zone and allowed myself to see *anyone*."

Lyric held her breath. It was stupid to pray he would see her, but she wanted him to want her.

Asa cupped her chin and lifted it, bringing her gaze to meet his. "But I'm glad I met you this way. I'm glad we've gotten to know each other. I'm glad it was you."

"Me too," she whispered.

"Is there a chance you'd let me take you out after we get out of here?"

"Yes." Her answer was quick. This was everything she wanted, and she didn't have the willpower to push him away.

His gaze dropped to her lips, and he swallowed hard. "I guess kissing before the first date is off-limits."

"Yes. I mean, no." She shook her head, rattled by his words. Goodness, she couldn't think straight with him this close.

He leaned in until his lips were just a breath from hers. "Are you sure?" he asked, his whisper deep and rough as if he were holding back.

Lyric swallowed hard. She might pass out from lack of oxygen before Asa kissed her. "Yes."

He dipped his head to press his lips to hers. She inhaled a deep breath, fighting against dizziness as Asa filled her senses. He kissed her hard and soft, adoring and sweet, fiery and promising. Her head swam with a high like none other.

A kiss had never seared her like this before. Asa's arms wrapped around her, pulling her onto her toes as she moved her hands up his chest. She clung to his shoulders as his lips moved against hers.

When he pulled away, she gasped for breath, thankful for the reprieve. She needed to figure out which way was up.

His strong hand slid slowly from the nape of her neck down and over her shoulder, leaving a scorching trail on her skin. "Full disclosure. I know I should step away from you right now, but I really don't want to."

Lyric chuckled. "Same."

He inhaled two more deep breaths before pressing his mouth to hers again. She wrapped her arms around his neck and lifted onto her toes. She wanted more, but would she ever have enough? Asa was goodness and light, and she wanted nothing more than to sink into the safety he offered.

Finally, he broke the kiss and cleared his throat. His fingers threaded with hers, and he took a deep breath. "The soup is getting cold."

"Right. Let's eat." Lyric turned and let her fingers fall from his, immediately missing the contact. She needed a million tasks to distract her from Asa's all too tempting kisses. More than the amazing kiss, he'd told her in beautifully arranged words that she was special. He was taking a chance and making a big change in his life with *her*.

She took deep breaths, trying to calm her racing heart. No one told her that opening her heart could be the best feeling she'd ever known.

14

LYRIC

sa scrolled on his phone for a few seconds before dropping his spoon into the empty bowl.

"Three cans of soup wasn't enough?" Lyric asked.

He tilted the phone so she could see the screen and pressed a button. A live forecast played over the radar.

The meteorologist waved in front of the map. "I'm afraid we're in for another round tonight. This band is sweeping in fast, and it's already left destruction in Idaho this afternoon. Expect high winds and more downed trees. If you've been lucky enough to keep the power on, prepare to lose it during this round. Remember to keep a stock of clean water and get those generators ready. Under no circumstances should you try to brave this storm. Stay where you are and stay safe."

"Wow, that's pretty ominous," Lyric said.

Asa laid the phone down and picked up his bowl. "We don't have much to worry about here, but not everyone is prepared for things like this." He picked up her empty bowl and headed to the sink.

Lyric wrapped her arms around her middle. Asa was right. Even if she'd been stuck at her place during this storm, she wouldn't have been nearly as comfortable as this. "I bet you see the worst of the damage when things like this happen."

He stepped to the sink and started washing the dishes. "I usually don't have much downtime to think about it. Going from one job to the next helps keep my mind off it."

Lyric walked toward him, but he didn't look up from the dishes he was scrubbing. When she stopped beside him, the muscles in his jaw tensed.

"I hate that you have to see all that," she said. "But I'm glad you do what you do. Not everyone is that brave."

It had taken years before she could look back at the rock bottom she'd been living in and see the good in anything. She'd been a part of the wreckage Asa and the other police officers had to deal with every day, and the guilt was thicker than the snow burying her car in the driveway.

She took the opportunity to watch him. All she'd known for years were selfish people, yet this guy was perfectly safe and comfortable during a natural disaster and wishing he could be out in the storm helping people.

When he finished washing the dishes, he dried his hands on a towel and rested his palms on the edge of the counter. A low scoff vibrated out of his chest, and he looked over to her. "I'm glad you're here. I know we wouldn't have even met if it wasn't for the storm, but now that I know you, I'm worried about what could have been if you'd been stuck out here alone. Is that crazy?"

Lyric's chest tightened. He did know her. He just didn't remember. "You wouldn't be worried about me if you never knew I existed. I would be just another stranger in this storm."

He pulled her to him and wrapped an arm around her back. She fell into his warm embrace as he pressed a kiss to the top of her head.

She nuzzled into the warmth of his chest as her throat constricted. He wouldn't be concerned about her at all if he remembered her. She'd be another nuisance he'd been forced to deal with. Another problem he'd taken care of that kept him busy. Another inconvenience who stole time from his family.

"Asa, I'm sorry," she whispered.

His strong hand brushed over her hair. "You didn't do anything. We'll get out of here, and I'll get right to work. There's plenty to do, even in the aftermath of a storm like this."

Good grief, the lump in her throat was growing, making it hard to speak. "I'm sorry you're not with your family."

He held her tighter. "They're okay. Jacob is a good kid, and my mom is always prepared for things like this. Yeah, I wish I was there too, but if I wasn't here, I still wouldn't be at home with them. I'd be working."

Turning her head, she wiped the tear that was sneaking out of the corner of her eye on his shirt.

"Are you tired of being stuck here?" he asked.

A soft chuckle bubbled out of her chest. "Not really. Stranded with a handsome man in a luxury cabin isn't something to complain about."

Asa hummed. "Handsome?"

She swatted his chest and lifted her head. "Don't act like you didn't already know you're hot."

"Oh, I've progressed to hot now. Keep going. You think I could be sexy before dessert?"

If he only knew. Asa was the perfect mix of masculine and model. The beard that was filling in fast only upped her attraction.

At this rate, dessert sounded dangerous.

Asa rubbed his beard. "Speaking of dessert. How do you feel about s'mores?"

Lyric arched an eyebrow. "Does anyone have negative feelings about s'mores? They're probably the best treat ever."

Asa grinned. "A woman after my own heart."

With a wink, he stepped around her toward the pantry. "I saw everything we need earlier. Meet me at the fireplace with plates and skewers."

"Skewers?"

"I saw some in the silverware drawer," he called over his shoulder.

After taking a moment to shake off the chill his wink had given her, she grabbed the things they needed. Somehow, Asa always knew how to cheer her up when she was sinking into a pity party about the unfairness of her situation.

Stranded in a snowstorm: not great.

Stranded with a stranger: not great.

Stranded with Asa: great and terrible at the same time.

Sinking to her knees at Asa's side in front of the fireplace, she started opening the snacks. "Are you a slightly toasted or burnt to a crisp kinda guy?" she asked.

"Perfectly toasted. It takes patience, but it's so worth it when you get that even gooeyness all the way through."

Lyric laughed. "Are you serious? How long does that take?"

Asa snatched the skewers from her. "Laugh it up, but you'll see. This first one is for you."

She scoffed and reached into the marshmallow bag. "Fine. Then my first one is for you. If I have to try yours, you have to try mine."

Asa scrunched his nose. "Do I have to? I can already tell you it'll taste like ashes."

She flipped the marshmallow and moved it closer to the flame. "How does Jacob like his marshmallows?"

That earned her a heart-stoppingly handsome grin. "Perfectly toasted, just like me."

"Did you teach him the art of toasting?"

"I didn't actually. He's a patient kid. Way more patient than I was at his age. He likes to build model cars, so he's used to focusing on one thing for hours at a time."

"Hours?" Lyric mouthed "Wow" as she pulled the stick closer to inspect the doneness of the marshmallow on the end. A black, bumpy crispiness had formed over the entire thing, hiding any trace of white that lingered in the middle. "I think it's done."

She swung the stick toward Asa, and the marshmallow slid right off the end, crunching against the front of his shirt.

"I'm sorry. I'm sorry!"

Asa grabbed the collar and pulled the front of the shirt away from his chest as the gooeyness slid down. "It's okay."

"Did it burn you?" Lyric asked as she grabbed a plate and tried to peel the marshmallow off his shirt with the skewer.

He put his marshmallow and stick down beside hers. "Nah. I have good reflexes."

"Tell me about it. I've never seen anyone move that fast." She picked at the sticky mess on his shirt, but it kept spreading.

Asa held up a hand. "Wait. Let me get it."

Lyric rested back onto her heels as he reached behind his head. Grabbing the collar of his shirt, he pulled it off in one quick motion.

And just like that, his bare chest was on full display. Suddenly, she wasn't too upset about almost charring his skin with molten goo.Knowing he had broad shoulders was one thing. Knowing everything beneath his shirt was stacked with muscle was serious torture.

He balled up the shirt and stood. "Looks like this shirt gets another wash. Seriously, my clothes have never been so clean."

"Uh-huh." Lyric stared up at him, holding the plate of marshmallow mess like she had no idea what to do with her hands.

"We're gonna need a redo on both of those." He pointed to the mess on the plate. "I'll be right back."

"Uh-huh." Lyric watched him walk away before covering her gaping mouth. Being stranded with Officer Asa Scott was definitely a good thing.

15

ASA

Asa left Lyric in the living room with her jaw on the floor. He didn't care one bit about his looks, but working out was a part of the job he enjoyed. It helped that Jacob was starting to show interest in running. He could run laps around the gym while Asa lifted weights.

Tossing his shirt into the washing machine, he set it for a short cycle and headed back to the living room.

Lyric sat in front of the fire holding a marshmallow over the flames, carefully watching it as she slowly rotated the stick.

"A watched mallow never toasts," he said as he sat beside her.

"I'm giving the perfectly toasted thing a try. If I have the patience, that is. It's starting to look really tasty."

He grabbed the bag and put another on his skewer. "Once you try it, you'll never go back."

Lyric rolled her eyes, then returned her gaze to the task at hand. "We'll see about that. This is a lot of work."

"The best things in life are worth the hassle."

That earned him a look. She tilted her head and inhaled a deep breath. "Someone else told me that once."

"Really? Was it good advice?"

She looked back to the fire, and a small wrinkle formed between her brows. "It was. Still is. I guess that means I need to trust you on this one."

Asa bumped his shoulder against hers. "You should probably trust me all the time. Just sayin'."

"Do people always trust you?" she asked, a hint of sadness lacing her question.

"Not at all. It's not because I don't try."

"It's because you deal with criminals all the time."

"It's not just that. I have to get along with judges, attorneys, probation officers, dispatchers, and other first responders. Sometimes, it's easy. Sometimes, I take out my frustration on a punching bag after work."

Lyric tilted her head until it rested on his shoulder. "How do you always know the right thing to do? Is that something you're born with or do they teach it in a class?"

Asa lifted her chin with a finger until she was looking up at him. There wasn't a hint of the smile he'd come to crave. "I don't always know the right thing to do, and I don't pretend I know it all either. There are some things I feel strongly about, and I'll fight for those truths. But there are still a lot of things I don't know, like why you're sad right now."

She shook her head. "I'm not sad. Just thinking too much." She pulled her marshmallow away from the flames. "I think it's ready."

"Take a bite and find out."

She slid the mushy marshmallow off the stick and took a bite. After a few chews, she let out a humming sound. "You win. It's delicious."

Asa turned his stick over the fire. "I'm just glad you like it. You want this one with the chocolate and graham crackers?"

Lyric popped the rest of the marshmallow into her mouth and shook her head. "That one's yours," she said around the mush she chewed.

"No, it's yours too. Get the crackers ready."

She grabbed for the plate where she had crackers and chocolate laid out. He pulled the marshmallow away from the flames, and she squished it between the two halves.

"Man, this looks too good." She took a bite, and her eyes rolled toward the ceiling. "It's amazing. You have to try this."

Asa held up a hand. "No, it's for you."

"Please," she said as she held the s'more out to him.

"Okay, but I'm making you as many as you want." He took it and bit off half the remaining s'more.

Lyric wiped her mouth. "It's amazing, isn't it?"

Her gaze fell to his lips, and he had to focus on swallowing the bite he'd been chewing. Lyric had quickly taken over his thoughts and was testing every ounce of his willpower. Now that he knew what it was like to kiss those lips, he wanted more.

She looked up at the bandage on his head. "I should change that. Let me get the first-aid kit."

Within seconds, she was on her feet and jogging out of the room. Asa rested his head in his hand. What was he doing? So, they were stranded together. Alone. Were any of the feelings he was having real?

They sure felt real. Every time he looked at Lyric or she made a point to take care of him or joke around, he felt it all the way down to his bones.

Was it the same for Lyric? Would their lives be so different when they left the cabin? Could a relationship work? Did Lyric even want one?

Asa stood and paced on the area rug. Did she even want it to work? She could be a serial dater. She could be in it for just a fling.

But Asa wasn't a fling kinda guy, and he wouldn't ever be. When he made up his mind about Danielle, he was all in. It didn't take him long to realize she was the one for him either. They'd been high school sweethearts, and there hadn't been any of the typical on-again, off-again stuff. He'd known they were meant for each other from the beginning.

It might help him know what to expect if he had any other dating experience. Still, the pull he felt toward Lyric was familiar. It was the same way things had started with Danielle.

Jogging back into the room, Lyric settled down on the couch with the kit. "I think this might be the last time it needs changing."

Asa swallowed hard, trying to clear the lump in his throat. He sat facing her on the couch. "Yeah. I don't think it'll bleed anymore."

Her delicate fingers gently pulled back the tape and gauze from his head. He couldn't tear his attention away from her face. Her dark eyes focused on his injury, and she bit the side of her bottom lip. He had plenty of time to memorize the lines of her jaw, the angle of her nose, and the shallow dimple in her cheek.

With the bandage off, she put it to the side and started measuring out gauze and tape. "Pretty sure this one is gonna leave a scar."

Asa didn't need a reminder. Every moment from the time he hit that tree was seared into his memory. Lyric Woods made sure of that.

She taped the new bandage on his forehead, but her fingers lingered on his skin, brushing down his beard and over his jaw.

Her gaze met his, and he couldn't hold back anymore. Leaning in, he captured her mouth with his. His hand slid up her neck and into her hair as she latched her arms around his shoulders.

Everything about Lyric was wild and unchecked. She pulled him in and wrapped him around her finger without a single word. She looked at him with kindness, and every defense he had melted in her wake.

Being alone with her without any distractions was dangerous. It didn't help that he was shirtless and every brush of her hands over his shoulders left a fire in its wake.

Lyric jerked back, pressing her hand to her mouth.

"What? What's wrong?"

"Your phone," she whispered.

As if on cue, the phone in his pocket buzzed. Had it been ringing?

He pulled it out and checked the screen before showing it to Lyric. "It's my mom."

She nodded and stood. "I'll give you some privacy."

He hadn't meant to imply he wanted her to leave, but she probably needed a breather as much as he did.

Asa answered the call but kept watching Lyric as she walked away. "Hello."

"Hey. Just checking in. I think Jacob is officially

exhausted, and I thought you might want to say good night."

"It's barely eight." Jacob didn't usually stay up late, but eight was a little on the early side.

"He went out and played with some kids in the neighborhood earlier. I guess trudging through snow all day is hard work."

"How are you?" Asa asked.

"Peachy. I made apple butter today and got those canned for the year. The power came back on around eleven this morning."

"That's good. Did you have enough gas for the generator?"

"You know I did. You check that thing like the gas in it might just disappear one day. Oh, here's Jacob."

"Hey, Dad."

Asa rested back against the couch. "Hey. How was your day?"

"Fine. Just hung out with Tyler and Max."

The kid always got to the point. Short and sweet. "Sounds like a good day."

"It was. Miss you."

"I miss you too, bud. Chief said I should be out of here in the morning, but I'll probably have to go straight to work. Can you take care of Granny until I get home?"

"No problem."

Jacob had a protector's heart. It had been ingrained in him from the beginning. Asa had seen him take up for other kids when he was a toddler, and he still had that same fortitude when standing up to bullies.

"See you tomorrow," Jacob said.

"You be safe. Love you," Asa's mom added.

"Love you too."

Asa ended the call and started looking for Lyric. He found her in the laundry room starting his shirt in the dryer. "Thanks for doing this."

She turned to him but quickly looked at the floor. "It's not a problem. Actually, you being shirtless is the problem."

Good to know he wasn't the only one whose attraction was through the roof. "Should I put on the robe?" he joked.

She looked up at him and smirked. "You don't have to, but maybe keep a healthy distance when you have those muscles on full display."

He crossed his arms over his chest and leaned a hip against the doorframe. "Noted."

"Everything okay at home?" she asked.

"All good. Those two keep busy. Is there anyone you need to call?"

Lyric shook her head. "Nope."

"No one at all?" It was hard to believe she didn't have anyone who cared about her. She clearly had a heart for helping others.

She fidgeted with her fingers for a moment before sighing. "Okay. I should probably let my neighbor know I'm okay since I haven't been home."

Asa handed over his phone and pushed off the doorframe. "I'm going to check on the generator. Take all the time you need. And, Lyric?"

Her gaze lifted to his face, and those dark eyes pierced him like a knife to the gut.

"Thanks for bandaging my head. And everything else you've done."

A small smirk lifted her cheeks. "Happy to do it."

He turned and headed to get his coat. Maybe the shock of the cold outside would take his mind off Lyric.

16

LYRIC

Slipping into one of the bedrooms, Lyric turned her phone on and looked up Wendy's number. Last they'd talked, Lyric was coming to the realization she would be snowed in at the cabin.

Really, she wasn't giving her neighbor an update. Lyric was the one who wanted the update. Russell might be stuck at the apartment complex with nothing to do but wait around to throw that eviction notice in her face.

Wendy answered on the third ring, laughing as she said, "Hello."

"Hey. How's everything?"

"Fine. Just trying to survive. Jaycee is here, and I think we've eaten everything in the apartment."

Lyric rubbed a hand over her chest, trying to massage out the ache. If she'd been snowed in at the apartment, she'd be out of food by now too. "You can grab something from my place. I know I have a jar of peanut butter and some bread."

Wendy laughed again. "Thanks. We might do that." She gasped. "How are you? I've been so worried."

"I'm fine. My boss said we could eat the food here since the renters wouldn't be coming."

"We?" Wendy asked. "Who's with you?"

Why did Lyric's throat close? It should be so easy to say his name, but giving air to the words would take the private life she'd been living with Asa and make it public.

Why did she want to keep it all to herself?

"A man had a wreck near the cabin, and he's been staying here too."

"Girl! Please be careful. Men are pigs."

Not this man. Asa had been nothing but kind and courteous to her. "I know. I'll keep my guard up, but so far, he's been very nice."

"I can't believe you're stranded with a stranger. How scary is that?"

Not a stranger exactly.

"Is this his phone you're calling from?" Wendy asked.

"Yeah. I'm out of minutes."

"Do you have any idea how worried I was when you weren't answering my calls?"

"Sorry, but it's hard to keep everything floating."

Wendy sighed. "I know. Sorry, girl. If it helps, Russell hasn't been by looking for you again."

A breath that had been trapped in Lyric's chest escaped with a rush. "Thanks. I was hoping that was the case."

"I've got your back. We'll take you up on that peanut butter offer and hold down the fort here."

"Thanks. I appreciate it. I should be back tomorrow."

"Stay safe. Bye."

Lyric cradled the phone in her hands and sat on the side of the bed. She'd been terrified to be stuck here, but now she didn't want to leave. The real world was waiting for her with a daunting eviction notice, but things here were straight out of a fairy tale.

She and Asa had formed an understanding team. They helped each other out, shared the workload, and encouraged each other through everything.

A door closed outside the bedroom, and she stood to take Asa's phone back to him. It dinged in her hand, and she instinctively looked at the screen.

Jacob: Love you, Dad. Good night.

She clutched the phone to her chest. Everything inside her said Asa was a good man, and as desperately as she wanted the safety and care he could give her, she didn't deserve it. She'd already given him plenty of reasons not to trust her, whether he remembered or not.

Clutching the phone, she made her way back to the living area. Asa was in the kitchen closing up the snacks from their s'mores dessert.

"Everything okay?" he asked.

"Yeah. My neighbor is running low on food, so I told her to help herself to my pantry."

"Your pipes are treated, right?"

"Yeah, my landlord stays on top of stuff like that." She handed him the phone. "Thanks for letting me make a call. You got a text a minute ago."

Asa looked at it and quickly responded. "Jacob. He worries a lot."

"He must have gotten that from his mom. You seem like the cool, calm, and collected type."

Asa huffed. "Not always. You should have seen how not cool, calm, and collected I was when she was going through cancer treatment and it wasn't working."

Lyric started tidying up the kitchen area. "I can't imagine how hard that would be."

"The worst part was feeling useless. There was literally nothing I could do to help her, and for someone who likes to be in control of all situations, it was like having my arms tied behind my back while she suffered."

A fire burned in the back of her throat. She didn't have anyone in her life she loved like that, except Kendra. It was difficult to even imagine what Asa had been through.

Lyric closed the space between them and wrapped her arms around Asa. Resting her head on his chest, she listened to the steady beat of his heart as the tension in his shoulders melted away.

"It's in the past. It took a long time to get over it, but I had to trust it was all the Lord's plan. Once I figured that out, I stopped looking at it like something had been taken from me and started looking at my life and reminding myself about the good I still have."

Lyric raised her head. "Will you tell me about him?"

"Jacob?"

"Yeah."

Asa liked talking about his son, and Lyric wanted to soak up anything and everything about the man who had taken up all the space in her thoughts since they'd been stuck in the cabin together.

Well, she didn't feel stuck, since she was enjoying herself, but Asa would probably rather be with his family, with good reason.

Asa told her story after story about Jacob and the things he loved and had done over the years while they cleaned up the kitchen together. They worked seamlessly in the same spaces until everything was in its rightful place.

The dryer beeped in the laundry room just as Asa put away the last clean bowl in the cabinet. "Right on time."

Lyric gathered the dirty rags and followed Asa. He pulled his shirt out of the dryer and slipped it on.

"Shoot. Looks like the show is over," Lyric said.

Asa rolled his eyes. "I'm not the walk around with my shirt off kinda guy."

She tossed the rags into the washing machine. "It's a shame."

With a smirk, he slid his arms around her waist and nuzzled his face against her neck, kissing the sensitive skin. "Should I expect you to spill breakfast on my shirt in the morning?"

A shiver raced down her spine, spreading all the way into her toes. "Um, maybe."

Lifting his head, he chuckled low and pushed a lock of her hair behind her ear. "Do you need to get anything out of your car?"

She blinked a few times, trying to focus on his question with him standing so close. "Um, I don't know."

"You might have to leave it here for a few days. Money? Weapons? Anything you wouldn't want someone to be able to steal if they decided to break the windows?"

"Oh, I guess I have both of those in there." The gun had been a gift from Kendra and her husband. They often worried about her living alone where she did, though Lyric had never had any trouble at her apartment and wasn't sure she could use the thing if worse came to worst.

"I'll shovel the snow away, then you can tell me where the stuff is."

"I'll help," Lyric said.

"You don't have to. It won't take me long. To be honest, I just need a distraction."

Lyric bit her lips between her teeth. He was trying to be a gentleman, and the realization had her heart warming. Abstinence was one of the values she'd adhered to since getting sober and finding Christ, and despite the circumstances that allowed for plenty of temptation, Asa's will was stronger.

Who knew self-control was so attractive? As if she needed another reason to like him. There were already so many.

"I insist. I want to help," Lyric said.

"I think I saw an extra shovel around back. I'll grab it and meet you in the front." He started to walk out of the laundry room but turned to face her. "And please bundle up before we go out there. The wind is brutal."

Lyric nodded, stunned by his thoughtfulness. "Got it."

THE ICY COLD stung in Lyric's chest as she tossed another pile of snow away from her car. The vehicle was completely hidden, and they'd been shoveling for nearly a quarter of an hour without a sign of it.

Lyric rested the scooper end of the shovel on the ground. "I'm not sure it's here."

Asa didn't stop shoveling. "It's here. We just got way more snow than I realized."

She looked up at the dark sky where tiny flakes were still falling, mocking her as they gradually added to the pile she and Asa were trying to move. Her teeth rattled together as she turned to inspect the pile of snow they'd relocated. Yep, still a huge pile, just in another place.

"Please go inside. I can handle this," Asa said.

Her words were shaky as she said, "I'm fine."

He stopped and studied her for a few seconds before stabbing his shovel into the ground and walking toward her. He took her shovel and did the same before bending down to lift her into a cradle hold.

"What are you doing?" she said, hanging onto his shoulders.

"Taking you inside. I can't watch you shiver any longer."

"Asa, I really don't need—"

"Shoveling snow is not important. You are."

She stared at him as he carried her onto the porch and inside the cabin. Her desire to help came from a deep need to prove herself, but Asa had touched a need she hadn't even known existed.

He thought she was important. He thought she had value. She buried her face in his neck, unsure if the moisture in her eyes was from the stinging cold or Asa's sweet gesture.

Once they were inside, he didn't stop at the door. He carried her to the couch before resting her on her feet. He pulled off her jacket and grabbed a nearby blanket, wrapping it around her. When she was seated, he knelt in front of her and pulled off her boots.

"Asa," she whispered.

He looked up at her with a softness in his eyes that melted the cold that had settled in her skin. "Yeah?"

There were too many thoughts running through her head. A whirlwind of appreciation and kindness that she didn't understand tangled her words in her throat.

"Thank you." She mouthed the words, but they didn't make a sound.

Asa must have understood. He stood and pressed his lips to her forehead. "I'll be finished shortly. Just get warm."

She snuggled into the blanket as soon as Asa disappeared. Closing her eyes, she said a heartfelt prayer of thanks to the Lord for sending help when she needed it most.

~

LYRIC BLINKED and stretched her aching legs. Her vision slowly cleared, and she looked around in the dim light. She'd fallen asleep on the couch, and every muscle was protesting.

Asa lay back in the reclining love seat. His arms were crossed over his chest, and his eyes were closed in peaceful sleep.

Lyric rested her head back and sighed. There was a good chance they'd be able to leave the cabin today, and things would go one of two ways. Asa would want to keep their relationship going, and she'd have to tell him the truth. Or he'd figure out that the feelings from the last few days weren't real, and she'd never hear from him again.

Was she going to be strong enough to do the right thing if he wanted to keep seeing her? How was she going to handle the heartache when he walked away?

She slowly pulled the blanket off and stood without making a sound. She had no idea when he'd gotten in from shoveling snow, and it was her mission to let him sleep as long as possible.

She took the opportunity to watch him as his chest rhythmically rose and fell. The bandage on his head did nothing to mar his looks. His short hair was slightly tousled, and the scruff on his cheeks gave him a rugged look.

Taking advantage of his deep sleep, she moved to his side and gave in to the urge to thread her fingers in his hair. He'd taken the initiative and kissed her both times, and she wouldn't be brave enough to make the first move when he was awake. Leaning down, she pressed her lips to his forehead next to the bandage before sneaking out of the room.

In the bathroom, she splashed her face with cold water and used one of the toothbrushes she'd bought for the guests. They'd racked up quite a list of things to pay Brenda back for after this was over.

Once she felt semi-clean, she stripped the beds she and Asa had slept on and tossed the sheets into the wash. She made her way through half of her usual cleaning list before Asa stretched on the love seat.

"Lyric?"

"Morning!" she called from the kitchen.

He slowly made his way across the big open room, stretching his neck from side to side. "How long have you been up?"

"A couple of hours."

He slid his arms around her and cuddled her close to his warm body. Relaxing in his arms, she savored every second of his sweet embrace.

"Good morning. How did you sleep?" he whispered against her ear.

"Best sleep I've had in ages," she said. It was the truth. The cold had zapped her energy, and she'd been toasty warm by the low fire. "Are you ready for breakfast?"

"I could eat. I need to check on the generator."

"I'll make something for us. You go do that."

He pressed a quick kiss to her cheek. "I won't be long."

The cracking of her heart might as well be a gunshot in the room. This perfect life would soon be gone. She'd been so blissfully ignorant to this kind of happiness before, and life after would be colorless and dim in comparison.

She mixed batter for pancakes and started them on the griddle. The heaviness in her gut threatened to pull her to the floor as she worried over what she would tell Asa.

He walked back into the room and hummed. "Something smells amazing."

"Pancakes. Nothing special," Lyric said.

Asa stepped up behind her as she flipped a pancake. He wrapped his arms around her. "Do you have everything you need when you get back home? Did your neighbor say you had power?"

Ugh. Reality was determined to interfere this morning. "She didn't have power last night, but hopefully it's on today."

Asa's phone rang, and he lifted it to his ear. "Hello."

"She okay?" Asa asked the person on the other end of the line as he stepped away from Lyric and leaned against the bar. "Good. I'll ride with you to check on her after I get the truck towed."

The call was quick, and Asa was pocketing his phone just as Lyric finished plating a stack of pancakes.

"Everything okay?" she asked.

Asa reached for the small bottle of syrup. "Yeah, Mrs. Grant lost power when we did, and she can't get out to get wood for her fireplace. They're clearing this road to get to her, so that means we're getting out of here this morning. Probably within the next hour, from what my friend said."

An hour? She needed more time. It was time to come clean, and she wasn't ready.

She stood frozen, until Asa turned around with a plate filled with pancakes and handed it to her. "Let's eat." He gestured toward the table, indicating she should lead the way.

Moisture filled her eyes as she sat at the table, and she quickly brushed it away. Asa blessed their food, but she didn't hear the words. The only sound she heard was the pumping of blood rushing in her ears.

Before she took the first bite, Asa reached over and laid a hand on hers. "Hey, what's wrong?"

"Nothing." She shoveled the first bite into her mouth to hide her lie. They didn't have to talk if they were eating, right? She could at least put it off until after breakfast.

As soon as Asa finished the last of his pancakes and let his fork clink on the plate, Lyric was on her feet. "I'll clean up." She grabbed their plates and rushed to the kitchen.

Asa was close behind her, determined to help. She kept her head down and focused on cleaning, until he spoke.

"Are you sure everything is okay? You seem quiet."

It was time to face the music. Lyric turned around and dried her shaking hands on the dish towel. She only had to get the first words out. The rest would be easy.

"We've met before."

Asa's eyes widened. "We did? Where? When?"

Lyric took a deep breath and straightened her shoulders. "You arrested me ten years ago."

17

ASA

The words punched him in the gut. Of all the ways he could have imagined meeting Lyric before, arresting her wasn't one of them.

He pinched the bridge of his nose and prayed this was all a dream–a nightmare. Ten years was a long time, and she was still young. What could she have possibly done back then?

"I did a lot of bad things," she whispered shakily.

"What kind of bad things?" The ball of unease in his middle was growing and writhing. He should have kept his mouth shut. He probably didn't want to know.

Her chest rose and fell quickly, and her whole face was turning red. "I was drunk. And I threw a brick through a store window."

Asa's eyes widened as he studied the woman

standing in front of him. She didn't look like a vandal. She looked like the woman who had tended his wounds, cooked him meals, and shared her life with him for the last two days.

But he'd been trained not to be deceived by appearances, hadn't he? He saw the worst deceit every day, and it didn't look anything like Lyric.

"What else?"

Her shoulders tensed, rolling forward as if she wanted to curl up and hug her knees to her chest. "Just those things...that time."

Asa's brows lifted. "There were other times?"

"Well, *you* only arrested me once."

Clearing his throat, Asa tried to push down the growing unease in his gut. "But someone else arrested you the other times?"

Lyric nodded. The motion was almost imperceptible.

He rubbed his jaw and leaned against the counter. She'd been so good to him. It was hard to reconcile the destructive young girl with the kind woman who'd gone above and beyond to help him. The disconnect between the two had him questioning everything he thought he knew.

"But I'm clean now. Sober for a little over five years."

Asa knew enough addicts in his line of work to know they could rarely be trusted. Even knowing how easy it was for addicts to pull the wool over someone's eyes, it didn't seem like a lie when Lyric said she was sober.

"Your family?" he asked.

"I pushed them away. Or they left me. I'm not sure which happened first, but it's for the best. I hurt them. A lot."

It took everything he had to understand what Lyric was telling him. "What made you quit?" he asked.

When Lyric didn't answer right away, he reached for her hand and brushed his thumb over her skin. "Relax. We're just talking."

"I almost died," she whispered.

The words were small and scared. The thought of Lyric being on the precarious line between life and death made him sick to his stomach. He didn't have a good response, so he kept quiet, hoping he'd be able to settle his mind and his heart while she did the talking.

Lyric leaned against the counter beside him, and that sweet scent he'd come to love was in the air. It was everywhere. *Lyric* was everywhere, and there was no getting away from her now.

"Rock bottom is an ugly place. I overdosed. I was in a coma, and when I woke up, Kendra was there."

"Kendra Bates who works at Deano's?" His mom had mentioned Kendra knew Lyric, but he hadn't expected this to be their connection.

Lyric chuckled, but the sound was sad. "Yeah.

That Kendra. It doesn't surprise me you know her. She's friends with everyone in town. Anyway, she was sitting beside the bed when I woke up in the hospital, and she said she was there to save me."

Asa held his breath, praying for that same saving grace. "And she did?"

Lyric kept her chin down. "Pretty much."

"How?"

"She became my sponsor."

"Kendra is an alcoholic?" The sweet older woman who served him breakfast at least three days a week didn't look like the alcoholics he ran calls on regularly.

"She is. She's been sober for thirty years."

Thirty years? That was a lifetime. No wonder he didn't know about that part of her past.

Lyric rolled her eyes. "Don't rewrite everything you know about her. She doesn't deserve that."

"I wasn't." He had a hard time believing it. He still couldn't picture Kendra as a struggling alcoholic.

"At first, she was the one I called when I needed help."

"What about now?"

"She pointed me to Jesus. It took a long time for the idea to sink in, but I wanted to think I still had a chance–that I could be forgiven. I know nothing can erase what I did, but Kendra told me God would forgive me."

Asa sighed. It had been a while since he heard a testimony as powerful as Lyric's. "She's right."

Lyric was still looking at her hands folded in front of her. As hard as this conversation was for him, it was probably even more difficult for her.

She inhaled a deep breath and pushed it out quickly. "I get it. I know you don't remember me, but I remembered you because you stood up for me."

"I did?"

"To the judge. I got community service instead of more jail time."

Ten years ago, he'd believed in second chances. Now, he was a little jaded and a lot less lenient. Years of facing the worst of the world left him with little hope.

Seeing the turnaround Lyric had made reignited that hope in him.

Asa's phone rang, and he pulled it from his pocket on autopilot. Dawson detailed their ETA, and the call was over within seconds. "They're almost here."

"Asa, I'm sorry. I know you have every right to be mad at me, but I didn't mean to keep this from you. I didn't know how to tell you, and I was scared."

He pulled her in to his chest and brushed a hand over her hair. "We have a lot to talk about, but you can relax. I'm not mad. Just confused. It's a lot to take in."

"I know. I'm sorry."

"I'm glad you told me." While Lyric's old life wasn't something that made him want to cut ties with her immediately, it did mean he had to be careful. If he was going to bring a woman into his and Jacob's life, it had to be someone he could trust.

Telling him the truth had taken guts. Was the confession a sign of her integrity? He desperately wanted to believe it was.

But he knew what addiction could do to families. He'd seen countless addicts do unexplainable things. They would strike a match just to watch it burn. He couldn't subject his family to that. Was it a possibility for Lyric? Would she relapse?

Asa lifted her chin to face him. "I want to know everything. No secrets."

Lyric shook her head frantically. "None. I promise I'll tell you the truth. I just don't want you to think I'm that person anymore."

"I get it. We don't have a lot of time to talk now, but give me your number so I can call you when I get off work. I expect to be on overtime until the storm mess is cleared up."

She brushed her sleeve over her eyes and rattled off her number. Asa saved it in his phone and tucked it away.

"I have a prepay phone, so if I don't answer, it's probably because I don't have minutes."

Asa's heart rate spiked. Prepaid phones were popular for criminals, and he tried to push that little fact to the side and focus on what Lyric promised him—the truth.

"I told Dawson I'd ride up to Mrs. Grant's place with him, but one of the other officers can give you a ride home tonight and arrange for you to get your car when the roads are clear and the snow thaws."

Lyric kept her head lowered. "Yeah. I'll get my things."

He reached for her hand as she started to walk off. "Lyric?"

"Yes?"

"We'll get through this. I'm trusting you."

She bit her lips between her teeth. "Thank you. That means a lot."

He let her hand go, but she didn't look convinced. Her eyes held that same defeated look as they did when the terrible conversation started.

One thing at a time. First, they needed to get out of here.

The next hour was a swirl of numbing cold. The storm was over, but the snow and destruction were everywhere. The mounds of snow hindered every job as they cleared the tree and got Asa's crushed truck attached to the wrecker.

Lyric stayed in the cabin, but out of sight wasn't out of mind. Nagging thoughts of her were just behind every move Asa made.

When the road was clear and everyone was ready to head out, Asa trudged down the drive to the cabin. So much had changed in the last few days, and more change was coming. He had big decisions to make, and hopefully, Lyric would open up and trust him to handle the truth. When all the cards were on the table, hopefully he'd know what to do. He was a father first and foremost, but what if Lyric wasn't a good fit for their family?

He hesitated at the door as if the extra second would reveal something spectacular, but it didn't. No amount of time waiting in the freezing temperatures would turn back time and erase the connection he'd found with Lyric, and it wouldn't remove her crimes either. It was all mixed together–black and white jumbled into a hazy gray.

When he'd stalled long enough, Asa went inside. There wasn't a vast temperature change walking in like there had been when he first arrived, but the power had been off a while with little heat circulation on the main floor.

His attention was drawn immediately to Lyric. Wearing her coat and scarf, she scrubbed dishes in the sink. The water had to be freezing since he'd unplugged the hot water heater from the generator hours ago.

The wind pulled the door closed behind him, and the slam echoed through the large open room. Lyric's chin jerked up, and her eyes were wide in fear.

"Didn't mean to scare you. I think we're almost ready to go."

She dried her hands on a towel and tossed it into an open garbage bag with other rags she'd used to clean. "Okay. I'm almost finished."

The door opened behind Asa, letting in another gust of cold air.

Dawson looked up at the vaulted ceiling and whistled. "Where's the restroom in this place?"

Asa pointed to the hallway. "Just around the corner."

Dawson gave him a two-finger wave and spotted Lyric. His stride halted. "Lyric Woods?"

Lyric bent to tie up the bag without a second look at Dawson. "Long time no see."

Dawson gave Asa a wide-eyed look and whispered, "Lyric Woods?"

Asa had no idea how Dawson and Lyric knew each other, but just knowing they shared any past at all had his fists clenching. He had too many strong, jumbled feelings where Lyric was concerned, and he didn't need his friend muddying the waters even more.

Ignoring Dawson's obvious looks, Asa turned to Lyric. "I'll carry that. Where do you want it?"

"I need to ask one of the officers if we can drop it off at the dumpster at the bottom of the hill."

Asa took the bag and headed outside. He handed

it off to Officer Guthrie and turned back toward the cabin.

Lyric was shutting down right before his eyes. If she decided the new and fragile relationship they were building wasn't worth the risk of telling him the truth, they might not get much of a chance after they parted ways today.

Asa walked in just as Dawson strode back into the room whistling a chipper tune. He stopped when he saw Asa. "Is she here?"

"I guess so. Jason is taking her home, and he's still outside."

Dawson rushed to Asa's side. "Dude, you didn't tell me it was Lyric!" Dawson whisper-screamed.

Asa stood and crossed his arms over his chest. "How do you even know her?"

"She's Jeremy's age. They went to school together."

The crushing weight on Asa's chest dissipated a little bit. "So she's about twenty-eight?"

"Should be. I haven't seen much of her in years, but Jeremy said she got into some trouble a while back."

"You could say that." Asa eyed the door, praying Lyric would reappear so he could talk to her again.

"What did she say?" Dawson asked.

Asa shook his head. "Nothing I want to talk about."

"But you'll tell me later, right?" Dawson nudged Asa's shoulder.

Lyric walked back into the room and gave him a small, guarded smile. She'd pulled her dark hair up into a low ponytail, and her beautiful face was on full display. Dark eyes, pink cheeks, and red lips.

Dawson waved at her as if she hadn't given him an icy greeting. "Hey, Officer Guthrie is gonna take you down the mountain."

Lyric shoved her hands into her pockets. "Thanks."

Dawson started toward the door. "Follow me."

Asa cleared his throat. "I'll walk her out."

"I'll be in the truck," Dawson said before ducking out.

Alone with her in the cabin, Asa could feel his heart beating in his chest. Fast and hard, the thumps distracted him from everything he needed to say.

"You okay?" Lyric asked. Her words were as cold as the temperature outside.

"Yeah. I just wanted to check on you before we head out."

Lyric bit her lips between her teeth and nodded. A second later, she met his gaze. "I'm fine."

"I'll call you as soon as I can. We can talk."

"Right," Lyric whispered.

So, that was it? That was their grand farewell? Fire blazed inside him, and he wanted to scream. Why did it have to be this way? Why did things have to change? Why was she pulling away? Was there more to the truth more than what she'd told him?

She turned and reached for the door.

"Lyric–"

"Hmm?" she asked quickly.

There were a million reasons he should say his good-byes now and walk away from her, but it could never be that simple–not between them. Not when he'd be seeing her face and hearing her voice every time he closed his eyes for many nights to come.

"I'll call you. I promise."

Was that all he had to say? It was all so stupid that he couldn't think straight.

Lyric sighed. "We'll see."

And just like that, she walked out of his life.

18

LYRIC

L yric tightened her grip on the plastic grocery bags that weighed her down on both sides. She rarely bought so much, but it had been such a long time since she'd stocked up on groceries that her cabinets were bare.

She wasn't sure which payment was worse–the blow to her wallet or the arm workout.

After panting all the way down the sidewalk, Lyric released a big sigh when she reached the door of her apartment building. Her apartment wasn't far from the store, but walking it with groceries in tow was tougher than she'd expected. She still hadn't picked up her car from the cabin.

With her hands tied, she backed into the door and did an ungraceful turn to dodge it as it slammed closed behind her. Now, the stairs.

She was grateful there was only one flight.

With the way her weekend was going, she wouldn't be surprised if the remaining steps to her apartment started multiplying right before her eyes. The ache in her back throbbed, and her heels were screaming. It wasn't even noon yet, and she wanted a nap.

Would Kendra fuss at her if she skipped church today? Just this once, she wanted to fall onto the couch and stay there until tomorrow.

"Three, two, one," Lyric panted as she crested the top of the staircase.

A man cleared his throat, and Lyric looked up to find Russell standing beside her door. He looked everywhere but at her.

No. No. Not today. Anybody except her landlord.

"Mr. Porter." She would have probably led with a better greeting if she wasn't on the verge of passing out.

"Miss Woods." He cleared his throat again. "You're three months behind on rent now."

"I know. I'm sorry. Can I pay you part when I get my check tomorrow?" She had five dollars in her purse right now, but she wasn't about to offer it to him. That wouldn't go over well if she gave him a fiver when she was carrying forty dollars in groceries into the apartment he owned.

Russell shuffled his feet. "If you can't pay it all, I'm going to have to rent to someone else."

All the blood in her body was rushing to her feet,

her fingers were close to falling off, and she couldn't get her lungs to do their stupid job.

Russell scratched his head and looked at her door. "I mean, I get applications from time to time, but I don't have any openings. I figure I need to rent to someone who will pay."

"I get it." The words were a hollow whisper. She couldn't feel anything anymore. Her fingers weren't cold, and her feet weren't throbbing, but her head was spinning.

"If you can't pay by Wednesday, you need to be out by Friday." With that friendly farewell, Russell scurried down the stairs.

A half breath escaped her parted lips. Why couldn't she get it together? Why was it so hard to rebuild her life from the ground up? It had been five years. Why hadn't she been able to pull herself out of the hole yet?

Fumbling her keys, she finally got the door unlocked and the bags inside. She hefted them onto the small counter in the kitchen and stared at them. There wasn't any point in taking the groceries out of the bags. She'd be packing everything within these four walls into boxes and bags starting tonight.

This morning, she'd had a home but no food. Now, she had food but no home.

Everything was messed up, and she wanted to scream until her throat was sore.

Instead, she crumpled to the floor and rested her

back against the cabinets. Sunday mornings were quiet in this part of town, and Lyric listened to the beat of her heart. Stupid, useless heart. All it did was pump blood that kept her alive. Why did she even need to be alive? She didn't have anything.

Lyric burst into sobs at the first memory of Asa. He'd said she could have him, but that was a lie. She didn't have anything, and she missed him–missed the carefree and happy time they'd spent together last week. She'd gone from cloud nine to rock bottom in two days flat.

Her phone dinged with a text, but she didn't move. It was either Kendra or Asa. Kendra texted her every Sunday morning offering her a ride to church, and she'd been avoiding Asa's texts. True to his word, he'd texted her as soon as he got off work. She hadn't worked up the courage to respond yet.

Lyric wouldn't be going to church or even answering the text. If she had more than five dollars in her pocket, she'd make a run to the liquor store right now.

Her chest swelled with each heaving breath. Where was God when things got tough? Was He in the church with the Christians? Would He be with her on the streets later this week? Why did she feel so far away from Him when she needed someone so badly right now?

She wasn't sure how long she'd been sitting on the kitchen floor when someone knocked on the door. If she stayed quiet, whoever was on the other side would go away.

Kendra's words were muffled through the door. "Lyric, I know you're in there. You can either let me in or I'll let myself in."

Shoot. Kendra had a key.

"You have five seconds," Kendra warned.

Not bothering to beg for more time, Lyric pushed off the floor and wiped her eyes on her way to the door.

There wasn't any shock when the door opened. Kendra looked Lyric up and down and snapped her fingers. "Get dressed."

"I'm not going."

"I didn't ask if you were going. I said get dressed."

Lyric wailed as the tears started anew. Kendra's arms were around her in a second, and the door was closed behind her, locking them away from the world for a moment.

Kendra rubbed a soothing circle on Lyric's back. "Shh. Shh. It's okay. Everything is okay."

"No, it's not. Russell is kicking me out."

"When do you have to be out?" Kendra asked, clearly unfazed by the revelation.

"Friday."

"Then we'll find you a new place or the money to keep this one before then. Right now, you need to get dressed." Kendra grasped Lyric's shoulders and pushed her away.

"I'm not going to church. I just found out I'm being evicted!"

"You're going to church."

"Ugh!" Lyric huffed in anger. "Why?"

"Because it's better for you than anything else you could be doing this morning. Trust me."

Lyric didn't wait a second before turning toward her temporary bedroom. She'd get dressed in record time and get church over with so she could wallow in pity for the rest of the day.

LYRIC FLIPPED THROUGH THE HYMNAL. The words, notes, and lines were a confusing mess on the pages. She'd never learned to read music, but her mother had a gift. Stupidly hoping to pass her talent along to her daughters, she'd named her first daughter Melody and her second daughter Lyric. Too bad neither of them had pursued their mother's dream.

"Welcome. Welcome. Open your hymn books to page 537, and we'll start with one of the classics this morning."

Lyric's mouth moved, forming the words without sound as the congregation sang around her. Did God really walk with her as the hymn said? If He did, why was she still so brokenhearted? Was she selfish in hoping He would drop everything else to hold her when she felt like crumbling?

After the first chorus, Lyric gave up pretending to sing. It wasn't in her heart this morning.

Kendra reached out and grabbed Lyric's hand, squeezing it tight. She did have one person. She would always have Kendra beside her. And as much as Lyric wanted someone to blame, she knew questioning God wasn't the answer to her problems. For all she knew, He was working out the fine print of her future right now. It was scary to hope, but she desperately needed something to hang onto.

When the worship service was over and Brother John stood in front of the church, Lyric began squirming in her seat. Shame and regret nagged at her. She'd spent the morning huffing at God for landing her in the situation she was in, and she wanted to hide or run away. The Lord could see her. She knew it. And He knew her heart when no one else did. Why did He have to have a first-class seat to the wreckage of her life?

Brother John's deep voice filled the room. "Our Father sent us a Savior. That means you needed saving. That means I needed saving. We can't do any of it on our own."

Lyric hunched her shoulders. She was definitely doing it on her own, but she was supposed to let God help her. How could He help her? How did she get herself on His list?

"Jesus's name means rescuer, and His mission was to save us from our sins. Jesus didn't die for you to be lukewarm about Him or the sacrifice He made for you. Jesus didn't come to put you in your place. He came to prepare a place for us to call home for all eternity."

Tears slid down Lyric's cheeks and landed on her best pair of pants, soaking into the fabric and disappearing as if they'd never been. She'd accepted Jesus into her heart, but everything about following Christ was still so new to her. She shouldn't doubt Him anymore.

Brother John's loud voice lowered, and he looked out over the congregation. "He has never lost a battle, and your battle is His battle. He'll never leave your side."

Kendra's arm wrapped around Lyric's shoulders, pulling her close. She had a battle ahead of her, but she wasn't fighting alone.

When Kendra first told her she didn't have to beg or borrow for God's forgiveness, it hadn't made sense. It didn't seem possible, especially since convincing regular people to trust her was always an uphill battle. There had to be a price, right?

Now Lyric could see that the price wasn't hers to pay. It had already been paid, and she'd been willing to give up mere hours ago. God never gave up on her. She shouldn't give up on Him.

When the service was over, Lyric wiped her eyes before turning to Kendra. "Go ahead. Let's get it over with."

"I'm not going to say I told you so."

"You just did."

Kendra grasped Lyric's shoulder. "I don't want to be right. I wanted you to hear God's Word this morning."

Lyric went in for a full-on hug, breathing in the thick smell of Kendra's hairspray. It was a scent Lyric had come to associate with happiness and with good reason. She couldn't ask for a better friend.

19

ASA

Asa stared at the photo on the screen just as he had all week. No wonder he hadn't recognized Lyric when they'd met at the cabin. She didn't look anything like the young girl in the mugshot. Blue makeup was smudged around her eyes, her hair was matted, and her smile was mischievous.

It didn't add up. Why had their paths crossed twice? Was it a second chance? Was it his second chance or hers?

The door to the office slammed, and Asa hurried to minimize the window on his monitor.

Dawson sighed. "Are you still pining over Lyric? Why don't you just call her already?"

"I'm not pining, and I did call her. A lot." One of those things was the truth, but he wasn't so much pining for her as he was missing her.

Dawson flopped down into the nearest chair and pointed a granola bar at Asa. "Dude, you need to perk up. This gloominess is bringing me down. Are y'all gonna talk about things or not?"

Asa looked at the screen again. The window was hidden, but he could still picture Lyric. The image morphed between the messy girl and the beautiful woman. "I don't know."

Dawson leaned over the arm of the chair, crowding close to Asa. "How can you not know? I mean, you like her or you don't."

"I do like her, but it's complicated."

"You might even *love* her."

Asa shoved his friend and scoffed. "I'm not in fifth grade. Don't sing the song." He glared at Dawson, daring him to say another word about Lyric.

"I don't know what song you're talking about."

"I have work to do. If you're staying in here, don't talk."

It took a full three seconds before Dawson started whispering, "Asa and Lyric sittin' in a tree."

"That's it." Asa stood and shoved Dawson out of his seat.

It had been days since Asa left the cabin, and none of his calls or texts had been answered. What would he even say if she answered?

Sorry. I really have been on overtime all weekend.

I don't care about your past.

I miss you.

It all sounded stupid–just as stupid as the rap sheet he'd memorized.

Dawson waited. "Soo is that a yes?"

Asa turned back to his computer. "We should all do a little less talking and a lot more working."

"You are such a wet blanket."

"I'm not a wet blanket." Well, he wasn't completely sure, but he didn't want to be one.

"Are too."

Asa pointed at the door and used his most intimidating scowl. Too bad Dawson wasn't afraid of anything.

Dawson sighed. "Fine. I'll go, but will you please call her? I know she has a past. I know she's trying to do better now. I know she's not Danielle. Just don't lose out on something good because you're too scared to take a chance."

"I have called her, and it seems like she doesn't want to talk. Plus, I have Jacob to think about."

Dawson held up his hands. "I get that. But Lyric hasn't had a run-in with us in a long time. Jeremy said she's working at Blackwater Restoration. You said she's been sober for more than five years. That's a long time for an alcoholic."

"How is it any longer for an alcoholic than it is for anyone else?" Asa asked. He got it. He knew the statistics, and he knew the repeat offenders they came in contact with all the time. Addicts tended to be unpredictable.

"Stop trying to turn things around. The point is that you need to chill out."

Asa pinched the bridge of his nose. "Telling someone to chill out never works."

Jason Guthrie walked in and tossed a form onto the desk. He eyed Asa, then Dawson, before narrowing his eyes. "What are you two up to?"

"Solving world hunger," Dawson quipped before shoving the end of the granola bar into his mouth.

If Asa took his job seriously, Jason held the law above all else and added a heaping helping of cynicism to it. He might have been the youngest officer, but that didn't stop him from hanging over everyone like a prison warden.

Overall, Dawson and Jason were opposites that needed constant supervision.

Jason pointed at the paper on Asa's desk. "Boss said for you to take care of that."

"Got it," Asa said, picking it up and waving it in the air.

Seriously, the guy needed to take a step back. No one here needed another supervisor.

Jason gave Dawson another glare before walking out.

"He needs a hobby," Dawson said, pointing his snack at the door.

"Why don't you set him up on a date. He'd leave us alone if he had a girlfriend."

Dawson gasped. "I would never saddle some poor woman with that stick in the mud."

Asa scanned the documents Jason dropped off. "Then take him fishing. I don't know."

Dawson huffed. "I'd rather lick wet paint, thank you very much."

Flopping the papers down on his desk, Asa leveled Dawson with a stern look. "Is there something I can help you with?"

"Right. Back to your dilemma. You've been moody lately."

"I have not been moody," Asa said.

"Have too."

Asa's face heated as his irritation mounted. He was having a tough enough time figuring out his feelings for Lyric, and this wasn't helping.

Dawson slapped his hand down on the desk. The thud echoed in the small office. "Call her. Make yourself happy." He didn't look back as he walked out.

MONDAY WAS the most Monday of all Mondays, and to top it all off, a headache was pounding behind Asa's right eye. The weekend held the record for the most hours he'd ever worked, and he was on the verge of a twelve-hour rest before he would be called back to the grind.

He parked the rental truck in front of his mom's house and rested his head against the seat. He'd give last week's paycheck to be able to drift off into the hardest sleep of his life right now.

When he lifted his head, the clock on the dash read 4:47. Rubbing a hand over his face, Asa slipped out of the truck, preparing for Jacob's excited energy that waited just inside the house.

The phone in his pocket buzzed, and he stopped in the driveway to take the call.

"Hello."

"Mr. Scott? This is Mrs. Huntley, Jacob's teacher."

Asa turned his attention to the side door of his mom's house. "Is everything okay?"

"Oh yes. I just wanted to let you know Jacob seemed a little sad in class today. He's usually so happy. The change in his mood was concerning."

"Sad? Did he say anything?" He'd never gotten a call from Jacob's teacher before. His mood must have been terrible to warrant a call.

"He didn't. I asked him how he was feeling after lunch, and I checked him for a fever. I thought he might be getting sick. Has he seemed okay this afternoon?"

"To be honest, I just pulled up at my mom's house to pick him up. I haven't seen him yet."

"Oh, okay. It's probably nothing, but I wanted to

let you know. I never have a single problem out of Jacob. He's a good kid."

Asa rubbed his face again. The unexpected call had jolted some life back into him, but his shoulders tensed as he tried to piece together what might be going on with Jacob. "I'll have a talk with him in just a minute."

"I'm sure he's fine. He's allowed to have bad days. They're just so rare for him."

Mrs. Huntley was right. Jacob rarely had bad days. The kid was so full of kindness and energy that he hardly ever seemed sad. "Thanks for the heads-up. I appreciate it."

He pocketed the phone and stepped inside, immediately looking for Jacob. Asa's mom stood in the kitchen washing dishes in the sink.

"Hey, you're home early."

Asa scoffed. "This is the time I normally get home from work."

"Not lately." She dried her hands on a rag. "How are you holding up? I know the hours have been long."

"I'm fine." He rested his hip against the counter by the sink. "Just got a call from Jacob's teacher. She said he seemed sad today."

Asa's mom jerked her head up. "Really? He's been fine since I picked him up from school."

"I'm gonna check on him. We're heading to Beau's shop to work on the car."

"If he was sad before, he'll be happy to hear that. It's all he talked about last weekend."

Fixing up old cars was something Asa had always wanted to do with his own dad. Unfortunately, his dad hadn't ever wanted anything to do with him or his mom. When Jacob started showing interest in cars, Asa made a point to spend the time with his son.

Those old dreams and disappointments of his childhood vanished. Nothing could beat hanging out with Jacob, and the only one who had missed out was Asa's dad.

Asa knocked on Jacob's bedroom door.

"Come in!"

The room had as much furniture as his bedroom at home. Model cars sat along shelves around the room, and his socks were tossed on the floor at the foot of the bed. Jacob had spent quite a few nights at Granny's house over the years when Asa's job required long hours.

His kid shouldn't need a second bedroom, but it was a weight off his shoulders knowing his son always had someone who cared for him.

"Hey, Dad." Jacob didn't look up from the paper in his lap.

"You have a lot of homework?"

"Nope. I'm almost finished. What's up?"

Asa sat on the corner of the bed and waited for Jacob to finish the math problem he was working on.

When he looked up, Asa saw the sadness his teacher had been talking about.

"Everything okay?" Asa asked.

"Yeah. Why?"

Apparently, the mystery would stay unsolved for a while. "Just wondering. You still up for working on the car at Beau's garage?"

Jacob thumped his book closed over the page of problems and bounced on the bed. His eyes widened along with his smile. "Really?"

Well, that escalated quickly. "Yeah. If you've finished your homework, maybe we can stay an extra hour today."

Jacob shoved his math book into his backpack by the bed and scrambled to his feet. "I'm done. Let's go."

"Wait for me, unless you plan on driving," Asa said as he stood.

Jacob rounded on him and gasped. "I can drive?"

"Absolutely not. That was a joke. I'm not ready for you to drive yet."

"You let me drive at Blackwater Ranch one time," Jacob reminded him.

"Yeah. That was a work truck in a wide-open field. The road is a whole other ballgame."

Jacob's shoulders sank a little, but his smile didn't fade. "Fine, but next time we're at the ranch?"

"You can certainly drive if we get a chance," Asa finished.

Jacob pumped his fist in the air and pushed his feet into his socks. "I'm ready." Seconds later, Jacob darted out of the room and down the hallway.

By the time Asa made it to the kitchen, the door was slamming behind Jacob as he ran outside.

"What got into him?" Asa's mom asked.

"Excited about going to Beau's," Asa said.

Jacob peeked his head back inside and said, "Sorry. Didn't mean to slam the door," before disappearing again.

Asa chuckled and turned to his mom. "See you tomorrow. Love you."

"Love you too, son."

By the time Asa got to the truck, Jacob sat still and silent in the passenger seat.

"Dad, I'm sorry," Jacob said quietly.

Asa let his hand rest on the gear shift and didn't speak.

Jacob wrung his hands in his lap. "I thought you were going to cancel tonight. Mrs. Huntley kept asking me what was wrong, and I told her it was nothing."

Oh, man. Jacob had been upset all day, all because he thought he couldn't count on his dad to be there for him.

Asa rubbed a hand over his face and tried to breathe through his constricting throat. "Buddy, I'm sorry I've been working so much lately. We're short-handed, and—"

"I know. I really get it. I know the town needs you, and I know you need the job so we can have money. I don't want to be selfish, but—"

"But it's okay to be upset when things don't go your way. That's a part of being human."

"Yeah, but I feel bad for doubting you and being selfish."

Asa wrapped an arm around Jacob's shoulders and pulled him in. "I feel bad for letting you down lately. Trust me, I'd rather be spending my time with you. I look forward to working on the car just as much as you do."

"Really?" Jacob asked.

"Really."

Satisfied with the outcome of the talk, Jacob bounced in his seat. "Well, let's go."

Jacob talked the whole way to Beau's garage. His class was working on a home design project at school, and he detailed every feature his group had put into the model and why. The kid was so observant and smart, Asa never worried about Jacob's future job opportunities. If he stayed this focused and determined, he'd have his pick of any career he set his mind to.

A light dusting of snow was falling when they pulled up at Beau's garage, but Jacob jumped out of the truck and ran inside before Asa got his seatbelt unbuckled. Inside, Jacob quickly located Beau and said his hasty hello before darting off to the last bay where the old Mustang they'd been working on waited.

Beau wiped his greasy hands on a rag and pushed it into his back pocket. "Long time, no see."

Asa and Beau went back to the diaper days. With moms who were best friends, they'd started elementary school with a solid friendship that sometimes flipped to competition. Teachers tried to separate them into different classes, but Asa and Beau found ways to keep in touch.

Asa offered his hand to Beau. "Busy times."

"Tell me about it. I can't keep up lately."

"You thinking about taking on another hire?"

Beau shook his head. "Nah. Can't afford it yet, but at this rate, maybe soon."

"Give it about six years and that one will be knocking down the door looking for a job," Asa said, pointing at Jacob.

"Man, if only they were all as good as him. I have to babysit most of the guys around here. At least Jacob knows what he's doing."

The metal door screeched as Beau's sister walked in. Olivia had been just as much a part of Asa's life as Beau, and she'd treated Asa like a brother since day one.

She held onto the grocery bag she carried with one hand and threw the other in the air. "Asa! How's it going?"

"Pretty good. What about you?"

Her dark hair was longer than she'd kept it when they were in high school, and she'd finally started smiling again recently. When her mom died a few years ago, Asa, Beau, and Dawson had done all they could to pull her out of her grief. He couldn't imagine losing his own mom, but Olivia and Martha had been inseparable—more like best friends—for as long as he'd known them.

Olivia brought her arm down around Asa's shoulders and gave him a side hug. "I'm makin' it. Is Jacob here?"

"Yeah. I'd better go see if he needs help."

Olivia lifted the bag. "I brought dinner for Beau. There's enough for you and Jacob too."

"Thanks. We'll take you up on that. Jacob isn't going to be happy about stopping for a meal."

Shoving the bag at Beau, she stepped past Asa. "I'm going to say hey."

"Hold on a second," Asa said. "Do you know a woman named Lyric?"

Okay, so it wasn't any secret he'd been thinking about her in every spare moment since they parted ways, and the lack of replies on her end was letting him know she wasn't that into him.

"Yeah. There was a girl named Lyric in a different grade in school. I don't know her personally, but I know of her. I mean, who could forget a name like that?"

"What else do you know?"

Olivia shrugged. "Not much. I haven't heard about her since I graduated. No news is good news, right?"

Asa started walking toward the bay where Jacob waited. Olivia just hadn't heard the news about Lyric's arrests. That part wasn't good news.

He gave Olivia what he hoped was a friendly smile. "Thanks for letting me know."

"Why do you ask?" Olivia questioned with a little too much lift at the end.

If he didn't keep his mouth shut, word would get out that he was asking about Lyric before he had a chance to talk to her and figure out where they stood. "No reason."

Olivia narrowed her eyes. "I can do some investigating. What do you need to know?"

"No, that's okay. Thanks for the offer though. I better tell Jacob to come eat before he gets elbow deep in grease."

He had no doubt Olivia could investigate. The problem was, he had Lyric's number, but it wasn't doing him any good if she wouldn't answer.

20

LYRIC

Lyric rested her hip against the checkout counter at Deano's as Kendra handed a customer his change and a ceramic mug. Kendra's job wasn't glamorous, but she was a bright spot in the morning for so many. Deano's was a popular hangout for the older men, and she kept their mugs full while they chatted.

"I'll have that out to you in just a minute," Kendra said.

The slender old man tipped his hat. "Thank you, ma'am."

When he was out of earshot, Lyric scooted back over to the checkout counter.

Kendra stuck the order in line with the others. "Where were we?"

"I was telling you about striking out at The Landing." It was the last apartment complex in town. Now the last of her hope was gone.

Kendra wrapped her warm hand around Lyric's. "Don't do that."

"Do what?"

"Give up. We won't stop until we find something."

"I can't pay first and last month's rent," Lyric reminded her friend.

"If all else fails, you'll sleep at my place."

Lyric kept quiet. Kendra's daughter, son-in-law, and granddaughter were living with her and her husband right now. There wasn't even a couch open at Kendra's small house.

As if sensing Lyric's thoughts, Kendra squeezed the hand she held. "We'll put an air mattress in the living room."

Boots thudded against the floor behind Lyric, and she stepped away from the register.

"You two have a good day," Grady said on his way to the door.

"Bye," Kendra and Lyric sang in unison.

Lyric turned back to Kendra, leaning in to whisper as the bell above the door chimed at Grady's exit.

"I think it's safe to accept the fact that I'm not going to find a place before Friday, but I'm not imposing on you. You have three extra people in your house as it is."

Kendra's eyes widened, and Lyric followed the line of her gaze toward the door.

Asa stood as still as a statue less than three feet from her—tall and imposing, as if he owned the place.

Lyric's face heated, and her lungs constricted in her chest. He'd slipped in when Grady was on his way out, and she hadn't heard him come in. And from the look on Asa's face, he'd heard everything.

Embarrassment, shame, and longing warred within her. She'd desperately wanted to see him these past few days, but reality tarnished the desire. Things had changed between them, and they were strangers again.

It was better this way. At least, for him.

It was funny and sad how just a few words could change everything.

Yet, here stood the reminder of all the things she couldn't have. Lyric had been careful to stay out of relationships since her resolution to stay sober. The program advised against dating within the first year of sobriety. New members were encouraged to focus on their goal and learn to stand on their own before pursuing a relationship. As if a year was enough time for a former alcoholic to learn to stand on her own two feet. Here Lyric was, five years later, and she was still single and newly homeless. She'd done her time, but it hadn't been enough.

Not only was she homeless, but now Asa knew

about it. Why hadn't someone told her rock bottom had a basement?

"Morning," Asa said as he stepped up to the counter.

The heat of his gaze tickled up the side of her neck. She couldn't look at him. Facing her failures was too hard.

"Morning," Kendra said in her sweetest voice.

Lyric traced a crack in the linoleum countertop and kept her head down.

"Good morning," Asa said.

Lyric looked up at him and immediately regretted it. Why did he have to be so handsome? Why did he have to look at her with those kind eyes the way he did when he'd held her in the cabin? Why did he have to be here reminding her of all the things she'd lost?

"Morning," Lyric whispered.

He leaned toward her and lowered his voice. "How are you?"

"Fine. Thanks for asking. You?"

Asa took a deep breath. "Been better."

An awkward silence settled in around them. Could this reunion be any worse?

"What can I get you?" Kendra asked.

"Just coffee to go," Asa said.

"You can't sit a while this morning?" Kendra questioned.

"Nah. I have to run."

Kendra chuckled. "Fun stuff, huh? A dollar fifty."

Asa pulled his wallet from his pocket. "Always."

"How's your mom and boy?" Kendra asked.

"Good as gold."

Kendra handed him a to-go cup. "You tell Betty I said hello."

"I will."

Lyric stayed still as Asa walked around her to the drink station and filled his cup. A few seconds later, he was walking past her toward the door.

"Thanks, Kendra."

"Anytime." She waved and turned to grab an order from the ready bar.

He stopped and turned to Lyric. "It was good to see you."

Ugh. Could her heart break any more? It was bad enough seeing him, but it made things worse to know he was really a good guy and she hadn't dreamed it all up.

"You too."

His gaze darted to the door then back to her as if he wasn't sure which way to turn. Finally, he turned toward the door and walked out. The stupid cheerful bell chimed at his exit.

When Kendra returned after dropping off the order, she wrapped an arm around Lyric's shoulders. "You okay?"

No, she wasn't okay. She was sad and tired and hurt.

"It's okay to say no," Kendra reminded her. One of the best things about having an awesome sponsor like Kendra was that Lyric didn't have to pretend to always have her act together.

"I missed out on something great because I used to be a screwup. So, no, I'm not okay."

Kendra wrapped Lyric in a full hug. "I know you really liked him. Maybe there's still hope for the two of you."

Lyric pulled away. "I know you want to encourage me, but don't get my hopes up. I think that dream is dead."

"Does he have your number?" Kendra asked.

"Yeah."

"Maybe he'll call. He's been busy."

"He has called."

Kendra's eye widened. "Oh, and how did that go?"

Lyric traced the same line in the linoleum countertop. "I haven't answered."

"Oh, honey. Talk to him. The next time he calls, just talk to him like you did at the cabin."

"That time at the cabin was all make-believe. He didn't know me then."

"He did know you. He just didn't know who you used to be. He knew who you are now, and those are two different people."

"I can't shed my past like a second skin. It doesn't go away."

"Really? Because my past is dead. It can't hurt me anymore. I became a new person. If I hadn't put my new self together, I would have stayed broken."

"How did you do it?" Lyric asked.

"I only had to take the first step. The Lord carried me after that."

Lyric sighed. "I don't know what the first step is. I guess finding a place to stay would be a good one."

"Maybe the first step is something smaller. Don't worry. You won't be on the street on Friday."

Lyric checked her watch. "I've gotta go. My shift starts in twenty minutes."

"I'll ask around about a place for you today," Kendra said.

"Thanks. I don't know what I'd do without you."

She might not have everything, but having a friend like Kendra was something she wouldn't take for granted.

Maybe Kendra had the right idea. Lyric could ask around while she was working today. She saw lots of people at the thrift store. One of them might know something about a place to rent.

21

ASA

A sa watched the barista pour coffee into a cup behind the counter at Sticky Sweets. Coffee made him think of Lyric, and thinking of Lyric made him think about how he'd fumbled over his words like a pre-teen this morning at Deano's.

He hadn't even been able to string an intelligent sentence together, and he'd been sweating a little extra under his Kevlar vest.

There was also the little tidbit about her getting evicted that he'd overheard. Was she really being evicted? He could run back by Deano's later and ask Kendra, but what good would knowing be if he couldn't help?

"Dude, are you even listening?" Dawson said as he bumped Asa's shoulder.

"No." That was one of his problems lately.

Listening when he shouldn't and not listening when he should.

"Ugh. Now I have to start the story over."

The line cleared in front of them, and they told the young girl their orders, then stepped out of line to wait for their food.

Dawson crossed his arms. "As I was saying, Beau thinks I'd look stupid with a mustache, but Mom says I'd be cute."

"Your mom always thinks you're cute."

Dawson shot Asa a glare. "Are you saying I'm *not* always cute?"

"No comment." Asa scanned the customers in the bakery. Why was he always looking for Lyric? He didn't need another opportunity to make a fool of himself, but he missed her. It was messed up, but he hadn't figured out how to handle the situation with Lyric. Never talking to her again didn't sit right with him for a number of reasons.

First, he hadn't gotten a chance to say all the things he wanted to say. They'd been rushed out of the cabin, and he still didn't have all the answers.

Second, he missed her. He wanted that special connection back, and he wasn't convinced it was just part of being stranded together. Lyric wasn't some ordinary woman. If she'd talk to him, could they start over?

He still hadn't figured out how her criminal record would fit into his life. If she wanted a relationship with him, Jacob was part of the deal. Could Asa trust that she wouldn't relapse? There wouldn't be an answer to that question. Could he live with that? Subject his son to the possibility?

"Earth to Asa," Dawson said.

"What?"

"Your order is ready."

Asa turned to see Tracy, the bakery owner, holding up a tray.

"Thanks. Sorry about that."

"No problem. Enjoy," Tracy said before turning back to her work.

Asa sat at a table, and Dawson joined him a minute later.

"What's got you distracted?" Dawson asked.

"You know about any places up for rent?"

Dawson's brow lifted. "Like a storefront or a house?"

"House. Apartment would be better."

"Who's it for?"

Asa hung his head. "That's not important."

Dawson gasped. "It's Lyric!"

"Keep your voice down," Asa chided.

Dawson leaned forward and whispered, "It's Lyric."

"I'm not saying who it is."

"Why does she need to move?"

"I don't know."

"It's Lyric," Dawson repeated.

"I didn't say that."

"You didn't have to."

"Do you know a place or not?" Asa asked.

Dawson sat straighter and picked up his sandwich. "I don't, but I'll keep my ears open."

"Thanks."

Dawson wouldn't spread gossip, but Asa hoped his friend would find something. It would give him a reason to call Lyric. Until then, he needed to figure out what he'd say if he did find a place for her.

On their way out of the bakery, Asa asked Tracy and the other baristas if they knew of any places to rent around town, but he didn't have any luck. He'd also asked at the bank and the post office before his shift ended. By the time he picked up Jacob from school, the odds of finding a place for Lyric were looking slim.

Thoughts of calling Lyric had taken over his brain, leaving no room for anything else in his head. He sat at the dinner table with his mom and Jacob and tapped his fork on the side of his plate.

"Dad, what are you doing?" Jacob asked.

Asa looked up to find his mother and Jacob staring at him. "What?"

His mother pointed to his plate. "You've been tapping your fork."

No wonder he was a bad poker player. He had obvious tells. Tapping when he was thinking was one of the more annoying ones. "Sorry."

"Tough day at work?"

His mom kept her questions about his job simple, and he chose to gloss over most of it for her sake. Blackwater wasn't overrun with crime, but there were a number of things that kept him awake at night. The Howards and the Pattons were trying their best to kill each other off on a regular basis, and the Wilson brothers had an endless list of ways they could torment people.

"No, it was good. How was your day?"

"Wonderful." His mom's answer to the question was always the same, and people in town occasionally called her Ms. Wonderful.

"Can I play Fortnite before we go?" Jacob asked.

"Sure. I'll come get you when I finish helping Granny clean up." The three of them took turns in sets cleaning up after dinner when they ate with Asa's mom. Three people in the small kitchen was too crowded.

Jacob took off toward the living room as Asa started stacking plates.

"Anything I can help with?" his mom asked.

"What do you mean?"

"Whatever's got you thinking so hard."

Asa carried the dishes to the kitchen, and his mom was right behind him. With the door closed between them and Jacob, they could talk without being overheard.

"You remember Lyric?" Asa began.

"Of course. I need to get her address so I can send her a thank you card for taking such good care of you."

"She was really nice, and we had a great time while we were snowed in."

His mother's hands halted above the dirty dishes in the sink. "Are you dating her?"

There was a hint of excitement in his mom's voice. What did he think about her reaction? Excitement was his top emotion when he thought of Lyric most of the time, but there was also doubt, shame, and indecision grappling for the number-two spot.

"No. I actually hadn't talked to her since we left the cabin until today. I ran into her at Deano's."

"How is she doing?"

"Well, I overheard her talking to Kendra. I think she's getting evicted."

"Kendra?"

"No, Lyric."

"Oh, goodness. That's awful."

Asa rubbed the back of his neck. Stressing about Lyric had his muscles aching. "Um, I don't think I told you this, but Lyric has a criminal record."

"What? Is that why she's being evicted?"

"No, no. She used to be an alcoholic...and an addict. It sounds awful, but she said she's been sober for over five years."

His mother rubbed her forehead. "Wow. Sober for five years is quite an accomplishment."

"Yeah, and it could also disappear in an instant."

The wet rag was whipping toward his face before he had a chance to block it.

"Asa Henry Scott. I did not raise you to be judgmental."

"I know. I know." He still had his hands up. "Normally, I'm the first person to give the benefit of the doubt, but this is personal. What if I start dating her and she gets to know Jacob? What if Jacob and I let her into our lives and she relapses? What if we love her and she leaves us when things get tough?"

The doubts poured out like water. He still hadn't figured out which way was up when Lyric was thrown in the mix.

"I think there are any number of what-ifs you can ask about any situation. If you were dating someone who wasn't an alcoholic, wouldn't there still be a chance you could fall in love and things still didn't work out?"

"I get it."

"Do you?" his mother asked. "Because all I'm hearing is that you care about her, but you can't accept that she made mistakes. If we were all bound to our mistakes forever, the world would be a dark place."

Asa swallowed. It had been a long time since his mom had taught him a lesson.

She turned her attention to the dishes and started scrubbing them with soapy water. "You need to learn to accept people as they are. Not even Danielle was perfect."

"I know she wasn't perfect, but there were no secrets with Danielle. Nothing was ever going to surprise me."

"That's all well and great, but what about now?"

He sighed. "Surprises aren't my favorite."

"That's rich coming from a man who enters buildings where gunfire has been reported."

"I haven't done that in a long time."

"Thank goodness. My heart couldn't take it."

Asa fell silent as he dried the dishes beside his mom. The one thing he'd been wanting to ask her hadn't come up yet, and now he didn't know how to say it.

His mother spoke first, relieving him of his mission. "She can stay here."

Asa didn't have a spare room, but his mom did. In fact, she had two. While it wasn't his place to offer the room to Lyric, he'd hoped his mother would pick up on his intentions.

"Are you sure? I don't want you to think you have to do this."

"I'm not worried about Lyric bothering me. Kendra has mentioned her before and has only said good things. It sounds like she needs a helping hand."

"Thanks."

She turned to him and smiled. "I'll be glad if she

decides to stay. It'll be good for you to be around her more."

Asa chuckled. His mom made it sound like Lyric was the good influence. "I was thinking the same thing."

22

LYRIC

Lyric crawled on her hands and knees to a box on the other side of the bedroom labeled for bathroom items. She had one day to get her things out, and without an actual residence to move these boxes to, they'd mostly have to be donated to the thrift store. Condensing her life into the few boxes that would fit in Kendra's place was like round two of packing. It didn't help anything that she'd taken the day off to get it done. She needed the money, and the bitterness over the move had a black cloud settling over her head.

A knock on the door startled her, and she stopped to listen. If it was Russell, she wasn't answering. She had eighteen hours left, and she wouldn't be leaving until then.

Whoever was at the door knocked again. Now wasn't the best time for a visitor. She was sweaty from packing, and she hadn't changed out of her pajamas.

"Lyric."

Asa! Of all people. Why did it have to be him when she looked like she'd just rolled out of bed?

She stumbled to the bathroom and pulled the ponytail from her hair. The tangled mess fell over her shoulders. That wouldn't work. She twisted it into a more contained bun and scrunched her nose at the sickly pale reflection. She'd been doing a lot of crying and not a lot of eating these last few days, and it showed.

Asa knocked again, and Lyric hurried to the door. She took a calming breath and opened it.

Of course, Asa looked like he'd just finished chopping wood and was now ready for his lumberjack-romance book cover photo shoot. Ugh. Figured.

She locked her fingers in front of her and stretched a smile. "Hey." What else was she supposed to say? *What are you doing here? How do you know where I live? Why are you torturing me with your perfectness? I miss you?*

"Hey. Um, are you busy?"

"Yes. I mean, no." She wanted to invite him in, but she didn't even have a cup to offer him a glass of water. She'd packed those up this morning.

"Can we talk?" he asked.

She wanted to talk, sort of, but was there a way to forbid certain topics? Her eviction, her criminal record, the perfect time they'd spent together at the cabin—all of those were dangerous areas that she didn't want to enter right now.

"Sure." She stepped aside, allowing Asa to enter the room. "Sorry. I'm in the middle of moving."

Asa looked around for two seconds before turning his attention to her. "Where are you moving?"

"Um. I'm staying with Kendra. Temporarily."

Asa rubbed the back of his neck and looked at the floor. Maybe he was nervous too.

Finally, he looked at her and dropped his hands to his sides. "I'm sorry. Things got weird after you told me about how we'd met before, and I panicked. I probably didn't say the right thing."

His apology made her want to cry. She hadn't expected it. He was visibly nervous, and it warmed something in her tired heart. If he didn't care a whole lot, he wouldn't have tracked her down to talk.

"I'm the one who should be apologizing. I should have answered your texts. And I was weird at Deano's. I'm double sorry."

"Wow. I've never had a double apology before," Asa said as a grin formed on his lips.

Unable to contain the relief that swept over her, she tried to hide her own grin. "I'm trying to make a serious declaration of my stupidity. This is not a laughing matter."

He pulled the collar of his flannel shirt over his mouth to hide his smile. "Sorry. Go on."

Lyric took a step toward him and gently tugged his shirt from where it covered his mouth. "I've never been so stupid before."

She could hear her heart beating loud in the quiet room, and Asa was close enough to touch. She'd been avoiding his calls and texts because losing him had been so heartbreaking the first time. She didn't want to relive it again.

But now, Asa had tracked her down and given his own apology, even though he hadn't done anything wrong. He wasn't just saying he cared. He was showing it.

Asa was a good man, and he'd gone out of his way to find her. Few men would have given her a second thought.

This was bad, but oh so good. "I'm sorry," she whispered again.

He only hesitated a moment. "You're forgiven. If you're not into me, just say so. I'm a big boy. I can take it. I think."

"That's not it at all. I was just...I thought you'd be happy to be rid of me."

Asa scoffed. "Far from it. I can't stop thinking about you. I do think we need to talk some things out, but I'm willing to listen if you're willing to let me in."

Oh no. The emotions were swelling in her throat and tingling behind her eyes. She couldn't cry now.

Be strong. No tears.

She cleared her throat. "Thank you. I understand why you freaked out. I mean, you're the picture of lawfulness, and I have a lawless history. But I want you to know that I'm not like that anymore."

"I believe you. I have to," he said resolutely.

"You don't *have* to, but I'm glad you do."

"We *will* talk about that soon, but can we talk about something else first?" Asa asked.

She was suddenly aware that they'd been standing near the door this whole time. She gestured to the couch. "Sure. What's on your mind?"

When Asa didn't move toward the seat she'd offered, worry began to creep in. She'd gone from super happy and comfortable with Asa to totally embarrassed in a split second.

"I overheard you telling Kendra that you're being evicted."

"Yep. That about covers it." No sense in denying it. He heard it himself. Her entire body warmed as the panic set in.

Asa fidgeted before continuing. "I haven't been able to stop thinking about it."

"It's fine. Kendra has offered to let me stay with her until I can find a place."

He rubbed a hand over the back of his neck. Was he as nervous as her? "Well, I was talking to my mom last night, and she has a spare bedroom. She said she'd like for you to stay with her until you find something."

Lyric stared. Everything stopped. Her lungs quit working. What did he say?

"Mom is nice. She helps me out with Jacob, and she works at the antique store in town."

Lyric's lips parted, but she couldn't push any words out–only a breath.

"She said she'd love to have you," Asa said.

"But she doesn't even know me."

"She knows enough. She's heard me talk about you. She said Kendra has said good things about you before."

"I—I don't want to impose."

"It's not imposing. My mom willingly offered."

Lyric held up a hand, still stunned enough to fumble her words. "Are you sure?"

"Yes. Positive."

"I can't afford much, but I'll give her whatever I can until I pay off what I owe."

Asa shook his head. "No, Mom doesn't want money."

"I have to pay her."

"She has an extra bedroom, and she lives alone. You living there wouldn't put her out one bit."

"But nothing is free." That was one thing she'd learned in life. Payment wasn't something you could get around.

"Help her out a little bit around the house and she'd be more than happy. Mom is simple. She loves her family, and she likes helping others. She's not going to take your money."

"But–"

"Save up to afford your own place."

She'd been dreaming about talking to Asa again all week, but none of the imaginary conversations she'd thought up had gone like this. They'd all ended horribly with her walking off with her imaginary puppy dog tail between her legs.

"Why are you doing this for me?"

Asa took her hand and threaded his fingers with hers. "Because I care about you, and I believe in you. If you're going through a hard time, I don't want you to go through it alone." He looked up at the ceiling. "And because I care about you."

Lyric chuckled. "You said that already."

"Good. Just making it clear."

The tightness in her chest was different from the heartbreak of the last few days. This was a healing ache, sewing the ripped pieces back together.

"I care about you too," she whispered.

"Good. Um, I guess I should be upfront and tell you the offer to stay with my mom doesn't mean you have to date me or even like me."

"Oh, good. You can go now." Lyric playfully gestured to the door.

Asa tried to hide his smile. "I don't know where we left off, but can we start over?"

"I'd like that," Lyric agreed.

"I want to see where things go for us. If you want that too."

"I do." She was speaking without thinking again. Asa would call it impulsive. She called it following her heart.

"I'm not looking for a fling. I want something real and forever."

The word forever caught her off guard. He wanted forever, and he still wanted to date her. He was a single father, and she knew his life wasn't entirely his own. He had a son to think about before making every decision. Did that mean he thought Jacob would like her? Would she like Jacob? What if she didn't? What if he didn't like her?

"Sorry. Didn't mean to scare you with that big word."

Lyric squeezed his hand. "No, it's okay. I don't want a fling either. I want...forever." The word sounded sweet on her tongue and oh so tempting.

Don't hope too much. Don't hope too much. That would be her constant chant.

"There's one rule," Asa said.

"I can follow rules."

Asa chuckled. "Can you?"

She put a hand over her heart. "Promise."

"Here's the deal: leave the past here."

Her hand still rested on her heart, and the rhythmic beating sped up. It was exactly what she'd been trying to do since she decided to be sober. Leave the past behind? She could do that. She had to.

"Okay. I will."

He looked around the sparse apartment. "Have you had lunch?"

"No." Her appetite had been absent since the eviction notice.

"Can I take you to Sticky Sweets?" he asked.

"I'd love that, but I really have to get this stuff packed up."

He squeezed her hand. "I'll help you. After we eat."

Lyric looked down at her pink sweatpants. "I need to change."

Asa released her hand and leaned back against the bar. "I'll wait here."

"Five minutes. Ten tops."

Lyric ran toward the bedroom, practically giddy. That date he'd asked her to go on when they were still at the cabin felt like a forgotten dream. This wasn't the exact date she'd envisioned. It was better.

23

ASA

Asa brushed his shoulder against hers. They were same-siding in the booth because he wanted to be beside Lyric when she met his family. They were taking a step in their relationship that was usually reserved for weeks or months into a stable relationship and transplanting it to the beginning. Their first real date had been six hours ago when he'd treated her to lunch at the bakery.

"My palms are sweating." Lyric shook her hands in the air, trying to dry the stickiness.

Asa reached for one of her flailing hands and lowered it to the table. "You don't have to impress anyone here."

Lyric's gaze darted around the small restaurant. The Basket Case wasn't a classy place, but locals loved it.

"Stop it. You're making me nervous," Asa said, still holding onto her hand.

"I want them to like me."

"Mom already decided she likes you. Jacob is going to like you too."

Her heel tapped rapidly beneath the table, and he removed his hand from hers and pressed it to her knee. "What can I do to help with the nervous bouncing?"

Lyric turned to him with a smile. "I really shouldn't be nervous, but this is important. I know it's important to you too."

She had no idea. It was extremely important to him, but he also had a certainty about the situation that she didn't. He knew his mom and son, and they would love Lyric. "I'm not worried."

She took a deep breath. "So I shouldn't be either."

"Exactly."

"Okay." The tension in her leg melted away, and she leaned her head on his shoulder. "It's really nice to trust someone."

"You trust me?" Asa knew she didn't have many people in her corner, and that was because trust had been broken on one side or the other. Trust was always a fickle thing when an addict was involved, and knowing it was something they could talk about was a good sign.

"Of course. You're super dependable. I bet you're the best dad."

Asa turned his cheek and smelled her hair. She'd washed it right before dinner, and it smelled like citrus. They'd been packing all day, and he was happy to smell something besides cardboard. "I'm not the best, but I want to be."

"You're like the iconic super dad in movies."

"Are you trying to say I have a dad bod?" Asa joked.

"Not at all!" Lyric lifted her head and smiled up at him. "I bet you've always been Mr. Do-Gooder."

"I would say you're wrong, but then I'd be lying."

Lyric chuckled, but the cheerful sound quickly died. "I wish I could say the same about myself. I really do."

The hurt in her voice had his throat constricting. He wrapped an arm around her shoulders and pulled her closer. "Don't think like that. I thought we were leaving the past behind."

"We are. I just think I need to explain some things to you." She looked down at her hands in her lap. "My memories of that time in my life feel like they belong to someone else. I hate her–the girl I used to be. I knew better than to do the things I did. I did them anyway, and my life spiraled for a long time. Things were so bad that I thought that's the only way my life could be–bad. It was hard to hope for a better tomorrow when each day was a complete disaster. It was painful and scary."

Asa couldn't imagine how hard it might be for her to talk about the past. That was one reason he hadn't asked her to do it. All he needed to know was that she was dedicated to staying sober, but hearing her talk about her past gave him a better understanding of why she was here now and why she'd chosen the new path.

She looked up at him with her brow furrowed. "I just want you to know I'll never make those mistakes again. I learned my lesson, and I paid the price. I'm not going back."

"We don't have to talk about it if it's painful for you to relive, but I'm glad you told me."

"I'd like to talk about it more with you. Maybe in pieces because it's tough sometimes, but I think you deserve to know about me. It wouldn't be right if we blocked out that topic of conversation."

Asa smiled. "You know how happy it makes me to hear that you want to share things about yourself with me?"

Lyric playfully slapped his chest. "Stop saying all the right things."

"I mean, there's so much I don't know about you. Nothing about us has been traditional at all. I mean, you're meeting my family on our second date."

Lyric winced. "It might be a long time before you

meet my family. If ever." She shrugged. "That's a left-over wound from the dark days."

"They didn't keep in touch with you?"

Lyric shook her head.

That was something Asa couldn't understand. He couldn't turn his back on Jacob. Ever. Asa's mom wouldn't have done it to him either.

Still, he didn't know the circumstances in Lyric's relationship with her parents. She'd said there was a lot of hurt that hadn't been mended.

"Do you want to fix your relationship with them?" he asked.

"Of course. I made my amends to them, but at the time, they weren't very confident I would stay sober. After seeing the way they looked at me and pretty much shut the door in my face, I've been afraid to try again."

"Dad!"

Asa and Lyric both turned at Jacob's call. He dodged tables on his way across the restaurant. Asa's mother walked at her own pace behind him.

Lyric gasped, catching Asa's attention. She stared wide-eyed at Jacob.

"What's wrong?" Asa asked.

"He looks just like you," she whispered.

Asa heard it so often that he'd gotten used to it. Lyric's shocked expression morphed into a smile. The similarities between him and his son might help Lyric relax while meeting his family.

Jacob jerked to a stop by the table. "Dad, I finished another model!" He held up the blue car, careful to balance it on his palm.

"It looks great, bud." Asa gently lifted the model and inspected it. "Where are we putting this one?"

"I was thinking the second shelf, on the left side."

Asa had built the narrow shelves on Jacob's bedroom wall last year, and the kid had already filled them with a wide range of classics.

Jacob's attention fell from the car, and he peeked around Asa. "Are you Lyric?"

Lyric had the look of a deer in headlights. "Um, yeah. You must be Jacob." She stood and extended a hand to him, then tensed. Her pleading gaze cut to Asa just as Jacob took her hand. She whispered over Jacob's head, "I don't know what to do."

Asa's mom strode up to them with a beaming smile. "Hello, you two. Lyric, it's so good to finally meet you." His mom opened her arms and gave Lyric a full-on mom hug.

"Oh, it's great to meet you too. Thank you so much for letting me stay with you. I know I'm a stranger, but I promise not to be a bother, and–"

"Lyric." His mom held up a silencing hand. "This will be good for both of us."

Jacob stepped well inside Lyric's personal space and craned his neck to look up at her. "Granny gets lonely when I'm not around to entertain her."

Asa covered his mouth with a hand and scratched a pretend itch on his cheek.

The shiny model car in Asa's hand caught Lyric's attention. "Did you really make that?"

Jacob grabbed the model from Asa. "I did. This is my favorite. I have two already on my shelf!"

"Ford Thunderbird." Lyric lifted her hands as if pulled toward the car like a magnet, then linked her hands in front of her. "1959?"

"Yeah!" Jacob shouted.

"My dad had one," Lyric said. A grin spread over her face, and her gaze was glued to the model.

"No way!" Jacob rounded on Asa. "Dad, can we have one?"

"No, buddy, but maybe Lyric can tell us more about it over dinner." Asa winked at Lyric, hoping it was okay to volunteer her to talk about something that might be classified as "the past."

"I'd love to." The full smile on her face was genuine as she took her seat in the booth.

Jacob quickly sat across from her. "Tell me everything."

Asa hadn't made a move to sit. He was engrossed in the interaction between Lyric and his son. They talked like old friends who had missed each other.

His mom's hand rested gently on his shoulder. "Breathe, son."

Her words jolted him out of his daydream, and he slid into the booth next to Lyric.

The whole day had been a whirlwind. He'd worked up the nerve to talk to Lyric and offer her the room at his mom's, they'd had the define-the-relationship talk, then their first date, followed by hours of packing. Now, they were sitting together with his family at a popular restaurant in town. Lyric fit in, and watching her talk to his son like there weren't any obstacles standing against them gave Asa a surge of hope that he wanted to lock onto and never let go.

It was too early to tell, but maybe this crazy plan could work out.

24

LYRIC

Lyric piled her dark hair into a bun on top of her head. Looking in the mirror, she wasn't impressed with anything she saw. The bun wasn't going to work, faint shadows rested below her eyes, and her sharp collarbone jutted out from behind the scooped collar of her dress.

It had been a little over a week since she'd been officially kicked out of her apartment and two since Russell told her to find a new place. Two weeks without enough sleep was draining the life out of her.

Well, she was sleeping fine now that she was at Betty's. She still wasn't sure what to call Asa's mom. Asa and Jacob called her Granny, and it felt weird to call her something different than what they did, but Granny felt too familiar. Grannies were named for their position in the family, and Lyric wasn't family.

Lyric looked back at the bed she'd reluctantly rolled out of an hour earlier. It was so soft, and the sheets were like puffy air gliding over her skin. Moving and working this week had been exhausting, and her body couldn't get enough of her new awesome bed.

It wasn't *her* bed. That was something she didn't need to forget.

She tugged the hair tie out of her hair and shook it out. Now what?

Someone knocked on the bedroom door, and she gave herself a quick glance. They needed to leave in twenty minutes to make it to church on time. Her hair was a mess, and she hadn't put on her makeup and wasn't sure about the dress she'd put on.

Well, stalling wasn't going to help anything. "Come in!"

The door opened a crack, and Jacob stuck his head in. "Are you ready?"

"Almost."

Jacob opened the door all the way and walked in. "Good. Can I hang out in your room?"

"Sure, but it's probably boring in here. I'll just be putting on my makeup."

"I don't care." He pulled a Rubik's cube out of his pocket and flopped onto the bed on his back.

Jacob had welcomed her into her new home in a way she'd needed but hadn't expected. He wanted to be around her all the time, and he didn't always give her a choice about it. Asking if he could hang out in her room was more than she usually got. By gently pushing his way into her personal space, he'd forced her to open up and become comfortable in ways she never had before.

Lyric turned back to the mirror and pulled half of her hair up before letting it fall. She rummaged through her limited assortment of hair ties and grumbled.

"What's wrong?" Jacob asked.

"Nothing. Just trying to get my hair to do… something."

"I like it like that," Jacob said as he sat up on the bed.

"Like this? It's just all…" She waved her hands in the air, expressing the craziness she couldn't put into words.

"It's pretty. You should leave it like that."

She chuckled. "I will for now while I look for some shoes that might match this dress." Saying a prayer of thanks that she hadn't been forced to give up two-thirds of her things, she knelt on the floor in front of the small closet.

Nothing was going to go with this dress. She didn't want to change, but none of her shoes matched. She'd found the dress a few weeks ago at the thrift store, and she'd been so excited to wear it that she hadn't thought about shoes.

Sitting back on her heels, she sighed again.

"What's wrong now?" Jacob asked.

"Sorry. Nothing is wrong."

Jacob climbed off the bed and sat on the floor beside her. "You sure?"

She looked at Jacob, and the expression on his face melted her heart. It was the same expression Asa used when he saw her struggling and had decided he was determined to help.

Lyric swallowed the lump in her throat. "I'm a little nervous about going to church."

"Why? You said you go to church."

"I do, but I used to go to church in Silver Falls."

"But you told Dad you wanted to go to church with us."

The conversation hadn't exactly gone that way. Asa had asked her in private if she wanted to come to church with them, and Jacob had overheard and practically accepted the invitation for her.

"I do want to, but it's a new place, and I'm just a little scared."

Jacob sat up straighter. "I used to not want to go because Dad made me sit and be quiet, but now I like it. My friends are there, and the old people are really nice. They love me."

Lyric chuckled at Jacob's description of the church. He was doing a good job of selling it, and she had no doubt they all loved the outgoing kid. Her on the other hand? They had plenty of reasons *not* to like her.

Jacob patted her arm. "Just say hey to everybody, and they'll love you too."

If only life was as simple as Jacob made it out to be. She wouldn't blame these people for not accepting her. Not after what she'd done.

She wrapped an arm around his shoulders. "It's easy to love you, kid. Me? I'm not everyone's cup of tea."

Jacob scrunched his nose. "You mean that hot tea stuff Granny likes? Why would you want to be tea?"

Lyric laughed and hugged him tighter. "You're a barrel of laughs. What I mean is, I'm not as loveable as you."

"Why not?"

"Well, I haven't been loved as much as you have, and that's okay. You deserve all the love."

"Don't your parents love you?"

That was a knife in her heart. They'd loved her immensely once, but now she wasn't sure where they stood. "Um, I think so."

Jacob lifted his head. "You think so? How can you not know?"

How much should she say? Jacob was always so open with her, and she wanted to be honest with him. But he wouldn't understand the reasons why a mother and a father might not be in their child's life anymore.

"Um, I haven't talked to them in a while."

"Dad always tells me I should know he loves me,

even if he's not always around to say it. Like, he tells me at least ten times a day, but he means when I'm at school and stuff. He still loves me even when he's not with me."

She hummed and brushed a hand over Jacob's soft hair. She liked that Jacob was a toucher. He liked hugging her, and she needed someone to hug. Win-win.

"I know your family loves you," she said.

Jacob leaned into her hand as she continued the rhythmic caress of his hair. "Sometimes, I wish I could talk to Mom," he whispered.

Oh boy. This casual conversation was going downhill faster than she could stop it. She knew the family talked about Danielle whenever they could, but Lyric didn't know the guidelines yet. Asa said they wanted to keep Jacob's mom's memory alive, but Lyric didn't have any memories of her to share.

"I bet she loves you too, even if she isn't around to say it."

He looked up at her. His expression was sad, but he wasn't on the verge of tears. "I bet it's like that with your mom too."

Lyric nodded slowly, willing her emotions to stay steady. Crying would only upset Jacob. "I hope so."

"I miss mine," he said.

"Me too," she whispered.

"Why don't you ask her if she still loves you?"

Lyric sniffed. "I could do that."

"You should. Then you'd know she loves you, and you wouldn't have to miss her like I miss mine."

"Okay." It was the only word she could muster. Anything else would break the dam holding back the sadness.

Jacob stood in a rush. "Anyway, you shouldn't be worried about church. Just stick with me, and you'll be okay."

Lyric stood and blinked back the moisture in her eyes. "Thanks. I feel better already."

Two quick knocks sounded at the open door. Asa stood in the doorway wearing light-gray slacks and a navy-blue shirt that matched her dress perfectly.

"Jacob, give her some space to get ready."

"I was! We were just talking."

Asa jerked a thumb over his shoulder. "Granny has muffins in the kitchen."

"Muffins!" Jacob darted past his dad and out of the bedroom in a flash.

Asa looked her up and down. She could feel the heat of his stare as his gaze traveled over her body.

"You're beautiful," he said boldly.

"Thanks."

Asa took a step into the room. "Would it be bad if I bothered you right now after I told Jacob not to?"

Lyric laughed and closed the distance between them, wrapping her arms around his waist. "He wasn't bothering me, and you aren't either."

Asa cupped her cheeks then slid his hands into her hair. "I love your hair like this."

"Your son said the same thing."

"Like father, like son."

Lyric smiled. "You have no idea."

"Dad! Lyric! It's time to go!" Jacob yelled from the other end of the house.

Lyric pushed up onto her toes and pressed a quick kiss to Asa's lips. "I have to get ready."

"You look ready."

"I'm not wearing shoes or makeup, and my hair is a mess."

"Leave your hair like that and forget the makeup. You might need the shoes though."

Lyric laughed and grabbed a pair of gray flats. Her feet might freeze, but it would be cute to match Asa on her first visit to a new church.

25

ASA

sa parked in front of the small church and killed the engine. After a week and a half driving a rental, he finally found a new truck.

Well, a truck that was new to him. It was only a few years old, but hopefully it would still be running strong when Jacob learned to drive.

Good grief, Asa's son would be driving in less than six short years, and he was not okay.

Jacob jumped out of the truck as soon as it came to a stop. "Come on. I want to be a greeter!"

The door closed behind the kid as he darted across the parking lot.

"Guess he didn't want to bring his Bible," Granny said, holding it up in the air as she scooted out of the passenger seat.

Lyric sat like a statue in the backseat, clutching her Bible to her chest.

"You okay?" Asa asked quietly as soon as his mom shut the door behind her.

She gave him a quick smile in the rear-view mirror. It was completely forced. "Yeah."

"Then why do you look like you just ate something bad but you're trying to spare the cook's feelings?"

Her smile morphed into something real. "It's not that bad. Just nerves."

He couldn't keep talking from the front seat to the back. He got out of the truck and opened her door. Lyric sat with her knees pressed together. The pale skin of her legs peeked out beneath the ends of the navy dress she wore.

Saying he liked the dress was one thing. It was the woman in the dress that gave him fits. He could barely think straight these days, whether he was with Lyric or not. Between her and Jacob, Asa's thoughts were busy for the foreseeable future, and he wouldn't change it for anything.

He propped a shoulder against the doorframe. "What's on your mind?"

She reached for his hand like a lifeline and threaded her fingers through his. "Lots of people in Blackwater know me, and not for good reasons. I don't feel comfortable going to church with the people I've let down. Quite a few of them only knew me at my worst."

Asa looked at the church on the small hill above the parking lot, then turned his attention back to Lyric. "I know a little bit about avoiding people. Most everyone in town knew Danielle. For a long time, I hated running into people I knew because they always brought up her name. I even avoided church for a while after she died. I lost a part of myself, and everyone wanted to talk about it."

"Oh, Asa," Lyric breathed.

He squeezed her hand. "When I finally got past it enough to go back to church, it wasn't so bad. I mean, someone still brings her up from time to time, but it's in a good way. At least, I can think of it like it's a good thing now. Back then, it all seemed bad."

Lyric nodded. "I might be overreacting. Maybe nobody cares."

"I know some people who care," he gently reminded her.

She smiled like she knew a special secret. "I know you care. A lot of people around here know what I've done. It's just scary."

"I know what you've done. I still care. Plus, if you had to be perfect to get in, the place would be empty. This isn't going to work until you realize people don't come here because they think they're better than you. They're all here because they're just like you."

Jacob jogged up to Asa's side, panting. "I forgot I told Lyric she could stick with me today."

Asa looked back to Lyric, who bit her lips between her teeth. She nodded and scooted out of the seat, keeping a hold on Asa's hand.

"Thanks, but I can stay with your dad if you want to do the greeting."

Jacob shook his head. "Nah. I just like saying hey to people, but I can do that inside. I'll introduce you to everyone."

Lyric looked up at Asa, but the panic from a moment ago was gone, replaced by a genuine excitement. "Okay then. I guess you can show me around."

Jacob reached for Lyric's hand, and she let go of Asa's to switch to his son's. He had a lot of reasons to be proud of his son, but the kid was kicking things up a notch today.

Asa followed Jacob and Lyric inside where Jacob did just as he'd promised. He introduced her to everyone he passed. It wasn't lost on Asa that his son introduced her as his friend. Jacob truly thought Lyric was his new friend. They played games together, she'd helped him with his homework a few times, and Asa had even found the two watching a football game together yesterday. Lyric probably didn't care one bit about the sport, but Jacob had explained everything that happened just as well as the commentators.

They finally made it to the pew their family

normally chose, and Jacob pointed to a seat. "Lyric, you can sit here. I sit there, and Dad sits there."

"What if I want to sit by Lyric?" Asa asked.

Jacob studied the pew. "Well, I guess she could sit here, and I'll sit there."

"But I want to sit by her too," Granny said, sliding into the conversation with a mischievous grin.

Scratching his head, Jacob frowned as he looked at the empty seats. "Well, I guess you could sit behind her."

Asa's mom laughed and nudged Lyric toward the pew. "Y'all go ahead. I'll sit on the end."

Ms. Landry stopped next to them and rested on her cane. The woman glared at Lyric with narrowed eyes and scooted closer. Her words were high-pitched and scratchy as she said, "I know you from somewhere."

Lyric's eyes widened, and she froze.

"Yes, I do. How do I know you?" Ms. Landry asked, leaning on her cane and tilting her chin up to get a closer look through her bifocals. "Who do you belong to?"

"I—" Lyric stammered and pierced Asa with a pleading look.

No, no, no. He had to get her out of this. Ms. Landry only left her house to come to church on Sundays and Wednesdays, but she somehow had her finger on the pulse of everything happening in Blackwater. If she caught a whiff of Lyric's past, word would make its way through her phone tree like a bolt of lightning. "Ms. Landry, this is—"

"She's Lyric," Jacob finished. "My friend."

"Lyric?" Ms. Landry practically shouted. Though, the volume probably had more to do with her hearing loss than surprise. "I would remember that name. I guess I don't know you." She looked up at Asa and gave him a single nod. "Good to see you, Asa."

He breathed a sigh of relief and wrapped an arm around Lyric's waist. "Good to see you too."

As soon as the older woman walked away, Lyric melted into Asa's side. "I just knew she was going to say something," she whispered.

Asa pressed a kiss to her hair. "So what if she does? The past doesn't matter anymore."

Truly, it didn't. No matter how many times they were reminded of it, as long as they agreed the past should stay behind them, they could look forward to the future together.

Jerry Lawrence stepped into the row in front of them and gave Asa a quick nod. His daughter, Olivia, was right behind him, and her smile had enough wattage to light up an underground cave. If Lyric spent any amount of time with Olivia, the two would probably become fast friends.

"So, you must be Lyric," Olivia said as she sat and turned all the way around to prop her forearms on the back of the pew.

Lyric's shoulder tensed beneath his hand. "I am."

"I've heard so much about you," Olivia said.

"Only good things," Asa added. "Lyric, meet Olivia Lawrence."

If only he could transfer thoughts to Lyric right now. Olivia had been a family friend for as long as he could remember, but the relationship was strictly platonic. What were the chances Lyric would think he'd ever been involved with Olivia?

"Of course. Asa is one of the good ones, which I'm sure you've figured out by now." She pointed a finger and moved it between Asa and Lyric. "So, you two are—"

"Together," Asa added. "You can post that on the community chat."

A jolt of recognition ran up his spine. Was that the first time they'd openly admitted their relationship?

Olivia rolled her eyes. "You know I don't gossip like that. I'm just glad to see the two of you happy. Y'all are adorable together!"

Lyric looked up at him with a genuine smile. Apparently, she'd gotten the memo that Olivia was just overly friendly and not catty.

"Hey, Lyric!" Dawson plopped down in a seat beside Olivia and turned to face them.

"You two are just alike," Asa said.

Dawson looked Olivia up and down. "I'll take that as a compliment."

She waved a hand in the air and told Dawson, "I'm getting the scoop."

"Well, let me in on it." He extended his hand to Lyric.

Lyric shook it. "It's nice to see you again."

She'd barely gotten the last word out before Asa's phone vibrated in his pocket. No one would call him on a Sunday morning except work.

Sure enough, the telltale name showed on the screen. He looked at Dawson, who seemed to understand what was going on, then turned to Lyric.

"Is everything okay?" she asked.

"It's work. I need to check in." Standing, he snaked a path through the people talking in the aisles and headed for the side hallway. Once he was out of the crowd, he answered the call. "Hey, boss."

"We've got a twelve-car pile-up on the highway. I need all hands on deck."

"I'm on my way. I'm with Dawson. Want me to tell him?"

"Yes. Bring him with you," Chief said.

"Got it." Asa ended the call and wove back into the sanctuary. Olivia chatted with Lyric, but Dawson looked up as soon as Asa was in sight.

Jerking his chin toward the door to let Dawson know they needed to head out, he slid back into the seat beside Lyric. "Sorry about this, but I just got called into work."

Dawson stood. "You riding with me?"

"Yeah, I need to leave my truck for them." He pointed toward his family on the row.

"Go," Lyric said as she pushed at his shoulder. "Don't worry about us."

Asa hesitated. Leaving Lyric when she'd been so nervous didn't sit right with him.

But he'd never backed away from his duty.

Lyric pushed his shoulder again. "Go."

"Seriously, I'll take care of your girl," Olivia said as she stood. "I'll even sit by her."

Asa handed his truck keys to Lyric. "Can you get Mom and Jacob home?"

"Of course. Now, please go. They need your help."

He pressed a quick kiss to her forehead before following Dawson out the door and into the parking lot.

"What's the word?" he asked.

"Twelve-vehicle incident."

"Yikes. We better push the limit."

The two slid into Dawson's truck and pulled out of the parking lot. They were in for a long day and an even longer night of paperwork.

Spending a lazy Sunday with Lyric and his family would have to wait for another day.

26

LYRIC

Lyric watched Asa and Jacob from across the bakery. The two waited at the counter for their orders, while Lyric had found an empty booth with Betty. The after-church rush was crazy on Sundays, and it was a miracle they'd found a seat.

She'd missed the last few weeks of church. Sundays were usually check-out days for renters, and Brenda often called her to work.

Lyric's second visit to Asa's church was much easier than the first. Her initial concerns were long gone. Between Asa, Jacob, and Betty, she'd been introduced to everyone, and they'd all been kind to her. She'd spotted a few faces from the congregation in line at the bakery, and they'd waved.

She still kept up with Kendra and asked about her old church, but the move had been a good decision. Though the nagging question of how long it would last always popped up in the back of her mind. When she found a new place to live, would she continue attending Asa's church?

That was one way to get a sense of what he thought about their relationship. He'd said before that he wanted something permanent. Did he still think he wanted those things with her?

Jacob was talking, but Asa glanced over his son's head at her. With a small wink, he let her know she was still on his mind.

Swoon. The man was Prince Charming wrapped in a cinnamon roll—oh so sweet.

"Those two are like peas in a pod," Granny said.

"I know. Jacob seems so much like Asa, I can't imagine what traits he got from Danielle." It was becoming easier to talk about Asa's late wife. Lyric had seen pictures and heard casual stories about the woman, but it was still hard to piece together who she'd been as a person.

That didn't stop Lyric from wondering, and her heart broke just thinking about all his late wife was missing. Instead, Lyric was here, trying to be a part of their lives without stepping on those memories.

"He's a lot like her. She was smart and inquisitive. But looking at them..." Betty shook her head. "Jacob is a mirror image of his dad."

"I bet Asa was a cute little boy."

"You have no idea. His dad left us before Asa

turned two, and I don't know what I would have done without my boy."

No one ever talked about Asa's dad, and Lyric had been too afraid to ask. Danielle deserved to be remembered. Asa's absent father didn't.

Left them? How could he? Especially if Asa was anything like Jacob. Both Scott boys were making her days brighter, and she would do anything to keep them in her life. "I can't imagine someone leaving."

"He didn't want kids, and apparently, he didn't want me too much either. I got divorce papers in the mail and never saw him again."

"I'm so sorry."

Betty waved a hand. "Water under the bridge. My life is great."

Lyric winked at Betty across the table. "Same."

A second later, the memory of her own parents seeped into her thoughts. She'd been the one to abandon them. Granted, it was a mutual parting. They'd been great parents—given her everything. All she'd done was throw that love in their face.

"I miss my parents," Lyric whispered, barely audible over the chatter in the bakery.

Betty reached over and rested a hand over Lyric's. "It's never too late to mend fences, sweetie."

"I know. I talked to them once since I've been sober, and it went okay. I didn't reach out anymore because I hadn't proven myself to them. I didn't have anything to offer. Why would they trust me yet?"

"The rift between parents and children can be the most heartbreaking. I don't know your parents, but I bet they'd be overjoyed to see you now."

"Maybe."

"And you do have something to offer them. Hope. You are redeemed and forgiven. That's a gift we sometimes forget about when life is dealing us hard times."

Lyric flipped her hand and clasped Betty's. "Thank you. You're probably right. I just have to work up the nerve to make the move."

"I'll be here for you through it all. Asa and Jacob will too."

A smile strained Lyric's cheeks. "I have no doubt."

When Lyric turned back to where Asa and Jacob were waiting, she saw a familiar face stepping out of the order line. Wendy pushed a strand of hair behind her ear that had fallen out of her messy bun —a truly messy bun that didn't have any of the casual appeal some women could pull off. Her friend kept her head low, studying the receipt the cashier just handed her.

"Do you mind if I say hello to a friend?" Lyric asked.

"Go ahead," Betty said, pulling her glasses from

where they rested on her head and checking her phone.

"Be right back." Lyric moved through the crowd until she was beside Wendy. "Hey."

Wendy jerked her head up. She'd been stuffing change into her purse. "Oh, you scared me." Resting a hand on her chest, she heaved a deep exhale.

"Sorry. It's good to see you." Up close, Lyric studied her friend. Wendy didn't have on any makeup, but she wore a cute sweater and dark-wash jeans that fit well.

"You too. I've been worried about you since Russell...you know."

Lyric scrunched her nose. "Has someone moved in yet?"

Wendy's lips tightened into a thin line as she nodded.

"Figures. He was right. He needed a paying tenant."

"But I hate what happened to you. You did find a place, right? You could have lived with us if we had any extra room. I mean, Jaycee is a little rough around the edges. You two might not have gotten along well."

"I appreciate that, but I found a place." Lyric jerked her head toward the table where Betty sat. Asa and Jacob had joined her, and Asa was glancing their way.

"You want to meet them?" Lyric asked.

"You're living with *Asa*?" Wendy gasped. She'd met him once in the hallway when he'd been helping Lyric move her things out of the apartment.

"No. No. The lady is his mom."

Wendy sighed. "Oh, I was about to say, we all know moving in with a man is the worst idea, even if he's that handsome."

"You don't have to tell me twice. I made that mistake myself once, but I quickly found out I'd messed up." Now that she'd found the Lord and dedicated her life to staying on the straight and narrow, all those mistakes waved in her mind like red flags.

Wendy grinned. "We live and learn, right?"

A few weeks ago, Lyric would have said living the sober life doesn't get easier. Now, she couldn't help but hope that this was the break she needed to get on her feet.

"You doing okay still?" Lyric asked.

"Six months." Wendy held up her crossed fingers.

"You can do it. If you need any help, just call me."

"I know. You're the best." Wendy wrapped an arm around Lyric's shoulders. "I've missed you."

"I've missed you too." Wendy and Lyric had always been on similar paths, and cheering each other on had been vital for both of them. It was good to have a reminder that you were being held accountable to someone who cared.

"Wendy!" the barista shouted.

"I need to run. I got a new job at Julia's Flower Shop."

"That's great. I hope you love it." Wendy had been through her share of ups and downs trying to get sober. A job she loved would be good for her.

"I do. I'll call you soon. Tell Asa I said hey."

Lyric waved good-bye as she made her way back to the booth. Asa was eyeing her with gentle curiosity, but Jacob was the one who spoke first.

"Who was that?"

"An old friend."

"Was that Wendy?" Asa asked.

"Yeah. She said to tell you hey."

"She doing okay?"

"She just got a job at Julia's Flower Shop."

"Oh!" Betty gasped. "I always order flowers from Julia. She's a doll."

"I hope she likes it there," Lyric said.

When everyone else had filled their mouths with sandwiches, Asa mouthed to Lyric, "Sober?"

Lyric held up her fingers and mouthed back, "Six months."

Asa nodded and whispered, "Good. Did you tell her to call if she needs anything?"

Asa's concern for her friend was more than

Lyric's heart could take right now. Knowing he didn't look at Wendy like a lost cause was the tipping point.

She loved Asa Scott, and the whole package that came with him.

27

ASA

A sa quietly closed the back door behind him as he walked into his mom's house. He'd worked overtime, and there was a good chance Jacob would be in bed.

Instead of the silence he'd expected, feminine giggles came from the living room. Was that a snort?

Lyric and his mom were lying on the floor surrounded by piles of boxes and photos. Lyric was flat on her back with her dark hair spread out around her. She wiped tears from her eyes as she huffed through the last of her laughter.

Asa was more worried about his mother. She sat with her legs tucked beside her, and she lay slumped, facedown.

"What's going on?" he asked.

Lyric sat up quickly and wiped her eyes. "It's all

her fault." She pointed at his mom and fell into another fit of laughter.

"No, it's his fault," his mom said, pointing at Asa.

"You're going to wake up Jacob," Asa said.

Lyric shook her head. "No, we won't. We went to the park after school, and he's out like a light."

Asa crossed his arms over his chest and fought the grin tugging on the corners of his mouth. "You two are crazy."

Lyric's hand shot up in the air. "Guilty!"

His mother laughed harder at Lyric's confession. "Lock her up, officer!"

Asa rolled his eyes. At least they could joke about Lyric's past now. It couldn't hurt them anymore. "I'm going to check on Jacob."

The two women on the floor kept laughing as Asa peeked into Jacob's room down the hallway. He was sound asleep as Lyric said he would be.

Half a minute later, Asa was back in the living room, and his mom and Lyric were composing themselves. His mom piled photos into a box, while Lyric straightened photo albums into another.

Asa sat on the couch. "What's all this?"

Lyric brushed her hair away from her face as she handed him a photo. "We found this one of Jacob."

Asa chuckled as he looked at the memory. Jacob was probably two in the photo. Danielle had put him in the bath and walked back into the bedroom to get his pajamas. When she returned, she found Jacob standing outside the tub with his arms crossed over his chest and a frown on his face. "He hated bath time."

"Then he found out that he hated being dirty more than he hated bath time," Asa's mom said.

Lyric looked at the albums on the floor beside her. "We're organizing photos for Jacob. He told me he's forgetting her."

Asa's chest tightened. Lyric didn't have to say the name. They talked about Danielle from time to time, but Asa hadn't thought about Jacob's own memories of his mom.

"So, you're doing this for him?" Asa asked.

His mother pushed to her feet with a groan. "We have to move this party to the kitchen table next time. My old body can't sit on the floor."

"Sorry. I should have thought of that before I started unpacking them in here," Lyric said.

Lyric had initiated this project? Danielle was a part of Asa's past just as much as Lyric's mistakes were a part of hers, but she didn't seem uncomfortable with either topic anymore.

"Lyric, you want some hot tea?" his mother asked as she waddled to the kitchen, rubbing her hips.

"Sure, thanks."

Asa hummed. "Should I be offended that she didn't offer me any?"

Lyric climbed onto the couch beside him and

playfully swatted his chest. "No. We all know you think her hot tea is gross. I happen to like it."

Asa wrapped his arms around Lyric, and she nestled close to his chest. "Is it weird that you're so much like my mom?"

"Not at all. I love her, and she's mine. You can't have her back."

The L word caught him off guard, and he stopped rubbing her back.

Lyric tensed. "Sorry. I was just–"

"It's fine. I love that you love my mom." It made his heart pound like a jackhammer, but it was true. He was glad Lyric loved his family. They loved her too. He was sure of it. Himself included.

If someone had told him two months ago that he was going to meet a woman who would turn his life upside down the way Lyric had, he'd have laughed them out of Wyoming. But the joke was on him. He'd fallen hard, and there wasn't anything he could do to stop it. He didn't want to.

"I really do," Lyric said softly. "I–"

"I love you." Asa blurted the words–fast and bold.

Lyric pushed off his chest and straightened. The dumbfounded look on her face would have been funny if he wasn't still waiting to see if she'd run.

"I love you too." Her words were shaky but sure. "I love you. I love you and Jacob and Betty." Tears pooled in her eyes, as she pressed a hand to her mouth.

Asa halted her quick words with a kiss. He hadn't expected to love again, but Lyric made it easy. She was selfless and helpful. She was good to Jacob, and she didn't take anything for granted.

When the kiss ended, Lyric swallowed hard. "I love you."

Asa smiled as warmth filled his chest. "I love you too."

Lyric smiled, but her chin trembled. "I never expected someone to say that to me."

"What? I love you?"

"Yeah. Say it again, please," she whispered.

He laughed, happy to keep saying it as much as she needed. "I lo–"

Lyric cut him off with another kiss–one fueled by the genuine acceptance they'd perfected for each other. He threaded his fingers in her hair and inhaled a deep breath as his lips moved over hers. Man, he'd completely forgotten how amazing love could be, and with Lyric, it just kept getting better and better.

She started smiling and broke the kiss. "I'm sorry. I'm just so happy."

"I love seeing you happy."

"You make me happy. This makes me happy." She waved her hand around the room. "I really do love your whole family. That doesn't take away from how I feel about you. It just multiplies things."

The nagging thoughts fought to overcome the happiness. His family was great, but knowing Lyric was still estranged from hers put a subtle cloud over the moment. Why couldn't everyone see her determination? She was giving it everything she had, and in some cases, it still wasn't enough. Maybe her parents didn't know how well she was doing and how hard she was trying to be better.

"Your family is a lot like mine. Or how they used to be," Lyric whispered.

Asa hugged her tighter. "You don't talk about them much."

"Because I'm scared. I want them to see how far I've come, but I'm afraid all they'll see are my mistakes."

"You'll never know if you don't try," he whispered.

Lyric huffed. "Been there. Done that. Got the T-shirt. But maybe you're right. I do need to try again."

"What can I do to help?" he asked.

She cuddled next to him and rested her head on his shoulder. "I'm not sure. I think the holdup is that I don't know how to approach them."

"Maybe this is one of those times when you need to say what you mean, do what you can, and let God handle the rest."

"I think that's a good plan," she whispered.

"You want to pray about it?"

"Will you?" she asked.

"Of course." He wrapped his arms tighter around her and prayed. He asked for wisdom, strength, and peace. He thanked the Lord for the family they had and the family they might get to know.

When he finished, Lyric lifted her head from his shoulder and wiped her eyes.

"Hey, we'll figure this out. Don't worry."

"I'm actually not worried." She grabbed his hand and squeezed. "You're a great man, and I'm amazed by your faith."

"I haven't always been so grounded. There were times when I wanted to doubt because it would be easier or because I was angry. In the end, it was the only thing that kept me going through Danielle's sickness and after she died. I had a son and a job. When things got tough, I trusted in the Lord, and I stopped worrying. I had to. It was killing me."

"I'm sorry you had to go through that. Jacob too."

Asa might not ever be able to tell Lyric how hard it was for both Jacob and him to grieve for Danielle. They were still grieving, but they were also hanging onto the things in life that made them happy.

"I had to let the Lord be in charge of my life. I was worrying myself into an early grave. When I gave it over to Him, I didn't check up on the promise. I just had faith that it would work out. It's still not easy, but it's a little better every day."

"Here you go," his mom said as she carried two steaming cups of tea into the living room. She handed one to Lyric and settled into the recliner. "*Little House on the Prairie*?"

"Sure," Lyric said as she wrapped both hands around the warm mug and snuggled closer to Asa's side.

"Really?" he asked.

"We watch it every night," Lyric explained.

"I think Mom has been waiting for this day her whole life. She tried to read those books to me when I was little, but talk about a snooze fest."

Lyric and his mom gasped at the same time.

"Don't talk about the Ingalls family like that," Lyric said. "They're doing their best."

"Are you saying they're real?" Asa asked with a smirk.

"Real enough," his mom said. "Now be quiet so we can hear."

Lyric giggled as his mom resumed the show. Asa rested his head back on the couch and closed his eyes. He needed to go home and rest, but everyone he loved was here.

28

ASA

Asa pulled into the Calvary Baptist Church parking lot and scanned the area lit up by the headlights. Not a soul in sight.

If he had to get held over on an already busy shift, at least he'd gotten a trespassing call and not the multi-vehicle wreck on the highway. He'd circle the building a few times, talk to the neighbor who made the call, and be back at the station before Jacob went to bed.

He'd rounded the building once before another cruiser pulled into the parking lot. Dawson radioed in, associating himself with the call.

Asa pulled up beside him and rolled down the window. "Want to do a perimeter check with me?"

"We'd better take a look at the parsonage too. That place has been abandoned for years. Probably kids messing around."

Asa stepped out into the cold night and shone his flashlight on the gravel and up toward the church. No signs of a disturbance at the front entrance or any of the windows facing the street.

"Let's go this way," Asa said, pointing his flashlight toward the right side of the church.

"I'll check the building. You check the woods," Dawson said as he ran his hand over a dark window.

On the back side of the church, the parsonage loomed in the field off to one side. What used to be a yard was now overgrown, and brush weaved in and out of the open windows and doors. The awning was drooping on one side, and the roof sagged in the middle.

Asa's light moved over the brush until it illuminated a trampled path leading to the old house. He stopped to get a better look at the disturbed grass, and Dawson doubled back.

Asa stilled the light on the trail as Dawson stopped beside him.

"You think someone's in there?" Dawson asked.

"Dispatch said the caller reported the trespassers behind the church. Maybe they're squatting in there."

Asa keyed up on the radio, announcing his call sign, then waited for the dispatcher's reply that she was ready for him. "Do we have a premise history on the parsonage?"

A few seconds later, Nancy from dispatch was

back on the radio. "Two calls for service: 2000 and 2001."

Asa wasn't surprised that there weren't other calls for service. Everybody in town knew Jeremiah Dunn bought it from the church in the late 1990s, and he and his wife lived in a house on the property adjacent to the church. Without an extensive history on the property, they didn't know what to expect.

"Show us going in," Dawson radioed back. "Signs of foot traffic. Negative vehicles."

Asa led the way up the path. Briars tugged at his pants legs, and a flurry of grasshoppers and moths fluttered in the spotlight ahead of him. He stopped to test the second step leading up to the half-rotted porch. It groaned beneath his weight, but it held.

A low noise caught his attention, and he stopped to listen. Was it a woman sobbing? Asa took a tentative step forward, trying to discern any other sounds.

"Let's go," Dawson whispered.

"Stop!" a man screamed from inside the building, followed by feminine whimpers.

A loud thud vibrated the boards beneath Asa's feet. He radioed to dispatch, "Subjects inside." He kept a hand on his weapon as he banged a fist against the rotting wooden doorframe. "Blackwater PD."

The muffled voice of a man silenced. Asa banged a hand against the door again. "Blackwater PD!"

He turned the old doorknob and pushed

against the door. It wasn't locked or latched, but there was resistance as he pressed his weight against it. The scratching of wood sounded on the other side, and shuffling noises came from farther inside.

The house didn't have electricity, but a light emanating from an interior room drew Asa inside as soon as he breached the entrance. "Blackwater PD!"

Curses came from the room with the light, and shadows jerked over the wall opposite the open door. Asa picked up the pace and pressed his back against the wall beside the open door. "Blackwater PD. Come out with your hands in the air."

Wood scraped against wood, but no one emerged from the room.

So, it was going to be the hard way. Asa inhaled a deep breath of damp, musty air and rounded the corner with a firm grip on his weapon.

A lantern in the corner of the room cast three bodies in shadows. Two men scuffled by a window, and a woman was tied to a wooden chair in front of them.

Trespassing was one thing, but the woman was clearly restrained against her will. She'd probably been abducted too, which meant these two were racking up more offenses by the second.

Dawson quietly radioed to dispatch from behind Asa using the police code for officers needing urgent backup, adding in the code for hostage.

"Stop it!" one of the men shouted, no longer trying to keep quiet.

Oh no. Asa knew that voice. Despite the darkness, he could pinpoint Bobby Wilson any day. The other guy had to be his brother, Zach.

Repeat offenders had at least one disadvantage: they were easy to identify.

The Wilson brothers had been the bane of Asa's existence since grade school, and he hadn't been a fan of the run-ins with them. They'd been raised to take what they wanted, to con their way out of anything, and to hate the cops.

Tonight, it seemed their plan was to test all three of those lessons.

"Put your hands where I can see them," Asa ordered.

The brothers continued to push and shove each other until Bobby, the bigger of the two, landed a shove to Zach's shoulder that knocked him off-balance. He stumbled into the wall and immediately popped right back up.

"I said no!" Zach yelled.

Bobby, the eldest brother, was usually the leader, but it seemed Zach had a dog in the fight tonight.

The woman in the chair whimpered. Her hair was messy and hung over her face. Pulling at the ties on her hands and shifting from side to side, she continued screaming behind the strap covering her mouth.

Bobby straightened and pulled a gun from his waist in one quick movement, leveling it at the woman's head. "Nobody move or she dies!"

A sinking chill ran from Asa's head to his toes. Bobby stood right behind the woman, and neither officer had a clear shot at him.

Don't do it. Don't do it.

Zach lunged for the gun in Bobby's hand, and the shot rang out in the small room just as a strong force pushed Asa backward. He hit the ground on his side and lost his grip on his weapon.

One of the brothers cursed as Dawson radioed to dispatch. "Officer down!"

The fire in Asa's shoulder spread to his chest and arm. Gritting his teeth against the building pressure, he raised his head and sucked in deep breaths through his nose.

Bobby shouted at Zach and busted the window with the butt of his gun.

"Stop and drop your weapons!" Dawson yelled as he moved to stand over Asa.

The pressure in his shoulder was morphing into a sharp pain. The initial shock was waning, but the adrenaline pumping in his system reminded him to get up.

Pressing the heel of his hand into the wound in his shoulder, he ignored the wetness and pushed to sit up. He stumbled once getting his feet under him, but he kept his focus on Bobby and the woman.

Bobby kept his gun pointed at Dawson until the second he turned and dove out of the broken window.

Asa shifted to the right with his weapon aimed at Zach. Dawson moved to the left as he radioed to dispatch.

"Known subjects. One fled the scene."

Zach cursed as his attention jerked between the woman and the officers moving to block him in on two sides. He shook his head before jumping out the window after Bobby.

Dawson fired, but from the spray of wood particles coming from the wall beside the window, he'd missed his mark.

"Asa?" Dawson asked without taking his gaze off the window where the two subjects fled.

"Go! I'll stay with her."

Dawson didn't hesitate. He pursued the men out the window without looking back.

Asa radioed to dispatch. "One female victim. Possible head trauma. Send medical. Officer Keller in pursuit of two armed subjects last seen headed northbound on foot."

Asa rushed to the woman and pulled the strap off her mouth. She sobbed, jerking her head from side to side.

"Ma'am, can you tell me your name? Are you injured?"

"Are they gone?" she asked as she continued to sob with her head down.

"Yes. I'm here to help you." He rounded to the back of the chair and used his knife to cut the ropes that restrained her hands. It took a few minutes and all the concentration he had left to break her free using only one good hand. "What's your name?"

She sniffed, and her voice shook as she said, "Lauren Vincent."

"Lauren?" Oh, man. Between the darkness and her hair covering her face, he hadn't even recognized the children's activities coordinator at the town library. She was one of Jacob's favorite people in the world.

"Asa?" When her arms were free, she wrapped them around his neck and clung to him as she sobbed.

He tensed his jaw against the stabbing in his shoulder and asked, "Are you injured?"

"I don't know," she wailed. "He hit me in the head, and I—I—" Lauren gasped and jerked away from him. "You're bleeding!"

Asa looked at his shoulder. The bullet grazed the edge of his vest. One inch to the left, and he might have gotten out of this with a bruise and a fractured clavicle.

Maybe he was the one who needed a medic. He couldn't tell if the night was getting darker or if he was losing his vision from loss of blood.

Lauren put her hands around his waist to hold him up. He was twice her size, and she used all her body weight to keep him standing. "You're swaying. Asa, sit."

Sirens wailed in the distance, but they were drifting away instead of coming closer. The cold in Asa's arm spread up his shoulder and neck. He widened his stance to keep his balance. "I'm fine."

Dawson's voice came through the radio. "Subjects eastbound on Moose Canyon Road in a blue Toyota Tacoma. Circling back to the church."

Nancy responded, "Cody, Silver Falls, and the sheriff's department en route."

The sirens faded in and out as Lauren guided him toward the seat she'd been tied to. "Please, sit."

"Blackwater PD!"

The words sounded so far away and muffled.

"Back here!" Lauren called.

Asa slumped against the wall as his legs buckled. Lights flashed in the dark room just before they were covered in darkness.

29

LYRIC

The sheet tangled around Lyric's ankle as she rolled onto her left side. How was she supposed to sleep when Asa was still at work?

He usually worked the day shift, and though it came with its own host of problems, it wasn't as scary as the night shift.

Lyric knew exactly what went on after dark. It was never good.

Blackwater was a small town, but that didn't mean there weren't bad people and problems. Don't ask how she knew.

She turned to look at her phone on the night-stand. It lay dark and useless. She couldn't think of a single reason that Asa would still be out this late that didn't involve some kind of trouble. There was a chance he'd forgotten to call her when he got off work, but that didn't seem likely. He always called.

Tossing to her other side, she squeezed her eyes closed and pictured Asa's face. Recalling how he looked at her always calmed her anxiety. From the short stubble on his jaw to the lift at the corners of his eyes when he smiled, she'd memorized every inch of his features.

Lord, keep him safe. If it's not too much...

No. Nothing was too much for the Lord.

If it's Your will, I pray Asa stays safe.

She sighed and turned onto her back. Would this be the rest of her life? He was a small-town police officer. Maybe she was worrying too much. There were more dangerous jobs out there.

Maybe.

The Andy Griffith Show theme song split the silence. Betty's ringtone for Asa and Dawson sent Lyric's heart racing. She sat up in the bed and stilled, listening for Betty to answer the call.

Because no one called this late with good news.

Betty's muffled acknowledgments filtered through the walls. "Is he okay?"

No, no, no. That meant he *wasn't* okay. Lyric tore off the covers and darted for the door. She'd just stepped into the hallway when Betty emerged, pulling her robe tighter around her middle. Shadows hid her eyes, but the firm set of her jaw betrayed her worry.

"What happened?" Lyric whispered.

"He was shot—"

"Shot!" The word ripped from her throat with a painful shriek.

"Shh. He's okay," Betty said.

"If he was shot, he is definitely not okay," Lyric whisper-screamed.

Betty rested a hand on Lyric's arm. "Dawson said he's stable. They're prepping him for surgery in Cody."

A breath caught in Lyric's chest. Shot. He couldn't be. Not Asa.

The grip on her arm tightened. "We can't fall apart. Asa needs us to be strong."

"Right," Lyric whispered. Though, nothing about the situation was right. Asa was a pillar of light in a world of darkness. He didn't deserve this.

"I'll wake Jacob, and we can ride together," Betty said.

Lyric nodded. Doing something would keep her mind occupied. "I'll drive."

Turning on her heels, she rushed back into the bedroom and flipped on the light. Grabbing jeans and a sweater, she focused on one task at a time. Getting dressed. Putting on shoes. Brushing her teeth and hair. When she was ready, she made her way to the kitchen and grabbed a few bottles of water and an apple for Jacob. He'd get hungry on the long drive after waking up this late.

"Lyric?"

Jacob's soft voice snapped her attention to the doorway. His brow furrowed and his eyes squinted against the bright light.

"Hey, bud." She crossed the room and drew him into her arms. The instinct to hug him overpowered everything else.

"Is Dad okay?" he whispered as he tightened his hold around Lyric's waist.

Swallowing the lump in her throat, she whispered, "I'm sure he's going to be okay, but we're going to find out for sure."

He pulled back and wiped his face. "Okay. I just don't know what to do."

Lyric brushed a hand over his dark hair that was so much like Asa's. "Put your shoes on. I'll take care of the rest."

Jacob nodded and headed for the shoe rack by the side door.

Lyric speed-walked back to her room to get her purse. Slinging it onto her shoulder, she mumbled, "This isn't what I meant when I said keep him safe."

"Don't go blaming the Lord," Betty said.

Lyric whirled around to where Betty stood in the doorway. Great. Caught in the act.

"I—I—"

Betty wrapped an arm around Lyric's shoulders and gently nudged her toward the hallway. "I know exactly how you feel. I ask the Lord to keep him safe all the time, and it feels like a slight right now."

Lyric's chin trembled as she let Betty lead her through the dark house. Clutching the strap of her purse, she whispered, "I'm sorry."

"It won't be the last time you question why bad things happen, but remember this is the Lord's plan, and it is good."

Lyric sniffed as they walked into the kitchen. Jacob stood by the door with his boots on and his arms crossed over his chest. What kind of an example was she setting if her faith fell apart at the first sign of trouble?

"I started the car," Jacob said.

Betty opened her arms to him. "Let's pray before we go."

Lyric wrapped her arms around both of them as Betty rested her forehead on Lyric's shoulder.

"Lord, we're all in Your hands. I pray You give Asa comfort and healing. Please be with his doctors and nurses, and we pray for our own strength and faith. Help us to lay our worries at your feet and trust Your plan. Amen."

Betty patted Jacob's shoulder. "Go get in the car. We're right behind you."

Lyric grabbed the drinks and snacks from the counter and turned to follow Jacob. Betty stepped into her path and took a few bottles from the armload.

"I'm glad he has you. I've been so afraid he'd have to go through life alone. He needs someone who will help when things get tough."

Lyric lifted her chin as determination steeled her spine. "You don't have to worry. I'm not going anywhere."

Betty nodded, accepting Lyric's resolve as they headed outside. The motion-activated porch light lit the billowing exhaust fumes as they climbed into Betty's car. Not a single living thing moved or made a sound in the quiet night. The banging of the car doors shutting thundered in the wide-open space.

Lyric settled in behind the wheel and looked at Jacob in the rear-view mirror before the cab lights dimmed. "Did you buckle up?"

"Always," Jacob answered.

The long, dark drive to Cody had all of them on edge. By the time they entered the parking deck at the hospital, Jacob was slumped against the window in the backseat.

Betty's phone beeped with a text. "Dawson said he's in recovery. The doctor should be in soon to let us know how it went."

"You go on in. I'll stay with Jacob while he wakes up. He might be groggy," Lyric said.

"No, you go. You're faster than I am, and you might get there in time to hear what the doctor says."

Lyric focused on looking for an available parking

space. The possibilities of what might be waiting for her inside the hospital had her throat closing.

As soon as the vehicle stopped, Betty shooed Lyric out of the car. "Go!"

She didn't need to be told twice. Lyric held onto the strap of her purse and jogged toward the hospital entrance. Inside, the entire front of the hospital was covered in windows, showcasing the few lights in the darkness outside. A woman with short, white hair sitting at the information desk looked up as Lyric approached.

"Hi, I'm looking for Asa Scott," she panted.

"The police officer?" the woman asked as she pushed her glasses up higher on her slim nose.

"Yes." She'd been so worried about Asa, but the whole town would be up in arms as soon as the sun rose. It was always a big deal when an officer was injured in the line of duty.

"He's on the third floor." The woman pointed to her left. "Take those elevators."

"Thanks," Lyric said over her shoulder as she followed the woman's directions. The elevator ride was torturously slow, and Lyric watched the numbers change.

When the ding let her know she'd arrived at the third floor, the doors opened to a crowded hallway. Officers and reporters crowded the small space, and the waiting room looked to be crowded as well.

"Lyric!"

She turned to see Dawson waving above the crowd and pushed her way toward him.

"This is crazy," she said as he rested a hand on her upper back, guiding her farther down the hallway.

"It's a big deal when an officer gets shot. Departments are here from three counties, and the news stations got the tip half an hour ago."

"Is he okay?" she asked, looking up at Dawson. Despite the chattering in the hallway, she zeroed in on his face as she waited for the answer.

He pushed a hand through his tousled hair. "I hope so."

They turned the corner, and Dawson led her to a young woman standing by the nurses' station. She looked up from her phone as they approached.

"Are you the family of Asa Scott?" she asked.

"His mother and son are on their way in. I'm his girlfriend." The last word trailed off. Was that title enough to allow her to hear the important update? It didn't hold enough weight. Asa was a part of her, and the distance between them was pulling her down like lead in her stomach.

"If you're in a time-crunch, we can relay the information to his mom," Dawson said.

An older man in a police officer uniform walked around the corner and set his sights on them. His hair was dark on the top and completely gray on the sides. His broad shoulders and straight posture gave him an air of authority.

The man extended a hand to the doctor. "Chief Wright, Blackwater PD."

"Doctor Sanderson."

Chief Wright turned immediately to Lyric and gave her a quick once-over before offering her his hand to shake. "You must be Lyric."

"Yes, sir." A cold sweat slid down her spine. Had she met him before under different bad circumstances? He didn't look familiar.

"How's our man?" he asked the doctor.

"The surgery went well. He received a blood transfusion, and we were able to repair the shattered clavicle with hardware. He will have rods and pins that will be in place for a while. He'll be transferred to the ICU after recovery." She checked her watch. "We'll keep an eye on his recovery until he wakes. You should be able to see him in a few hours."

"So, he'll make a full recovery?" Dawson asked.

"It will take a long time, but I believe he will. The wound was partially blocked by his vest, which very likely saved his life. He'll have a long road of physical therapy ahead, and there are likely to be more surgeries in his future, but Officer Scott is very lucky."

Lyric's shoulders sagged in relief. It wasn't luck. It was the Lord. How many times had she commented on Asa's body armor? She'd even lifted the heavy thing once and wondered if it would do its job in a pivotal moment.

"Lyric!"

Jacob darted into the hallway and barreled into Lyric, wrapping his arms around her waist.

She rubbed her hand over his hair. "He's okay. He's out of surgery, and we might be able to see him in a few hours."

Betty stepped up beside them and let out a long exhale. "That's great news."

"Praise the Lord," Chief Wright said.

Jacob pressed his face against her arm and sniffled. Lyric tightened her hold and whispered, "I love you, and I'm not going anywhere."

30

ASA

The stabbing in his shoulder jerked Asa out of a shallow sleep, and a blood pressure cuff tightened on his other arm.

They had just checked his vitals a few minutes ago. Why were they doing it again?

Squinting against the dim light filtering through the window, he blinked past the heaviness of his eyelids. So much for a few minutes ago. It was morning. If he'd slept this long, why was he still exhausted?

"Sorry to wake you, Mr. Scott. You need to take this." The nurse rattled off the name of the drug and what it was for, but he barely understood what she was saying through the fog in his head.

He tried to look down at his shoulder where the sharp pain pulsed. Layers of bandaging covered the entire side.

"Do you need pain medication?" The nurse checked her watch. "You're due for another dose."

"What is this?" he asked, pointing to the bandaging.

"You were shot. The surgery went well, but you still have a ways to go before you come out on the other side of this."

He remembered being shot, and he remembered waking up from the surgery. Why did it feel like it had all happened to someone else? He couldn't be the one tethered to a hospital bed by cords and tubes. He had things to do—people to take care of at home.

"Is anyone—"

"They're all in the waiting room. You're the talk of the town."

"The town?"

The nurse finally turned to him, but he could barely make out her shadowed features in the low light. "That waiting room has been packed out since well before my shift. Everybody's talking about Lauren Vincent and how you saved her."

"Lauren," Asa whispered. Then the important pieces of information started flooding in all at once. "Is my family out there?"

"Yep. They weren't too happy when visiting hours were over, but they've set up a home base in the waiting room." She looked at her watch. "I can probably let them in here for a little bit."

"What time is it?" he asked.

"Four in the morning."

"Can you see if one of them is up? Don't wake them if they're asleep, but I'd just like to..."

To what? He wanted to make sure his family was okay, but it sounded ridiculous when he was the injured one.

"I'll be right back." She padded out of the room and gently closed the door behind her.

"Is he awake?" a familiar voice whispered.

"Not yet."

Now, that voice was the one that got his heart pumping. Inhaling a deep breath, Asa opened his eyes and lifted his head.

Sure enough, Lyric sat in a recliner with her feet tucked in the seat beside her. Man, was she a sight for sore eyes. With her dark hair pulled up into a wild ponytail and a thin blanket wrapped around her shoulders, she looked almost comfortable.

Dawson tiptoed into the room still wearing his uniform. When he realized Asa was awake, he threw his hands in the air. "He lives!"

"It'll take more than one shot to keep me down," Asa joked.

Lyric was by his side in an instant. "Hey! I'll call your mom and let her know you're awake."

Asa lifted his hand, but the motion took way more effort than he expected. "No rush. I'm sure I'll be stuck here for a while."

Lyric was already lifting the phone to her ear. "Still, she'll want to see you awake."

Asa reached for her hand and gave it a squeeze. "I'm fine."

Lyric propped the phone between her shoulder and ear to quickly raise a finger in the air. "No, you are not fine. You are seriously injured, and she's been worried sick about you. We all have."

"That's a true story," Dawson added. "Dude, if you wanted attention, you could have just said so."

Asa tried to shift in the uncomfortable bed and grunted. Everything hurt. "Yeah, I thought about just letting a dog bite me."

Dawson's eyes widened, and he pointed at Asa. "Are you mocking me? I can't help it if dogs like to bite me!"

Lyric ended the call and pushed her phone into the back pocket of her jeans. "She's on her way. What's this about dog bites?"

"Dawson has been bitten twenty-three times."

"Why are you counting?" Dawson asked.

"It's not me. The news stations keep count."

Dawson hung his head and sighed. "I love dogs. Why don't they love me?"

Lyric gently brushed her fingertips over the bandage on Asa's shoulder. Her nostrils flared slightly with every breath. "I can't believe someone did this to you. It makes me so... angry."

"Welcome to the club, sister," Dawson said before taking a seat next to Asa's bed.

"It's part of the job. At least I'm still breathing."

"This isn't funny, you two!" Lyric almost shouted. She was really fired up.

"Hey," Asa said, squeezing her hand again. "It's part of the job. I knew that when I started. Though, I can't say I expected to be shot in Blackwater."

Lyric pressed her teeth into her bottom lip, and a crease formed between her brows. He hated to see her worried, but she sure looked good doing it.

"You'll be happy to know we caught the Wilsons," Dawson said.

"Oh yeah. It's all over the news." Asa had gotten wind of that part.

"Speaking of news crews. They're still swarming this place. They might have cornered your mom and Jacob," Dawson said.

Lyric pulled out her phone. "I'd better check on them. She said she was on her way from the cafeteria."

"No one needs to rush. I'm stuck here," Asa reminded them. "Hey, did we hear anything about Mason?"

"Who?" Lyric asked.

Dawson sucked in a breath through his teeth. "Nope. He's still MIA."

Lyric had a white-knuckle grip on his hand now. "Who is Mason?"

"The other Wilson brother," Asa said. "He wasn't there. At least, not that we know of."

She blinked a few times before whispering, "There's another one?"

Asa tugged on her hand, urging her to sit on the bed beside him. "Hey, don't worry about it. He's not a problem until he decides to be one."

"Then it might be too late," Lyric said as she sat beside him. Her hand covered her mouth, and her eyes turned glassy.

He pulled her hand to him, cradling it against his chest. "Listen, he's not a problem."

"Yeah, the other Wilsons are gonna hang out in jail for a while, and he probably doesn't want to join them," Dawson said. "I personally hope he decided to skip town and start a new life in Nantucket or somewhere equally far away and boring."

Lyric let her hand fall into her lap. "Only you would think Nantucket is a boring place."

Dawson lifted his hands. "I really have no idea where that is."

Asa shifted on the bed a little. His back was sore from lying in the same position for so long. He might not want Lyric worrying about the Wilson brothers, but he'd been playing over the events in his mind every minute he'd been awake. "Actually, what was up with Zach?"

Dawson rubbed his chin. "You mean how he pushed Bobby's gun away from Lauren?"

Lyric looked back and forth between them. "You think he saved her?"

"That's what it looked like to me. Bobby and Zach were fighting about something. Then Zach pushed the gun at the same time it went off."

"And you got shot instead of Lauren," Lyric finished, her words trailing off at the end.

"It looked like he was trying to protect her," Asa said.

Dawson rubbed his hands together. "I can't wait to hear what he says in the interrogations."

"Does that mean Zach might have been trying to stop Bobby?" Lyric asked.

"I wouldn't go that far. He's a Wilson, not a hero. Still, she's probably alive because of him."

Asa tried to sit up more, but the movement pulled in all the wrong places. "I need to talk to him."

"Easy, tiger. You're not talking to anyone but the doctors for a while," Dawson said.

Asa grunted. "What did we find out about why they restrained her?"

"She said they grabbed her as she was leaving work," Dawson explained. "They wanted information about her cousin, who apparently owed them money."

"They got a little more than they bargained for,"

Asa said.

Dawson looked around. "Dude, where is your mom? Did she get lost?"

Lyric stood. "I'll go find her."

"No, you stay. I'll find her." Dawson lifted his shoulders and puffed his chest out. "All in a day's work for a hometown hero."

"Good grief. Spare us the theatrics and go find my family," Asa said, pointing toward the door.

Dawson gave a stern salute before heading toward the door. "I'll check on you tomorrow."

Lyric's shoulders sank as soon as the door closed behind him. "I'm glad he was with you. I don't want to think about you going into that situation alone."

Asa rubbed his thumb over the back of her hand, focusing all his attention on the smooth skin instead of the pounding in his shoulder. "He's a good guy."

Lyric released his hand to wipe over her eyes. Her words shook as she whispered, "I'm just glad you're okay."

Asa rested his hand on her waist and pulled her down to him. She buried her face in the crook of his neck and sighed. He rubbed circles over her back for a few seconds before she rose up and pressed a kiss to his lips. He turned his head slightly and winced at the sharp pain.

"Ugh. I can't even kiss you properly without hurting you. I'm so sorry."

Asa chuckled. "Trust me. The next time I really kiss you, there won't be anything proper about it."

Her chin quivered, and she pressed her lips together.

Man, he knew what it was like to worry about the person you love. It was the last thing he wanted for Lyric.

"Hey, that was supposed to be funny. Or ambitious. Take your pick. Just anything but sad."

"I love you," she whispered.

"I love you too."

The door flew open, and Jacob darted into the room.

Lyric stood and opened her mouth, but his mom beat her to the punch.

"Easy!"

Jacob skidded to a stop beside Asa's bed. "Are you okay?"

"I'm great."

Lyric raised a hand. "Just to be clear, you're not great."

"I am." Asa reached for Jacob, guiding him into a gentle hug. "I have everything I love right here."

31

LYRIC

Lyric walked into Asa's living room and lifted the warm cup of tea to her face. The peppermint aroma filled her lungs and spread like energy through her limbs.

Asa looked up from the TV, and his entire demeanor changed when he saw her. He sat up straighter on the couch, and his eyes lit up like a kid on Christmas morning. The jolt of happiness struck her in the chest. No one had ever looked at her the way Asa did, and she'd never get enough of it.

He opened his arm to her as she approached. "Get over here."

She rested the steaming cup of tea on the end table and took the seat beside him. Draping her legs over his lap, she snuggled into his side and laid her head on his chest. "Did you figure out who did it?"

Asa wrapped his arm around her and pointed at

the TV where a romantic mystery played. "I can't believe you talked me into this. It's obviously that grouchy granny."

As much as she hated Asa had been shot, there were a few blessings in the aftermath. He hadn't been released to return to work yet, so her off days were spent cuddling on the couch—which had become her favorite thing to do.

After school, Asa and Jacob got to spend time at Beau's garage, and she got to join them whenever she didn't have to work. Both of the boys in her life were happier.

"I'm not so sure," Lyric said. "I was thinking the owner of the diner did it. He has a motive."

Asa's arm around her tightened, and he pulled her into his lap in one quick movement.

"Asa! You'll hurt your arm."

He brushed a stray lock of her hair behind her ear, sending a shiver down her spine. "My arm is good as new. The doctor released me to go back to work tomorrow."

"On light duty. You get to do paperwork."

"We'll see about that."

He slid his fingers into her hair and pulled her down to him, pressing his lips to hers.

If his looks sent sparks flying, his kiss was a wildfire. His lips moved over hers, stoking the flames in her middle. He adored her, and she poured all the love she had into every movement.

Loving and being loved was dangerously close to madness.

She broke the kiss and leaned back. "We can't do this all day."

"Who says? I could definitely do this all day."

A bubbling laugh burst from her chest as he pressed a trail of kisses down her neck. She gasped as his lips brushed an exceptionally sensitive spot on her skin. "I have to pick Jacob up from school in half an hour, and I won't be able to think straight to drive if you don't stop."

Asa's arms loosened around her. "Fair enough, but I want more of your undivided attention later."

Oh wow. The butterflies in her stomach were swarming. "Yes, sir." That was a request she could whole-heartedly agree to grant.

He brushed his thumb over her cheek. "I've actually been meaning to talk to you about Jacob's birthday. I was thinking we could have a party at the church. I haven't always done something big for his birthdays, mostly because he always asks if we can do things together instead of having a party and getting gifts, but I think he has a bunch of friends at school now and might like to have a party."

"That's a great idea. What can I do to help?"

"I'm not sure. You probably don't know this about me, but I'm not a good party planner."

Lyric giggled. "You don't say."

"I know. It's surprising, but I can't be good at everything."

"I'm not sure either, but I can figure it out. We'll need a guest list, food, a cake, presents. Oh! What do I get him?"

Asa rubbed his chin. "I was thinking about getting him a dirt bike."

"A dirt bike! Are you sure? That sounds dangerous. What can I get him? A helmet? A full body bubble suit?"

Asa laughed and pulled her to his side. "I was thinking the dirt bike could be his gift from *us*."

The pounding of Lyric's heart in her chest drowned out all other sounds. "From us?"

"Well, we do pretty much everything as a team now. Why not give a joint gift?"

Asa never did anything without thinking first, so he'd made the conscious decision to include her—to make her a part of something that meant the world to him.

A smile bloomed on her face, and she couldn't do anything to stop it. She didn't want to. "I love that."

"Planning parties together. Giving joint gifts. Are those big steps?" he asked.

"They are, but I want that. I want to do all these things with you." She waved her hand in the air. "I want it all. With you and Jacob."

Asa brushed his thumb over her chin. "I was hoping you'd say that."

He pressed a kiss to her lips, and she breathed in pure happiness. This was a life she didn't deserve, yet Asa never missed an opportunity to adore her.

Leaning back, she lifted her hands to her cheeks. "I love you so much."

"I love you too." He brushed a hand over her hair adoringly. "I can get a list of his friends from his teacher, and I'll talk to Tracy about catering. Jacob loves their cupcakes."

Lyric sat up straighter. "I can't wait! He's going to love this. I'll talk to Betty about it tonight. I'm sure she has some ideas too."

Asa linked his fingers through Lyric's, filling in all the empty spaces. "I'm glad you get along with Jacob and my mom."

"They're the best. I mean, you are too, but I guess I got double blessed when I got a boyfriend *and* an awesome family."

A wave of cold washed from her head to her toes, as soon as she said the words. She held the smile on her face, but the loss of her own family darkened her mood.

"Why don't you just call them?" Asa said.

"Call who?"

"Your parents. I can tell when you're thinking about them."

A sigh rushed from her chest, but it didn't ease the guilt. "I'm scared."

He wrapped her hand in both of his and held it between them. "If they're happy to hear from you and want a relationship, good. If not, then you still have us. I know we're not your real family, but it's as real as it can get without blood between us. You're ours, and we love you."

Lyric blinked through the moisture in her eyes. "You're right. I should at least see if there's a chance they can forgive me."

He released her hands, and she picked up her phone. She could press a few buttons and be talking to her parents. It was a simple action, but actually doing it was daunting.

"You could invite them to dinner at my place. I know how to heat chicken noodle soup out of a can."

She chuckled. "I can do it. I need to do it now or I'll chicken out."

Asa looked around. "You want me to give you some privacy?"

"No, I'd rather have you here beside me."

He rested back into his seat. "Then I'll be right here."

Knowing Asa would be there no matter how the talk with her parents went gave her the courage to make the call.

Her breath hitched as she pressed the phone to

her ear. No big deal. Just calling her estranged parents.

"Hello."

Lyric gasped at the sound of her mom's voice. She hadn't heard it in years, but the tone was so familiar, it wrapped around her like a warm blanket.

"Mom? It's Lyric."

There was a slight pause, before her mom responded. "Hey. It's been so long since I've heard from you."

"That's my fault. I'm so sorry it took me this long to call. I just...I just wanted you to know I miss you."

"I miss you too." Her mom's voice was hushed, but the words rang with truth.

"Um, do you have time to catch up a little?"

"Of course. Tell me how you're doing."

That small acceptance was all it took to lower the walls. She told her mom about her jobs and how she met Asa. She went on and on about Jacob, all too happy to share about the people she loved.

When she turned the conversation to her mom, the news was just as good. Her dad retired and loved spending time with Melody's kids. They had another grandkid on the way, and her mom was busy planning a baby shower.

Lyric glanced at the clock on the wall and gasped. "Oh, Mom, I'm so sorry to cut you off, but I need to leave to pick Jacob up from school."

"It was great to hear from you. I've missed you so much. Your dad has too."

"Can I call you again?" Lyric asked.

"Of course. Maybe your dad will be here next time."

"Thanks. I love you."

She blurted the words before thinking, and after a moment of panic, all the anxiety eased. She did love her mom. Why wouldn't she say it?

"I love you too. I'm so glad you called."

"Talk to you soon."

Lyric stood as she ended the call and rounded on Asa. "That was great!"

Asa was in front of her in an instant, wrapping her in his strong embrace. "I knew you could do it."

"Why do I want to cry? That's ridiculous," she said with a sniffle.

His calming hand rubbed circles over her back. "I've heard there's such a thing as happy tears."

Wiping her eyes, she looked up at him. "You've never cried happy tears before?"

Asa leveled her with a mischievous smirk. "Men don't cry."

"That is so not true. You're a total softie."

He gave her a wink before wrapping her up again. "Okay, maybe I've shed a tear or two, but you better keep it between us. I can't have people thinking I'm a wimp."

Lyric squeezed his large bicep. "I don't think anyone is mistaking you for a wimp."

Lyric's phone chimed, and she pulled it out of her pocket. "It's Wendy."

"Answer it."

"Okay, but let's head toward the car. I don't want to be late." She pressed the phone to her ear. "Hello."

"Hey, are you busy?" Wendy said through tears and gasps.

"No, I'm just going to pick up Jacob, but I can talk. What's wrong?"

Wendy sobbed and her breaths hitched until she could speak. "It's Jaycee. She's dead."

Lyric jerked to a stop beside her car. Wendy and Jaycee had been friends for years, both on different levels on the road to sobriety.

"Wendy, I'm so sorry."

"Can you come over? I need...someone."

"Of course. Let me get Jacob from school and drop him and Asa off at Beau's garage. It's on the way to your place. I should be there in forty minutes."

Wendy hiccupped and gasped. "Okay. Thank you."

"I'll be there soon."

Lyric hung up the phone and slid into the driver's seat. Asa wasn't released to drive, but they were hoping for clearance from the doctor at his appointment tomorrow.

"Is she okay?" he asked as he buckled his seatbelt.

"Her friend Jaycee died. I don't know any details yet, but last I heard they were roommates."

"Man, that's awful. I can go get Jacob. Go be with her."

"It's fine. It takes ten minutes to get through the school line, and the garage is on the way to her place."

Lyric backed out of the driveway and headed toward the school on the main road with pressure building in her chest like a shaken-up soda.

Asa reached for her hand and threaded his fingers with hers. "You want me to pray?"

"Yes, please." She hadn't realized what she needed until Asa said the words, but the one thing she and Wendy both needed was prayer.

Asa bowed his head and asked the Lord for strength and comfort for Wendy, as well as discernment for Lyric. He laid out everything they needed in clear and honest words.

"Lord, we know Wendy's sobriety is fragile. We pray she'll have the strength to resist the urge to fall back into her old life."

That was the part that terrified Lyric most. Was Wendy determined enough to withstand this storm or would she lose more than just her friend?

32

ASA

Asa stared at the incident report in front of him. There was something missing. What was the name of the man he'd talked to at the hardware store? The guy claimed he saw the subject running from the store across the street.

He flipped through his notepad. He'd recorded all of the witnesses' names, but had he really failed to get that guy's information? That wasn't like him. He was thorough, if nothing else.

"Boom!" Dawson shouted as he walked by. "I'm winning Jacob's birthday."

"I didn't know it was a competition," Asa said.

Dawson sat on the end of the desk, rubbing his hands together. "He's gonna love it. It's the present to beat all presents."

"Again, it's not a competition. Though I love your

enthusiasm. Can you apply that kind of determination when you have traffic duty at the school?"

Dawson straightened. "I have no idea what you're talking about. I am excellent at directing traffic."

"Yeah, maybe tone down the hip action."

"Are you saying my dance moves are a distraction? A danger to the public?"

Asa shook his head. "I'm wondering why you have dance moves at all. It's waving your hands. No hips involved."

"Maybe you're the one who isn't doing it right. The ladies love my moves."

"I'm sure they do."

Jennifer walked by and punched Dawson's arm. "They're just too scared to tell you the truth. An old lady could dance better than you, Keller."

Dawson gasped. "You take that back!"

Jennifer just grinned. She was one of the few women on the force, but she held her own better than half the men. Too bad her blonde hair and slim build made plenty of people underestimate her at first glance.

That was their mistake.

"I've seen your act. You have one move, and it's not a pretty one."

Asa sucked in a breath through his teeth. "That one had to hurt."

Dawson jumped to his feet and stalked off. "I'll

show you. I know how to Google. I'll be doing the twerkle by tomorrow."

Jennifer's eyes widened, and her smile faded. "Oh, no. What have I done?"

"There is no way he'll twerk in public," Asa said. When Jennifer didn't agree with him, he added, "Right?"

"Maybe check on him in the morning. He might cause a few traffic incidents if he attempts something like that." Jennifer checked her watch. "What are you even doing here? Your shift ended an hour ago."

Asa huffed. "That's a great question. Apparently, it's taking longer than expected to get back into the action around here. Everything takes me twice as long."

Jennifer chuckled. "Sorry. Glad it's you and not me."

Dawson stomped back to the desk. "I can do this one!" he said, turning his phone around so Asa and Jennifer could see a video of a woman in tight workout clothes swirling her hips around.

"Please, for the love of all things good, don't do that in front of the kids," Jennifer pleaded.

Asa laughed and glanced at the door as Lyric walked in carrying two boxes with a bag resting on top followed by Chief Wright.

Jumping up, he darted over to her. "Hey. What are you doing here?" He pressed a kiss to her lips as he took the load she was carrying.

"I found her wandering around with food, so I had to invite her in," Chief Wright said.

She brushed a stray hair from her ponytail behind her ear and looked around. Her hair was always incredibly soft, and Asa's fingers itched to touch it. Today, she wore it pulled up in a high pony-tail, exposing the tempting skin of her neck.

"I knew you were working over this afternoon, so I thought I'd bring you dinner."

"Wow. Thanks." He jerked his chin toward the break room. "You have time to eat with me?"

She shrugged and fidgeted her hands in front of her. "I guess so. Is that okay?"

"More than okay. Come on."

"I'll see you two later," Chief Wright said. "I have dinner waiting on me at home."

She fell into step beside Asa, as they headed to the break room. "I told Tracy I was bringing you dinner, and she insisted on sending—"

"Hey, stranger!" Dawson shouted when he saw Lyric. "What brings you here?"

She jerked a thumb over her shoulder toward Asa. "I brought dinner."

"For me? That's so sweet." Dawson reached for the bags in Asa's hands.

"Touch my food and die," Asa said.

"Actually, the doughnuts are for everyone. Tracy sent them," Lyric added.

"From Sticky Sweets? Did you get a chocolate

one?" Dawson asked, already drooling at the mention of doughnuts.

"Dude, just say thank you," Asa chided.

Dawson slung an arm over Lyric's shoulders. "She knows I'm joking. I'm glad you stopped by. With or without treats."

"Thanks." The tension in her smile was beginning to dissipate. Maybe she'd come by the station more often.

"What's it like being back here?" Dawson asked. "You know, not in handcuffs?"

"Dawson," Asa warned. Was he really bringing that up the first time Lyric stopped by to see him at work?

She looked around and shrugged. "It's a lot different. Brighter."

"And for the record, I didn't cuff her. She wasn't resisting," Asa added. He'd read that note in the report when he looked up her record.

Lyric rubbed a hand over his shoulder. "Such a gentleman."

Dawson laughed and waved a hand, coaxing Lyric toward the break room. "Come on. I'll show you my secret candy stash."

Asa let out a tentative breath. Maybe the past was really behind them.

～

ASA SCANNED the sea of kids and parents in the church dining hall. Jacob's party had been a hit, just as he'd expected. His mom and Lyric had gone above and beyond with the food, cake, and games.

One little girl lifted a toy bow and arrow before letting it fly toward the wall. The suction cup stuck right on the horse's rump where the tail should be. She twirled, squealing as her dad wrapped her in a congratulatory hug.

But where was Jacob? It was his party. He should be hanging out with the other kids.

Asa's gaze landed on Lyric across the room. She scooped sandwich triangles onto a serving dish at a nearby table, all while smiling and nodding at Mrs. Harding's story.

Lyric had no clue how much he loved her. He'd been trying to put it into words for months, but they all fell short. The woman had his heart wrapped up tight with a pretty bow on top, served to her on a silver platter.

He stepped up beside Mrs. Harding and wrapped one arm around her shoulders. She turned to embrace him and pat his back. The Hardings were like family, and Mrs. Harding had babysat Asa quite a few times in his younger years. She had five boys of her own and a nephew. It wasn't much different adding another boy to the mix.

"Jacob is a good one. He's growing up so fast. I was just telling Lyric about the day he was born."

Asa's shoulders tightened. "Oh? What about it?"

Mrs. Harding narrowed her eyes at him with a smirk. "Nothing. Just that you were indisposed."

Lyric whipped around to face them. Her dark hair fanned out around her before falling in light waves over one shoulder. "She said you passed out."

"It wasn't *that* bad," Asa defended.

"I heard you sat in a chair while a nurse fanned you. All while Danielle did the heavy lifting," Mrs. Harding said.

Lyric chuckled and bit her teeth between her lips.

Okay, not his brightest moment.

"It was stressful. There was a lot of yelling in pain going on."

Mrs. Harding patted his chest. "It was very tough first responder of you."

Asa grinned. Mrs. Harding never pulled her punches, but no one expected her to after raising six boys. "I've had more honorable days."

"You made up for it in spades since then. He's a good boy. Gonna be a good man someday too."

"I have no doubt," Lyric added. "Speaking of Jacob, have you seen him?"

"I was looking for him myself. People are starting to leave, and they keep asking where he is."

Lyric placed the last sandwich on the tray and pulled the plastic gloves off her hands. "I'll help you look for him."

They stepped out into the hallway by the dining hall, and Lyric slipped her hand into his.

Asa pressed a kiss to the soft skin on the back of her hand. "Thank you for making his party great."

"I think he had a blast. Oh, and he's gonna love our present when we get home."

Heat spread in Asa's chest. *Our* present. *Home.* He wanted more words signifying their union.

He wanted it all. With Lyric.

They turned the corner and found Jacob and Dawson sitting on the last two steps of a staircase looking at something on Dawson's phone.

Jacob jumped up when he saw them. "Dad. Lyric. Come here. You have to see what Dawson got me."

Oh no. Asa hadn't circled back around to the topic with Dawson. The present that would *win* Jacob's birthday could be anything. Dawson had no limits.

Jacob grabbed the phone and held it up in front of Asa and Lyric. "It's a car!"

"A what?" Lyric shouted.

"He found a '69 Porsche 911! It needs some work, and Beau said we could work on it at his place."

Asa stared at the image on the phone. Dang it, Dawson won. "That's insane."

"He said we can all work on it. He even said he'd take me when you're working or hanging out with Lyric. Isn't that awesome?"

Asa glanced at Dawson, who gave him a thumbs-up. Smooth move sliding in some time for him to spend with Lyric, but she'd been going with them to the garage and seemed to like watching and listening to Jacob talk about the ins and outs of car mechanics.

"That is super awesome," Lyric said. "Our present isn't going to measure up."

Jacob gasped. "You got me something?"

Asa ruffled Jacob's hair. "You really thought we didn't get you anything for your birthday? It's waiting at home."

"Let's go!" He started to run off before doubling back to tackle Dawson in a bear hug. "Thank you for my present."

"It's my pleasure, kid. You're the best man for the job."

Jacob ran back past Asa and grabbed his hand. "Come on. We gotta go."

"I'll be right there. You go say your good-byes to the people who are still here."

The quick pace of Jacob's footfalls bounded down the hallway, leaving Asa with Lyric and Dawson.

Asa clapped a hand on Dawson's shoulder. "Thanks for that."

"Anytime. I can take him over there tonight if you want."

"Actually, he's staying with Danielle's parents

tonight, but I bet he'll be ready to head to the garage by sunrise."

Dawson wiggled his eyebrows. "Does that mean you two get some alone time? In case you can't tell, I'm trying to move this train along."

Lyric chuckled and wrapped her hands around his arm, scooting closer to his side.

"I was hoping she'd let me take her out on a date," Asa said.

"A date? What is that?" she asked sarcastically.

"When a man and woman want to find out if they love each other—"

"We already love each other," Lyric said.

"Well, in that case, he just buys you dinner and takes you stargazing or something equally romantic."

Lyric looked up at Asa. "I'll take a rain check on the stargazing until after the weather warms up. It still gets chilly at night."

"Dancing?" he asked.

"Oh, are you going to Barn Sour? Can I come?" Dawson asked.

Asa tilted his head. "Seriously?"

"Come on. The more the merrier," Lyric said.

Okay, it seemed Lyric had a double dose of kindness tonight because Asa wasn't as willing to share her during the stolen moments they had alone.

"I might see if Olivia is up for going out."

"Yes!" Lyric said. "I think she's still here if you want to go find her."

"You don't have to tell me twice," Dawson said with a wink. "See you two later."

Lyric slid her hand down Asa's arm to grab his hand. "I need to get back to cleaning up. I'll have to go back to Betty's to change before we go out."

"Why? You look great." He took her in from head to toe and back up again. "Better than great, as usual."

She rolled her eyes. "You're just saying that."

"I only tell the truth." Man, would she ever understand how irresistible she was to him?

Probably not, but that wouldn't stop him from trying.

33

LYRIC

Of course, tonight was the night her hair would decide to call in sick. It was flat on top, and she couldn't get a single piece of it to hold a curl. With a sigh, she unplugged the curling iron and grabbed a clip. She'd pull it half back, and maybe no one would notice it was flat and lifeless.

The doorbell rang, and she paused. In the weeks she'd lived here, she hadn't once heard it chime.

Lyric raced down the hallway toward the front door. Everyone they knew used the side door. Even the mailman knocked on that one.

She turned the deadbolt and opened the door a crack to peek outside. "Asa?"

He stood on the small front porch with his hands behind his back. He'd changed into a button-down and dark jeans but kept his boots on.

Wow. How did he know the perfect combination to sexiness?

He pulled a bouquet of roses from behind his back and handed them to her at the same time he swept her into his arms. When he pressed his lips to hers, she pulled him in, resting the flowers over his shoulder.

He couldn't even wait to say hello before whisking her into a heart-stopping kiss, and she had no complaints. He whispered his greetings against her lips, adoring her with every movement.

She pulled back and righted the bouquet in her hands. "Let me put these in water."

He held onto her hand until it slipped from his grip. Why was walking away from him so difficult? She wanted every moment, every look, every word. She wanted Asa and his family filling up every second of her days.

She trimmed the ends of the roses and placed them in a clear vase she'd found in a cabinet. Taking a second to arrange them, she brushed the pad of her thumb over a silky petal. Remembering the card, she reached for it on the counter.

I love you. Three words aren't enough.

Inhaling a deep breath, she laid it back on the counter. She understood completely. The love she felt for Asa was more than attraction. Her love was mixed up with respect, commitment, trust, and loyalty. It was an all-consuming force built on a foundation of faith and forgiveness.

Rushing back to the front door, she zipped outside where Asa waited with her coat. She slid her arms into it and turned to lift onto her toes and press a quick kiss to his lips.

"Thank you for the flowers," she whispered.

"Thank you for throwing Jacob a party. I couldn't have done it without you."

Lyric waved a hand in the air. "It was nothing."

He took her hand in his and lowered it to his side. The dim porch light cast his face in shadows, but she didn't have to see his eyes to know they were fixed on her. "It's something that means a lot to Jacob and me."

"And I was happy to be a part of it."

He lifted her hand to his lips and pressed a kiss to it. "Are you ready to go?"

"So ready." She followed him to the truck and settled inside. It wasn't until the dark wrapped around her that she realized what they were doing. They'd been together at church and out in public before, but Barn Sour was a place where alcohol ran freely, even if they didn't intend to drink.

What were the chances they might run into someone from her past? Or someone who didn't think she and Asa fit together?

Asa held her hand as he drove and talked about the party. It wasn't until they pulled up in the parking lot at Barn Sour that he broke the tentative bubble around them.

"Okay, what's on your mind?"

"What do you mean?"

He parked and left the truck running. "You've barely said two words."

"I'm just nervous."

"No one is going to say anything. If they do, I'll lay down the law."

A chuckle lightened the heaviness in her chest. "You think it's funny."

"It's not funny at all, but I'm serious when I say it doesn't matter. You're with me, and I dare anyone to say a cross word about you."

She sucked in a shaky breath. "Why are you so good to me?"

"Why are you so good to me?" he countered.

Fair enough. She didn't know how they'd ended up together or even how to explain their relationship, but every piece of her mind, heart, and soul reached for Asa. He believed in her wholeheartedly.

He brushed a hand over her cheek and into her hair. "You belong to me and the Lord. You shouldn't be afraid of anyone."

She rested a hand on his arm and squeezed. The restrained power beneath her touch was one protection, but Asa's determination was another. He was reminding her of the invisible armor she wore every day. Why did she keep forgetting about it?

"You're right. Let's go have fun."

He jumped out and jogged around the truck to get her door. She accepted his offered hand and snuggled into his side as they walked in. Light and music burst into the quiet night, as soon as Asa opened the door. Inside, laughter, songs, and chatter wrapped around them, folding them into the lively atmosphere.

Asa led her toward an empty booth near the wall, but someone shouted his name. A man and woman sitting a few tables down waved their hands in the air, urging Asa and Lyric over.

"That's Lucas and Maddie. Want to sit with them?"

"Sure." She'd met the couple a few times, and though they'd talked about getting together to hang out, nothing had worked into everyone's schedules yet.

Maddie stood and wrapped Lyric in a spine-cracking hug. "It's so good to see you. Asher and Haley are on their way. He's playing tonight."

"Oh, yay! So many people have told me I need to hear him play."

"You've been missing out. He's a riot," Lucas added.

The Hardings were well-known around town, and their reputation preceded them. If you needed a hand, you called the Hardings. If you wanted a sponsor for a sports team, you called the Hardings. If you needed prayer or support, you called the Hardings.

Lucas and Asher were born into the Harding family, but their wives, Maddie and Haley, were just as well-known for their willingness to help others.

No wonder Asa was so close with the Hardings. They were raised in the same kind of loving families.

"Well, look at this!"

Lyric turned toward the familiar voice. Brenda made her way toward them with her arms spread wide.

"I heard you two were an item! Oh, this just makes me giddy."

"Aunt Brenda, what are you doing?" Maddie asked, sounding a lot like an embarrassed teenager.

Brenda wrapped her arms around Asa and Lyric. "I could just kiss y'all!" she said in her raspy Southern accent.

"Please don't," Maddie begged.

Brenda released them from the hug and clasped her hands in front of her. "I just knew you two were meant to be when you got stuck in that cabin together."

"Stuck in a cabin? I haven't heard this story," Maddie said, sidling up beside them.

"I'll tell you all about it," Lyric said.

Maddie waved a hand in the air. "Another time. I love this song. Dance with me!"

Lyric glanced over her shoulder as Maddie

pulled her out to the dance floor. The smile on Asa's face said he was more amused than upset about being left at the table.

Maddie whirled Lyric around until they were in position for a line dance.

"I don't know this one!" she shouted above the music.

"Yes, you do. It's the same concept as the electric slide. Just add some heel-toe action and a few more hip shakes."

Bursting into laughter, she tried to keep up with the moves. Although it seemed she was always a step or two behind. They laughed until their stomachs were sore before giving up on the dance. Asa and Lucas waited at the table and greeted them with a round of applause.

"The prettiest footwork I've ever seen," Lucas said.

"I don't know about the feet, but something else was pretty." Asa winked at Lyric and pulled out the chair beside him for her to sit.

The night passed in a blur of food, dancing, and music. As promised, Asher put on a good show, and Lyric learned a few new dances. By the time they called it a night, her eyelids were growing heavy.

"You ready to head home?" Asa asked.

Home. Nothing had ever sounded so sweet. "I'm ready if you are."

It took a quarter of an hour to say their good-byes to all their friends, and she shivered when they stepped out into the cold night. Asa's strong arm wrapped around her, enveloping her in his warmth as they headed to the truck.

"Did you have fun?" he asked as they fastened their seatbelts.

"So much fun." She let out a massive yawn. "I don't think I've stayed up this late in years."

"I'm pretty sure you stayed up all night when I was in the hospital," Asa reminded her.

"Oh yeah, I was happily repressing that awful memory."

He squeezed her hand. "Thanks for taking care of me. Again."

"It was my pleasure. Just don't get hurt anymore. I don't know if my heart can take it."

They pulled up in front of his mom's house, and she smiled as he walked her to the door where he pulled her into his arms again. When she tilted her head up to him, he pressed a warm kiss to her lips.

When he broke the kiss, he rested his forehead gently against hers and whispered, "I don't want to leave you."

"The feeling is mutual," she said, pressing another quick kiss to his lips.

When he leaned back and looked at her, a mischievous smile greeted her. They'd both been firm about one thing: marriage was the only way they would go home together.

He gently kissed her forehead and took a step back. "I love you. Good night."

She gave him a little wave and reached for the doorknob. "I love you too."

Marriage was a huge and scary thing she had no right to wish for with Asa, but that didn't stop the hope blooming in her chest.

34

ASA

A sa stepped into Deano's and took his place at the end of a long line. The diner was packed for a Thursday afternoon. Thankfully, he'd called in the order on his way over.

Jerry Lawrence turned and extended a hand. "Hello there, Mr. Scott."

"How are you?" Asa asked as they shook. "Taking care of my favorite chickens?"

Jerry tucked his hands under his arms and adjusted his stance. "Oh, you know that's all Olivia's doin'. She loves those things. That's why they lay the best eggs."

"I believe it." Asa had practically grown up at the Lawrence farm. Beau and Olivia's parents always had an extra seat at their table. After Martha Lawrence passed, Jerry spent less time at home and more time hanging out with the other men who sat around solving the world's problems at Deano's.

Jerry stroked his long, gray beard. "How's the shoulder healing?"

Asa stretched his arm. "It gets the job done."

"I tell ya, Olivia was worried sick there for a while. I bet she called either your mom or Lyric three times a day."

"You raised good kids. Beau and Olivia both helped out when Mom and Lyric were running things. I appreciate it."

Jerry shook his head. "They got it from their mama."

"Martha was a good woman, but I guarantee you taught them a good bit about how to offer a helping hand."

Jerry grunted and moved up to the counter where Kendra waited to take his order.

"Have a seat, and I'll get that out to you in a bit," Kendra shouted over her shoulder as she stuck the ticket in line for the cooks.

She turned back around and gasped. "Well, if it isn't my new favorite person!"

Asa's eyes widened, and he looked around. "Who?"

"You, silly! I can't tell you what a blessing it is to see Lyric so happy. I know you and your family have a lot to do with that."

Asa shook his head. "I don't know if I can take credit for that happiness, but I'm thankful for it too."

In the last few months, Lyric had shed all the hesitation she'd once carried. She took charge, volunteered to help people, and spent all her free time with Asa and his family.

The best part? She seemed genuinely willing to do those things on her own. The bubbly excitement in her voice when she told him about her days made him itch to call her a little too often.

"You're an angel in disguise, Asa. She is too. Most people just don't see it," Kendra said.

"Nothing to worry about here."

The bell above the door chimed behind him, and Kendra straightened. "I guess I'd better get your order." She turned around and stuffed plasticware and napkins into a couple of sacks filled with take-away boxes. Once they were loaded, she lifted them over the counter. "Y'all have a good night."

"You too." With food in hand, he side-stepped the people who'd just come in and made a quick exit before the men hanging out in the dining room called him over to chat.

He made it to his mom's house a little after six. If he and Jacob could eat fast, they'd have time to stop by Beau's garage before heading home.

Lyric skipped into the kitchen just as he'd placed the food containers on the counter. "Hello, handsome."

Food? What food? Every thought left his brain at the sight of Lyric. Her hair was pulled up in a high ponytail, and she wore an old Blackwater High School sweater and what she called her work jeans. They had splashes of black and orange paint on the thighs, and she'd told him the story about ruining her favorite pair of pants while painting football signs in high school.

The fact that she could still wear clothes she'd worn ten years ago still blew his mind. He'd gone up three pant sizes in the waist and length since then.

Lyric's eyes fluttered closed, and she inhaled a deep breath. "How do they make those cheese-burgers smell so great?"

Yeah, Asa had a few questions too, but they didn't have anything to do with the food. He spent too much time wondering how he'd run into Lyric at the exact right times and why she liked doting on him and his son so much.

She slung her arms over his shoulders and lifted onto her toes. "Have I told you how delicious you look in this uniform?"

"Only twice today."

She let out a light-hearted giggle. "How was your day?"

Asa pressed his mouth to hers, breathing in the joy radiating from her. Every brush of her lips on his sent a crackling fire racing up his spine.

Jacob's quick steps pounded down the hallway,

and Lyric pulled back before pressing two more quick kisses to his lips.

"So?" she asked as Jacob darted into the room.

Asa stared at her. "So what?"

"How was your day?"

Oh, she had asked that. He'd just lost all of his senses while Lyric kissed him. "Fine. Pretty boring."

"Boring is good," she said as she pulled plates from the cabinets.

"What did you get me?" Jacob asked, peeking in the bags.

"Everyone got burgers. Yours only has lettuce and mustard."

Jacob dug in the bag for the burger with his order written on the wrapper. "Awesome. Are we going to Beau's?"

"Homework?"

"Done," Jacob said.

"Then we'll go after you eat."

Jacob sat at the table and bowed his head to bless the food before tearing the wrapper off the burger and digging in.

"Oh! I have news," Lyric said. "I just got off the phone with Mom."

Asa leaned back against the counter and crossed his arms over his chest. "And?"

She rested her hands on his arms and looked up at him with a megawatt smile. "She and Dad are coming to visit tomorrow after I get off work. Is there any chance you'd be able to come?"

"Around five thirty? I should be able to make it. Where?"

"The Basket Case. I was thinking something casual."

"Did you tell them I'd be there?" Asa asked.

"I told them I'd ask if it worked with your schedule. They said if you couldn't come this time, they'd make another trip to meet you and schedule further ahead next time."

Asa rested his hands on her waist. "Are you sure you don't want this first time to be just the three of you?"

"I'm sure. You're a major part of my life. I'd like for Jacob to be there next time too. Maybe even your mom."

Things with Lyric had moved fast from the beginning. She'd met his mom and Jacob early, and everything else had progressed at a quick pace ever since. Meeting her parents felt like a big step, but he was more than ready to take it. "I'd love that. Let's plan on it."

She pressed a quick kiss to his lips. "Thank you."

Lyric's phone rang on the end table. She looked at it but didn't move to answer.

"That might be important," Asa said.

She checked the screen. "It's Wendy."

The mention of Lyric's friend had them both on

edge. Wendy had been on a downward spiral since Jaycee died, and Lyric had told her to call if she needed anything. Lyric had spent a few evenings with her friend, and she was pretty confident Wendy was on the other side of her grief the last time Lyric and Asa talked about it.

Would Wendy need something small this time or was she in trouble?

"Hello." Seconds later, Lyric responded in a cheerful tone. "Of course. What time? Okay, I'll see you then." She rested the phone on the table and moved back to Asa's side. "She wanted to know if I could give her a ride to work tomorrow."

"And are you?"

"Yep. Her car had a flat, and the tire should be in tomorrow, but she won't be able to get it from the shop until after work."

"So you'll drop her off on your way to the store?"

"Yeah. My shift starts at 7:00. Wendy has to be at work by 6:30."

Asa pulled the rest of the food from the bags. "That worked out perfectly."

"I'm glad it did. I know what it's like when you get in a bind and you can't find anyone who can help."

Asa kissed the top of Lyric's head. "You're not alone anymore."

Lyric hummed deep in her chest as she snuggled closer to him. "I love you."

He would never get tired of hearing those words.

35

LYRIC

The sky was still dark when Lyric pulled up to her old apartment complex. As upset as she'd been when she was evicted, she sure didn't miss it now.

Wendy jogged out of the building, tucking her coat tight around her. The wind swept her ponytail in all directions as she slid into the car and closed the door quickly behind her. "It's freezing out here."

Lyric looked over her shoulder as she backed out. "I know. I'm just glad it isn't snowing."

"Don't say that word." Wendy tossed her purse in the back seat and started adjusting the vents. "Need heat."

"This oldie hasn't had time to wake up yet."

Wendy patted the dash. "Same here, girlfriend."

"You still like working at Julia's?" Lyric asked.

"Yep. How's the thrift store?"

"Great. I love it."

Wendy smiled wide and bumped Lyric's shoulder. "Look at us! Adulting!"

Lyric laughed. "It's just as hard as they say it is."

"I'm so glad you found a place. You look happy."

"Betty is great, the bed is so comfortable, Asa and Jacob are the best. What more could I want?"

Wendy sighed. "You are living the dream life."

"I can't believe it either." Lyric covered her mouth with a hand. "I've never been this happy before."

"I'm happy for you. Job, check. House, check. Man, check."

"Family, check," Lyric added. "Technically, the house isn't mine, but I think I found a place I might be able to move to soon."

"Why would you move out? Just stay and enjoy it."

Lyric made a clicking sound behind her teeth. "I can't impose on Betty any longer than I have to. She's been so good to me, but I need to move out as soon as I can."

"If you say so. How's it going with Asa?"

"Amazing. It's better than I could have imagined. I've never been in love before."

"Oh, girl. You are in deep. You sure about this?"

"Never been so sure in my life."

Wendy rested her back against the seat. "Wow. This is big."

Lyric focused her attention on the road ahead. "I want bigger. I want it all. With him."

"Sounds like you've got it all."

"I feel like I do."

They pulled into the parking lot of the flower shop, and Wendy pointed. "Take me to the side door."

Another car was already in the lot, and Lyric parked beside it. "I can't believe you get to play with flowers all day."

"It's a dream." Wendy rubbed her hands together and breathed into them. "Thanks for the ride."

"Anytime."

"I do not want to get out in this cold."

"I don't blame you." Lyric grabbed her scarf off the dash. "Take this."

Wendy wrapped it around her neck. "You're the best." She jumped out and made a run for the door, only stopping to give Lyric a small wave.

Who knew starting her day by helping someone would be the key to happiness? Well, that and the dozen other things in her life that were going so much better than she deserved. Maybe Asa was right when he said she should give it all to the Lord. She'd done a lot of praying when things were spiraling, and He'd come through in numerous ways.

The clock on the dash read 6:37 when she pulled up at Blackwater Restoration. She had some time before her shift started. Her phone in the console rang, and she answered quickly.

"Hey, Mom."

"Hey. Your dad and I might be a little later than we expected this afternoon. Melody just called and said she had a last-minute meeting come up after work.

"That's okay. Do we need to reschedule?"

"Hmm. Maybe. Are you free tomorrow for dinner?"

"Let me talk to Asa and see if he is. I'd love for you to meet him while you're in town."

"Oh, yes. That would be good. I'll just wait to hear back from you."

"Thanks. I'll call him right now. I love you."

"I love you too. Talk to you soon," her mother said before ending the call.

With a few minutes left before her shift, she dialed Asa's number and turned off the car.

He answered quickly with, "Good morning, beautiful."

Wow. Who knew three little words could steal the breath from her lungs?

"Good morning to you too. I just talked to Mom, and she said they might have to reschedule dinner tonight. She wants to know if you're free tomorrow for dinner."

"I'll be there."

"Great!" She held the phone against her ear with

her shoulder while she looked for the store keys. Once they were located, she gripped the door handle, reluctant to leave the warmth of her car. "I'm just glad you encouraged me to call them."

"I'm glad you finally did it. What are you up to?"

"Getting ready to make a mad dash to the door at work." She took a deep breath and said, "Three, two, one."

Asa chuckled in her ear as she hunched her shoulders against the cold. It was unseasonably cold for early May, and spring or summer couldn't come soon enough.

She jogged around to the back of the building and froze when she saw the door. The wood was splintered, and the knob was completely gone, hacked away by an ax.

"Asa, someone broke into the store."

"What? Tell me what you see. Is there anyone around?"

"The door is destroyed. I don't see anyone."

"Go back to your car, and move to the parking lot down the street. Call 911 so dispatch can send out a call. Stay in your vehicle until I get there."

"Okay." She wasn't about to argue, so she turned on her heels and raced back to her car.

36

ASA

Asa jogged out of the station into the cold morning. He'd already called Dawson, but Asa met Jason Guthrie as he stormed out into the parking lot. Officer Guthrie's K-9, Ranger, stood alert at his side.

"10-22 at Blackwater Restoration."

Officer Guthrie turned on a dime, and Ranger followed him back to his cruiser.

Jason wasn't Asa's first choice for backup, but he'd take what he could get. Within seconds, Asa and Jason were on their way. Thankfully, the store wasn't far from the police station.

He wished Lyric would have stayed on the phone with him, but he would only be paying half attention to everything around him if she was in his ear. Knowing she would stay on the phone with dispatch gave him some peace.

She was fine. He kept telling himself that anyway. She'd moved her car away from the store like he'd asked. If someone was still in the building, Asa, Jason, and Ranger would find them.

Asa passed the ice cream shop a block down from the store and spotted Lyric's car. She was on the phone. Good. Nancy at dispatch was probably doing her best to keep her calm.

Asa parked and waited for Jason and Ranger. Dawson was close too, so they waited for him to arrive before stepping out of their vehicles.

"Show us entering the building," Asa said as he pushed aside the scrap that was left of the door. He knew the layout of the store from visiting Lyric at work, but the back room was unfamiliar territory. A wooden desk was pushed into one corner and boxes were stacked on every surface, leaving only a narrow pathway to the door leading to the storefront.

How would they know if something was missing? Donations came in at all hours of the day, and from the looks of it, there wasn't an inventory system keeping track of the items still shoved into boxes and bags.

"I'll take this side," Dawson said behind Asa.

"Ranger and I will check the register," Jason said.

Asa veered to the left. "I'll check this side." As far as he could tell, nothing looked out of place on any of the displays. Nothing was broken or shoved around.

"Signs of a disturbance in the office behind the register. No suspect," Jason told dispatch.

After half an hour scouring the store, Asa, Dawson, and Jason exited the back. Camille Harding, one of the owners, waited in the back lot. Her husband, Noah, had an arm wrapped around her shoulders. She wore a suit jacket and skirt that did nothing to protect against the cold wind. Her law office was only about two blocks away. She'd probably shown up right after they started the investigation.

"Anything?" she asked with a heavy dose of hope in her voice.

"There are signs of a disturbance in the office. The place is clear. We couldn't verify what, if anything, had been taken," Jason said.

"We'll need you to check out the office, as well as the rest of the store. Then you can give a written statement and fill out a report," Dawson added.

Asa called Lyric, and she answered on the first ring.

"Hey. Are you okay?" Her hurried words were teetering on the verge of panic.

"I'm fine. No one was inside, but Camille is going to check things out to see if anything is missing."

Lyric let out a deep exhale. "Thank goodness. I was worried about you because..."

"Because of what happened a few months ago?" he finished.

"Yeah. Just thinking about you going in there when someone might be inside. It reminded me how dangerous your job can be."

"It's not always highway robbery, sweetie. It's mostly the paperwork that kicks my butt."

She laughed. "Okay. I'll stop worrying now."

"Good. Can you come over here and give a statement?"

"Oh, yes. I'll be there in two minutes."

Asa walked around the building and met Lyric as she was parking. She ran straight into his arms, and he didn't care if anyone saw them. He'd known all morning she was safe, but holding her gave him room to breathe.

"You okay?" he asked, just to be sure.

"I'm fine. Is the store ok?"

"Looks like it. The only damage we found was the door. Camille is doing a walk-through of the office."

"Good."

"Let's get inside. You think you can give a statement?"

"Sure." She followed him inside where Camille was handing out cups of coffee.

When they'd completed the on-site investigation, Lyric stepped up to his side and wrapped her arm around his. "I'll walk you out."

"It's freezing."

"I have a coat," Lyric said, pointing to the rack by the door.

"Fine. You can just kiss me at the door and run back inside."

"The door of your car."

"I meant the door of the building," Asa said with a smile.

"I meant the door of your car," Lyric stated resolutely. "I don't want to let you out of my sight until I absolutely have to."

Asa didn't push back. Lyric's determination was something he loved about her. He wished she was more confident in her instincts. He'd chastised her about being impulsive before, but the truth was that Lyric just knew what to do sometimes.

They stepped out into the cold, and Lyric nestled close to his side as they walked. She'd parked right beside his cruiser, and they slid into the half-concealed space between their vehicles.

"Thanks for coming to my rescue."

Asa kissed her forehead. "Always. I'm glad you're okay."

"Me too. I know Camille is probably upset. I'll do what I can to help her today."

Rubbing his hands up and down her arms, he smiled. "You're a good friend."

That earned him a kiss on the cheek, and the contact was warm and then cold when she pulled away.

Dawson, Jason, and Ranger walked out, and Lyric backed up a step.

"They know we're together," Asa whispered. "It's kind of a given that I'd be making sure you're okay."

"I know. I just don't want them to think we're making out or something."

Asa choked on a cough. He never knew what Lyric was going to say.

Dawson walked up and slapped Asa on the back. "Nice work, soldier."

"Officer Scott," Jason said from the other side of Lyric's car.

Asa looked over Lyric's head. Why was Jason calling him Officer Scott when only Dawson and Lyric were around?

Asa squeezed Lyric's hand and whispered, "I'll be right back." When he walked around Lyric's car, his steps halted.

The German Shepherd was down. His nose pointed at the back seat of Lyric's car.

Asa looked up at Guthrie. It had to be a mistake. Ranger wasn't giving a drug signal at Lyric's car.

Asa couldn't move. Couldn't breathe.

"Officer Scott." Jason's tone was deep and formal.

"What are you two doing over there?" Dawson said. Within seconds, he was on the other side of the car, frozen right beside Asa.

"Son of a bacon bit," Dawson spat.

"Asa?" Lyric's call was laced with worry.

"Tell her to open it," Jason said.

"Are you serious?" Asa asked. The tightness in his chest squeezed, threatening to cut off all access to oxygen.

Jason glared at Asa and repeated slowly, "Tell her to open it."

Asa turned to Lyric. The look on her face was curious, but there wasn't any panic. She knew Ranger was a drug dog. If she had something in her car, she would be nervous, right?

"Um, can you come over here?" he asked.

Lyric came around the car. She glanced at Ranger and back up to Asa. "What's wrong?"

"Ranger is signaling drugs in your car," Asa whispered.

"What!" Lyric shouted. Her eyes widened, showing too much white. "I don't have any drugs in my car. Asa, you know that."

He did know that. At least, he'd thought he knew it, but Ranger hadn't given a missed signal since he graduated to the force.

"He wants you to open the car," Asa said, low and cautious, jerking a thumb over his shoulder to Jason.

"Asa, I don't have drugs in my car." Lyric looked right at him through every word.

He believed her. He really wanted to believe her. But what if she was a good liar? He'd met tons of them. Criminals looked him in the eye and denied their crimes almost every time.

What if he'd overlooked the signs because he wanted things to work out between them?

"Asa, I don't have anything."

"I know, but you have to open the car. Just show him."

She held his stare and nodded. The motion was small, barely perceptible. "Okay."

She unlocked the car and moved back. Ranger calmly stepped one foot into the back seat of the car and froze.

"Got a hit," Jason said.

"No!" Lyric shouted beside him. "It's not true. I don't have anything!"

Ranger backed away from the car, and Jason reached in. Asa didn't move as Jason held up a tan leather purse.

"That's not mine." Lyric grabbed Asa's arm. "I gave Wendy a ride to work this morning. It's hers."

Jason laughed once, cold and demeaning. "That's what they all say."

All that fire in Asa's chest was building—pushing against the walls.

It wasn't Lyric's purse. At least, it wasn't the one she'd been carrying around since he met her. She *had* dropped Wendy off at work this morning, but Lyric's word would mean next to nothing. She had a history, and the drugs were in her car.

Jason handed the bag to Lyric. "Open it."

"It's not mine!" Lyric's tone rose higher as panic gripped her. She held onto Asa's arm, half hiding herself behind him. "It's not mine!"

Asa could barely get the words out. "Just open it."

She gasped, and the inhale was shaky. He was protecting her. If she opened it, they could move to the next step of the investigation. If she refused, it wouldn't reflect well on her, whether there was something in the bag or not.

Lyric took the bag and opened the top with shaky hands, holding it out at arm's length.

Asa had never wished he could project thoughts into someone else's mind more than right now. He wanted to tell Lyric everything would be okay. He wanted to tell her to stay calm and follow his lead. He wanted to tell her he believed her.

Jason reached into the purse and shuffled things around before he pulled out a small bag.

Lyric exhaled hard and fast as if she'd been hit in the back. When she looked up at Asa, the dark-brown of her irises blurred. "I swear, Asa."

"You have the right to remain silent," Jason said.

Lyric took a quick step back. "No. No. It's not mine. Asa, please."

The pain in her voice cut his chest in two. This couldn't be happening. He trusted her, and he wanted to keep that trust so badly that he might have overlooked the truth.

"Lyric, just stay calm."

He reached for her, but she took another step away from him. "No. I didn't do anything."

When he reached for her the second time, she took two quick steps back.

"Is she resisting arrest?" Jason questioned.

As bad as this situation was, it could get so much worse if Lyric didn't stop and trust him. Whether she'd lied to him or not, he didn't want her to have another charge stacked on this one.

"Please, Lyric. Trust me." It was what he wanted more than anything. No, what he really wanted was to wake up from this nightmare.

Lyric stopped her retreat, but a tear fell over her cheek. "You trust me," she said slowly.

"I do," he mouthed. Clearing his throat, he reached out a hand to her. "Please come with me."

37

LYRIC

Lyric's hand shook as she placed it in Asa's. The warmth was familiar and terrifying at the same time. The tears that had been stinging her eyes pushed free like a broken dam.

Asa wrapped an arm around her, and she buried her face into his chest. The vest he wore beneath his uniform was hard and unforgiving.

"Don't cry. We'll fix this," Asa whispered.

"Officer Scott," Jason barked.

Asa rounded on him. "Back off. You can go now."

Jason huffed. "Not a chance."

"You're not taking her in. I am," Asa said. His tone left no room for negotiation.

Lyric tensed even more. This was not happening. Her head was spinning. Could she hide in Asa's arms until this was over?

"I said I'll handle this," Asa said low.

Lyric looked up enough to see Jason leading Ranger to a cruiser.

Dawson whistled. "Whew. I thought he'd never leave."

Asa picked up the purse from the gravel and closed Lyric's car door. He turned to Dawson, keeping Lyric tucked close to his side. "Meet me at the station. I need you to stick around. Call Olivia too."

"Will do." Dawson jogged to his cruiser, leaving Lyric and Asa alone.

Asa placed his hands on both sides of her face. "Everything is going to be okay. You just have to trust me."

She was still crying, but the sobs had stopped.

"We won't be able to talk for a while. Don't say anything while we're in the car or at the station. Okay?"

Lyric nodded. The only thing she wanted to do was talk to him, and she couldn't.

"Don't worry. I'll figure this out. I'm hoping Dawson can stall long enough that you won't have to actually be put in a cell."

She gripped his hand that cupped her face. She'd been in a cell before, but she'd been either drunk or stoned. She didn't even remember those hours. They hadn't kept her long any of the times she'd been arrested.

"I'm scared," she whispered.

"Don't be. I'll fix this."

"How? Jason saw it. It was in my car!"

Asa straightened and lowered his hands, keeping one of hers clasped in his. "Let's go. The sooner I can get things into motion, the sooner I can get you out."

Lyric followed him to his cruiser and got in the back seat. He texted on his phone before getting in the car, but she couldn't read his expression. Maybe he was letting Dawson know what he had planned.

The ride to the police department was only a few minutes, but it felt like an eternity. Not being able to talk to Asa had her questioning everything. Did he really believe her?

Jason would make sure she was charged. Lyric didn't know him personally, but he was a few years younger than her, and they'd gone to school together. He'd always been stern and boisterous. Today, he'd wanted to be the one to take her in, and she had no doubt he'd have to make some kind of report about Ranger's part in finding the drugs in her car.

Drugs. Wendy's. She'd looked and sounded fine this morning. Lyric hadn't asked her directly, but she'd assumed her friend was still clean. Had Wendy lied about the months she'd been clean, or had she recently relapsed?

Either way, Lyric had failed somehow. Wendy had come to her when she'd been struggling in the past. Why hadn't she said something this time?

They'd been together or talked almost every day since Jaycee died.

They pulled up at the police station, and a chill rushed down Lyric's spine. Asa got out and opened the door for Lyric, offering her a hand.

When she was standing, Asa whispered, "It'll be okay. Olivia is on her way."

She looked up at him and saw the assurance in his eyes. She nodded slowly, and he kept hold of her hand as he led her into the building. The entry area had a desk and chairs lined against one wall. They took a right and walked down a hallway. He turned into a room with offices where Asa usually swiped a card to let her in when she visited him at work. He gestured for her to take a seat in a chair before he started texting someone.

When he put the phone down, he sat in the chair beside her instead of the one across the desk. "Dawson is coming."

Dawson walked in and jerked a thumb over his shoulder. "You can go now."

Asa turned to her and squeezed her hand. "I'll be right back."

Lyric looked from Asa to Dawson and back. "What? You're leaving?"

"Olivia is on her way. She'll stay with you until Asa gets back," Dawson promised.

She swallowed a lump in her tightening throat.

"Okay." Letting go of his hand was the last thing she wanted to do, but he'd asked her to trust him.

Asa pressed a kiss to her forehead and turned to go.

Dawson hummed for a second before singing, "Everything's gonna be all right."

Surprisingly, Lyric laughed. The tears had stopped, and she appreciated Dawson's attempt to lift her spirits. She also remembered to pray, and closing her eyes helped her distance herself from the mess of reality.

Kendra walked in, and Lyric stood quickly. Kendra had her arms open as she approached. "It's okay."

"It's not mine," Lyric said as she fell into her friend's embrace.

"I know. Asa said he's handling things."

If he still trusted her after this, it would be a miracle. Even if she'd been telling the truth, she still somehow ended up with drugs in her car. What if they'd still been there when she picked up Jacob? What if they'd been there when she met her parents for dinner like she'd planned earlier?

Camille barged in with a sheen of sweat on her temple. "I'm here."

"Did you run?" Dawson asked.

"Practically."

"I'm so sorry," Lyric said quickly.

Camille held up a finger. "I'm your attorney. Don't say anything."

Dawson crossed his arms over his chest. "I'm not sitting in this office with you three if we can't talk."

Camille shrugged. "Maybe a little talking. How's the fam?"

"Great," Dawson said. "Little bro is in town this week."

Camille reached for Lyric's hand. "Don't worry."

"Thank you." She still wasn't sure what Asa and Camille had planned, and it seemed she'd have to wait to find out.

Kendra wrapped an arm around Lyric's shoulders. "I'm so glad he knows what to do."

Lyric let her head rest against Kendra's shoulder. "This is undoing all the trust I've been building." She'd have to tell her parents about this, and she'd lose them too.

Kendra rubbed a hand over Lyric's back. "Don't worry. You have plenty of people who believe you."

"They won't believe anything I say after this." Lyric pinched the bridge of her nose. "I'll lose Asa and Jacob too."

"Don't say that," Camille whispered.

Whether Lyric said it or not, things were bound to change now, and there was nothing she could do to stop it.

38

ASA

The cheery bell above the door jingled as Asa walked into Julia's Flower Shop.

"Walked" was a loose term. It took everything he had not to storm in, demanding justice and action.

Julia Letterman looked up with a smile on her face. Her blonde hair streaked with a lighter gray was pulled up into a curly bunch, and her light-blue eyes greeted him with sweetness. "Hello there. Looking for flowers for a special someone?"

He'd known Julia most of his life. She'd been his Sunday School teacher when he was ten. There was no way Julia knew Wendy had a problem. Was it a good thing that the older woman was blinded by kindness?

"Is Wendy here?" She had to be here. She didn't

have a car, but Asa focused on keeping his breathing calm as he waited impatiently for Julia's unknowing response.

Julia put down the thick, red ribbon she'd been tying. "She's in the back. Let me get her."

Asa rapped his knuckles on the counter. He hated leaving Lyric at the department. Wendy needed to hurry up.

Was this what Lyric felt when she jumped into action without assessing the situation first? The urge to follow Julia and look for Wendy himself was almost overpowering.

Wendy stepped out of the back room with a smile on her face that morphed into a look of terror when she saw him.

"Don't run," Asa said, reaching over the counter with an open hand. "We need to talk."

Wendy gripped the doorframe and stared at him. He'd seen the cornered cat look too many times. Wendy's brown eyes didn't veer from him in the slightest. He could almost hear the gears in her head turning, searching for a way out.

"It's Lyric. She's at the station. Can we go somewhere and talk?"

Wendy squeezed her eyes closed, knitting her brows together as her chin quivered.

Julia wrung her hands by the register. "What's going on?"

Asa didn't take his attention from Wendy. If he

looked away, she might vanish, taking Lyric's chance of freedom right along with her. "I can get her out, but you need to claim it."

Wendy hadn't moved to take this conversation somewhere private, and Julia's hand rose to cover her mouth.

It seemed they'd be having this conversation right here in the middle of the store.

Wendy's shoulders slumped, quaking slightly in defeat. "I didn't use."

"That's good," Asa whispered. "Lyric will be happy to know it. I'm happy too." They both wanted to see Wendy beat this life-long battle. Asa was just as invested in her sobriety journey as Lyric.

"I guess that doesn't matter, does it?"

"It does. This isn't a failure. You can still keep going. You're still clean, and you've done it during some of the hardest times. That takes strength."

Wendy turned to him, and her eyes glistened with the tears that waited to run down her face. "It's so hard," she whispered. "You don't know what it's like."

"You're right. I don't. But I have to watch Lyric struggle with the past, and it tears me up."

Wendy shook her head slowly.

"The past is gone, and you can let it go. It'll be tough, but you're not doing it alone. That's why we want to help you. But you have to help Lyric first."

Please let her help. Please let her help. He'd prayed

the entire drive over, and now it was time to do his part. He'd asked the Lord for guidance, and now he was asking Wendy for help while also offering help in return.

Wendy straightened and took a deep breath, but she didn't speak.

Asa kept his gaze locked on Wendy. "You're not starting over. You have us. We'll stand by you."

Wendy covered her mouth with her hand and walked into the back room, closing the door behind her. Julia held up a single finger to Asa before following her.

Patience. Patience. He could be patient, even while his heart was banging against the walls of his chest. Wendy had to come back eventually. She didn't have a ride, and her cell was in the purse she'd left in Lyric's car.

A minute later, Julia stepped out into the store and linked her hands in front of her chest. "Wendy said you need her to go with you."

"Yes, please. And I'd like to take her home after we finish our business."

Julia smiled at him, the shallow lines branching from the corners of her eyes deepening. "Please be good to her. I only know what she's told me, but she seems to be trying."

At least Wendy had someone else on her side. "You don't have to worry. I'll take good care of her."

Wendy stepped out of the back room a minute

later. Her eyes were pink, and she'd wiped off the makeup around her eyes.

When they were outside, Asa whispered, "Thank you."

Wendy looked up at him, but her face was void of expression. "I didn't mean to do this to her."

"I know. She's scared, and she needs your help."

Wendy looked at the ground. "She's a good person. She's always been there for me. Now, look what I've done to her."

"She's the best person to have on your side," Asa added. He'd gotten to know the real Lyric these past few months, and she had a heart of gold and enough dedication to accomplish anything she set her mind to.

If only she could help Wendy develop that same determination.

Wendy grinned. "I think she'd say the same about you."

"I'm here to help. With that being said, I can't get you out of punishments you deserve, but call me if you get into trouble. I can help you get back on your feet."

Wendy wiped her cheeks and inhaled a deep breath. "You two make a good pair."

Asa chuckled. "An unexpected pair, but a good one. One of the things I love about Lyric is that she'll fight for you."

Wendy tilted her head, and a small grin played on her lips. "Like you're doing for her right now?"

Asa nodded slightly. "She needs someone to believe in her, and I plan to be that person."

Wendy nodded to the car. "Let's go."

39

LYRIC

Olivia burst into the room filled with desks and cubicles like a tornado. Brushing her hair from her face, she panted, "I'm here. Where's the fire?"

Dawson pointed to Lyric and threw his cards onto the desk. "I fold. You know, this game isn't any fun when you have zero facial expressions. Give me something to work with here."

Lyric dropped her cards. It was Dawson's idea to play poker. She appreciated his attempt to distract her, but nothing was going to calm the icy panic in her middle.

"She doesn't want to play cards, Keller," Olivia said. Sighing, she grabbed a chair and scooted it closer to Lyric. "What's going on? Catch me up."

Kendra rubbed a hand in soothing circles over Lyric's back. What *was* going on? She'd been sitting for half an hour, and they hadn't cuffed her or put her in a cell yet.

Jason lingered at a desk nearby, tapping away at the keyboard. Was he writing a tell-all? A report? An article for the local newspaper? He had plenty of fuel to start a fire in her life. Was he silently planning her demise or was he waiting to see what cards Asa had up his sleeve?

Lyric cleared her throat. She'd already recounted the story for Jason and Dawson. Maybe she'd get through it without tears this time.

"I gave my friend a ride to work this morning."

"Which friend?" Olivia asked.

"Wendy."

Olivia nodded. She knew of Wendy. Lyric had asked anyone and everyone she knew to pray for her friend after Jaycee died. It was always hardest to stay clean when times were tough.

The prayers hadn't worked this time, and defeat swirled in Lyric's stomach like a whirlpool, sucking all the happiness into a dark hole. She hadn't saved Wendy. That fragile sobriety had cracked under the pressure.

"I dropped her off at Julia's Flower shop, then went to Blackwater Restoration. I was early for my shift, and the back door was destroyed."

Olivia's eyes widened, and she reached for Lyric's hand. "Are you okay? Was there anyone around?"

"I'm fine. I was on the phone with Asa, and he

told me to call 911 so dispatch could send officers out to investigate. I talked to Nancy while they did that."

Nancy had been a bright spot in a dark morning. The friendly dispatcher had kept Lyric updated on what was happening at the store all while keeping conversation light and hopeful.

Nancy came over to introduce herself a few minutes ago. She also brought Lyric the cup of hot chocolate that sat cooling on the desk beside Dawson's folded poker hand.

Olivia scooted closer, keeping her attention fully locked on Lyric. "Was everything okay?"

"Camille's office was destroyed. They must have been looking for cash, but she never keeps any in the store overnight."

"That's a relief," Olivia said.

Lyric picked at her cuticles and stared at her hands in her lap. "Then, Jason's dog smelled drugs in my car."

"What? Are you serious?" Olivia shouted, looking around with wide eyes.

Lyric huffed. "Afraid so. Wendy left her purse in my car. They weren't mine, but that doesn't even matter. They were in my car."

Olivia grasped Lyric's hand, holding it tight. "I'm sorry. That's a lot to process in one morning. The break-in, the drugs, Wendy. Oh, no. Does that mean Wendy—"

"I think so. I haven't talked to her yet." Lyric sniffed. "I thought she was doing okay."

"All we can do is let her know we're still here for her," Kendra said. "The last thing she needs is for us to give up on her."

Kendra's hand moved from Lyric's back to her shoulder. She couldn't give up on Wendy. What would her life be like if Kendra had given up? Or Asa? They both had reasons to doubt her—to label her a lost cause or decide she was more trouble than she was worth. Instead, they'd both stayed, and their support made all the difference.

Olivia leaned down to put herself in Lyric's line of sight. "Kendra is right. We'll be here for Wendy. In the meantime, what's going on here?"

Lyric shrugged. "I'm being arrested, I guess. Officer Guthrie is being oddly quiet over there, and Dawson is making jokes and playing card games to distract me."

Dawson hummed the tune of "You Got a Friend in Me" as he clicked at his computer. He really had done his best to keep her calm. It wasn't his fault her fragile world was crumbling.

"Where's Asa?" Olivia asked.

"I'm not sure. He said he was going to help and promised to be back soon. I don't know how he could fix this, but—"

"Don't lose hope," Olivia added quickly. "Now is

not the time to doubt each other. We're in this together, and I'm sure Asa is on your side too."

Lyric bit her lips between her teeth. Oh, how she hoped Olivia was right. With two jobs, a loving home, a man and his son she loved, and a new home in a church that had welcomed her with open arms, Lyric had so much to lose.

And her parents. She'd just gotten them back. The thought of losing them again sent a stabbing pain straight into her chest.

Olivia scooted closer until her knees bumped against Lyric's. "We are gonna pray, and you are gonna focus on breathing. Okay?"

Lyric nodded.

"Say it," Olivia demanded.

"We're gonna pray, and I'm gonna focus on breathing," Lyric repeated.

Olivia bowed her head. "Lord, You are in charge of everything, and right now I bring both Lyric and Wendy to You. They're hurting and confused and scared. I pray that You lift them up. I pray that You remind them of Your part in their lives. I pray that they let everything else going on in the world go and hit their knees at Your feet."

Lyric inhaled a breath that tingled throughout her body. Olivia knew exactly what to do. She guided all of Lyric's frustrations and worries to the One who could read her heart.

"Lord, we love You, and we trust You. Calm the

storms inside of us, and help us to help each other. Amen."

Lyric wrapped Olivia in a hug and held on. She'd known Olivia for a few months, and they'd grown to be good friends. Now, Lyric could see the Lord's handiwork in her life. He knew she'd need Olivia, Kendra, Camille, and Asa. He even knew she needed Dawson today.

She had plenty to be grateful for, and she wouldn't let today's events overshadow the good that the Lord had built in her life.

The door opened, and Wendy walked in with Asa right behind her. She wasn't restrained in any way, but her slow, dragging steps implied a heavy weight resting on her shoulders.

Lyric stood, and the whole room tilted. He'd gone to get Wendy. That was his plan. If Wendy claimed the drugs, Lyric could have her freedom.

Why was the realization bittersweet?

Wendy looked up at Lyric before turning her attention back to the floor. That one small glance revealed a hollowness in her eyes. She wasn't the same happy woman that Lyric had chatted with on the way to the flower shop only a few hours ago.

Lyric moved to meet Wendy, enveloping her in a hug that squeezed Lyric's heart.

"I'm sorry," Wendy said as she buried her face in the crook of Lyric's neck. "I'm so sorry."

"I'm sorry too. I should have been there for you more. It's been so tough for you lately."

Wendy pulled back and wiped at her eyes. "I didn't use. I just...had it. I don't know. I thought about it, but I couldn't bring myself to do it."

"I believe you. They'll probably test you. At least, that's what they did to me," Lyric said, hoping the information didn't strike some kind of fear in Wendy.

Instead, Wendy just nodded. "Okay. I really didn't use."

Lyric wrapped her friend in another hug with all the power of her relief. "I'm so glad."

Asa stepped up beside them. There was a guarded look in his eyes as he addressed Wendy. "We have a few questions for you."

Wendy sniffed and nodded. "Okay." She turned back to Lyric. "I'm really sorry about getting you into this."

"Don't worry about me. I'll be fine."

Wendy looked at Asa, then back at Lyric. "I guess I'll see you around."

Lyric reached for Wendy's hand and clasped it between hers. "I'm not going anywhere."

"But they'll release you now."

Lyric shook her head. "I'm not leaving you."

Dawson stepped up beside Wendy and extended a hand to her. "I'm Officer Keller. If you'll take a seat right here, we have a few things to talk about." He pulled out the chair Lyric had vacated and gestured for Wendy to take it.

Once Wendy sat, Lyric turned to Asa. Everything inside her was too full—too pressurized by the series of events.

Asa pulled her to him, wrapping her in the safety of his arms. "She'll be okay. It's a small amount. A misdemeanor. If she's clean, she might only have to pay a fine."

Lyric pressed her face to Asa's chest. Not being arrested was great for Wendy, but there was no way she'd have the money to pay a fine. The war of relief and sadness swirled in Lyric's middle.

"Thank you for this," she whispered.

"I would do anything for you. I knew from the beginning that it wasn't yours. I hate that Wendy got so close to a relapse, but I'm glad we found out before she went too far. There's still hope for her."

She wiped her face on his uniform and looked up to meet his gaze. The peace in his eyes calmed the shaking of her voice. "Is there any hope for us?" she asked quietly.

Asa cupped his hands around her face and threaded his fingers in her hair, directing her attention to him and only him. "I'll never give up on you."

40

LYRIC

Betty's tea was like a cure-all. Almost.

Kendra flipped through the photos on the breakfast table in Betty's kitchen, commenting on some and chuckling at others.

"That boy looks just like his dad," Kendra said, holding up a photo of Jacob. His dark eyes were the same shade and hue as Asa's, and the shape of his smile was a mirror image of his dad's as well.

"Spitting image. It's like raising the same boy twice." Betty sat on Lyric's other side and sipped her tea.

"Grandkids are the best, aren't they?" Kendra asked. "I thought my daughter was the best, but grandkids..."

Lyric accepted the photo Kendra handed her. It was a very young Jacob riding on Asa's shoulders. She could almost hear Jacob's laugh—the one she'd come to know well since she'd been living with Betty. She'd even heard his soft chuckles in her sleep once, only to check on him and find him sound asleep in his room at Betty's.

But Lyric's attention locked on Asa. The smiling man in the photo hadn't been smiling today. He'd been worried, torn, and confused. Her stomach rolled thinking about the hassle she'd caused today. Well, she didn't mean to cause it, but it had happened.

"You want more tea?" Betty asked.

Lyric couldn't muster a hint of a smile right now. Asa wasn't home from work yet, and she hadn't talked to him since leaving the station. He'd promised to meet Lyric at his house after his shift. They'd have time to talk while Betty picked Jacob up from school.

"Thanks, but I don't think I should have another." Three cups of caffeine would have her jittery for her talk with Asa. He'd promised things between them would be fine, but what if he'd said those things in the heat of the moment to keep her calm?

"You're welcome to stay, Kendra," Betty said as she lifted her purse strap over her shoulder. "Or you can ride with me to pick up Jacob."

Kendra stood and stretched her arms above her head. "I think I'll head home. Thanks for having me. It was so nice to catch up."

"You're welcome any time," Betty said as she embraced Kendra.

"I'll put these away." Lyric stacked the photos back into their places. They worked on the albums every time Jacob was at school or gone home for the evening, and they'd hopefully be ready soon.

Betty reached for the doorknob and looked back over her shoulder. "Tell Asa that Jacob and I are running by the church for a bit before we come back. You and Asa take the time you need this evening."

"Thank you. Thank you for everything." Lyric wasn't sure if a quick good-bye was waiting for her, but she wanted to hope he'd give her another chance. She'd never had so much to lose before, and the thought of everything with Asa, Jacob, and Betty ending tonight had her voice shaking.

After cleaning up the mess, Lyric slowly walked to Asa's house. It was only a few houses down the street, and she'd need the numbing wind later if her dreams of this beautiful life she was living got shattered.

She'd barely reached Asa's porch when his cruiser pulled in the drive. Of course, he'd be home early on the one day she needed time to think and process before their talk.

He pulled into the garage, and she met him there. He was out of the car as soon as it came to a stop.

"Are you okay?" he asked as he strode toward her and wrapped her in his arms.

Her heart lurched toward him, banging against the walls of her chest in an attempt to reach him. If she lost him over this, her life wouldn't be the same. She'd known true happiness, and a world without Asa and his family would be hollow.

"I'm okay." The tears threatened to come again, but she pushed them back.

Asa grabbed her hand and led her to the door. "Let's get inside."

Lyric knew his routine. After work, he shed the uniform as soon as possible, but tonight, he led her straight to the couch.

She sat beside him, but she didn't know where to start or what to say. "Thanks for saving me" would be a good start, but the words wouldn't come out.

Asa wrapped her hand in both of his. Seeing her small hand in Asa's now made her feel like a child being saved by a parent. He'd known what to do and say, and he'd kept her from spiraling today.

Now, she didn't know what came next for them.

He brushed circles on the back of her hand with his thumb. "I took Wendy home a few minutes ago. She said she'll call you tonight. We did a lot of talking while she waited for me to get off work. She's strong, but she'll still need help. I told her we're here for her."

We. That word sounded so good coming from him.

"You'll still have to come to the hearing, but Camille will be there to represent you."

Lyric bit her lips between her teeth. He was saying all the right things, and she didn't know how to process any of it. Kindness after kindness. That's all she'd known of him, but there had to be a limit. When would it be used up? What would come next to drag them back into the awful past?

Asa stood and pulled her to her feet. His strong arms wound around her, wrapping her in warmth. "I'm so sorry you had to go through that."

"I'm sorry I put you in that situation. I didn't know it was there. I didn't know Wendy had it. I–"

"It's over, and we're both okay. Wendy is going to be okay too."

Lyric buried her face in his chest. "What does this mean?"

"What do you mean?"

She looked up at him and tried to keep her expression neutral. Swaying him with tears wasn't her plan. "I mean, what does this mean for us? Your co-workers saw you bring me in today. They know we were dating."

"Were? We *are* dating. They know that."

"No, *you* know the truth because you know me and trust me. They know I have a record."

"This doesn't change how I feel about you. You didn't commit the crime."

"But I did." Whether it was today, yesterday, or five years ago, she *had* committed the crime.

"But not intentionally. You're not the bad guy we're after. You and Wendy are the ones we want to help." He cupped her cheeks and leaned closer. "That's what I love about you. You care about doing what's right, and you care about helping people who are struggling. I love that about you. I love *you*."

The tears came then, and she stopped trying to fight them. "You don't know what it means to have someone to fight for me. Everyone. Kendra and your mom. You all believed me, and you don't know what that means."

"I think I do. We're all guilty. We all make mistakes, but we've been pardoned. The Lord looks at us and sees His people, not our sins."

He picked up both of her hands and lifted them with his around them. "When you were begging me to believe you, I did. And the look on your face cut me to the core because I love you."

"I love you too." The whisper was low, but he was close enough to hear her loud and clear.

Asa's mouth quirked up on one side in an adorable grin. "You may be a good woman with a bad past, but you're my good woman with a bad past. I'll take you just the way you are."

Lyric wrapped her arms around his neck and held him tight. He lifted her off the ground and squeezed her until she couldn't breathe.

When he sat her down, she almost floated back up. The tightness in her chest was gone, and the weight on her shoulders had lifted. She sighed and asked, "What now?"

Asa shrugged. "I was thinking we could take the afternoon to ourselves. I'd like to beat you at Clue and eat canned soup."

Lyric narrowed her eyes at him. "That's not happening."

"The beating you or the soup?"

"Beating me. I know you too well."

He leaned closer and whispered, "I think that means I win either way."

"Asa, I—"

He cut her off with a searing kiss that left her breathless. Fast or slow, Asa's kisses always reaffirmed his love without words, but this one had the memories of what he'd done for her today. Memories that shaped their future.

If she ever looked back, now she'd have this to remember—unfailing love.

When he broke the kiss, he rested his forehead against hers. And smiled. "I love you. Sorry for cutting you off, but I wanted to say it first this time."

Lyric looked up at him with a smile. Her heart

was fuller than ever, and the joy overpowered all the stress of the day. "I think that means I win either way."

EPILOGUE
LYRIC

Lyric glanced over her shoulder. The fellowship hall at the church was full of her friends and family, but they were all busy chatting with each other.

Friends. Family. They were hers. Well, Asa's family wasn't technically hers yet, but her heart didn't know the difference. She'd been living with Betty—Granny as she insisted Lyric call her—for six months now, and every time Lyric mentioned getting her own place, Granny said there wasn't a point. Sometimes, Lyric brought it up just to be reminded that Asa might propose to her one day, and she would be an official member of the Scott family.

The moment her fingers touched the cupcake wrapper, Jacob appeared beside her.

"Can I have one too?"

Jacob didn't let her get away with anything, and

she couldn't tell him no now. Not when she'd been caught in the act.

She nodded to the cupcake table. "Grab one and meet me in the kitchen." Lyric chose a yellow one with white sprinkles, and Jacob picked blue.

As soon as the door closed behind them, Jacob asked, "Why are you sneaking? It's your party. You can have as many cupcakes as you want."

"I've already had two."

Jacob shrugged. "So?"

Lyric bumped Jacob's hip with hers. "I love that you don't judge me."

"I love that you let me have another cupcake. Dad said three was enough."

Lyric gasped. "Jacob! We're both in trouble now."

Stuffing the remaining half of the cupcake in his mouth, Jacob held up his hands. No evidence.

Lyric sighed. "I'm trying to be on my best behavior."

"Why? It's your birthday. You can do whatever you want."

"I don't know where you got that idea."

"You told me that like seven times on my birthday," Jacob reminded her.

The door opened, and Lyric tossed the last bite of her cupcake in the sink behind her where it landed with a thump. When Asa walked in, Lyric and Jacob were the picture of innocence.

"What are you two doing?" Asa asked, narrowing his eyes at the two of them.

"Nothing," Jacob said quickly.

Asa eyed them with skepticism. "Anyway, everyone is waiting on you."

Lyric frowned. "Why?"

"You have presents to open," Asa reminded her.

"Oh! I didn't think grown-ups got birthday presents."

Jacob grabbed her hand and started toward the door. "Come on! Open mine first!"

Lyric let Jacob lead her out into the main room. She blew a kiss to Asa as she darted past him, and his hand caught hers before slipping from her grasp as Jacob pulled her away.

Everyone had pulled their metal folding chairs to the middle of the room, and they all faced a table with half a dozen beautifully wrapped presents on it.

"Guys, you didn't have to get me anything!" Lyric clasped her hands to her chest and smiled at the crowd. She would still be wondering if this was a dream had she not eaten the amazing cupcakes. She'd never tasted food in a dream, so this must be real. Who knew reality could be better than anything she could have imagined?

Lyric reached for a box with blush-colored wrapping and a white bow.

"No! Mine first." Jacob was at her side in an

instant, handing her a present wrapped in blue paper.

Her breathing quickened as she tore it open. She didn't care what it was. She would love anything Jacob gave her. He put his whole heart into everything, and he'd taught her how to love in a new way. If the Lord chose to answer her prayers, she'd one day call him her son.

Lyric lifted the album out of the box and stared at it. The room grew quiet, and she stopped breathing.

"It's a photo album," Jacob said. "It's like the one you gave me, but this one is all about us."

Lyric brushed her fingers over the photo on the cover. Lyric, Asa, and Jacob stood with their arms around each other in front of Bluestone Creek. It was from the first time Asa and Jacob took her fishing, and their smiles were wide and full of joy. There was so much happiness in the photo that it stole the breath from her lungs.

She opened the album and flipped through a few pages. "Some of these are old." One photo caught her attention. She was maybe seven years old and sitting in the passenger seat of her dad's old Thunderbird.

Lyric searched the crowd for Asa and found him standing beside her mom and dad.

"Mom. Dad." Lyric stood, and Granny took the album from her.

Everyone took a step back, leaving Lyric and her parents less than five feet from each other.

"Happy birthday," her mom said.

Lyric didn't think. She wrapped her arms around her mom and buried her face in her mom's shoulder. They'd visited a few times, and having little pieces of them in her life only made her miss them more in the weeks when she didn't see them.

"Happy birthday," her dad said beside her.

"I didn't know you were coming."

Her dad wrapped her in a hug. "Asa called us a few weeks ago and invited us to the party."

Lyric looked for Asa, but she didn't have to look far. He was standing behind her with a barely contained smile.

She opened her mouth to thank him, but the words died in her throat when he slowly knelt before her.

Asa looked up at her and reached out his hand. Lyric grasped it, holding on for dear life.

"Lyric Woods, there is no doubt in my mind that we were meant to meet the way we did—each time. Our paths were meant to cross, and I believe our lives are meant to be shared. You've taught me so much, but the greatest lesson I've learned is that I should hang onto the best things in life. If you'll have me, I would be honored to love you for the rest of my life. Want to make this a forever thing?"

Lyric's smile was so wide she couldn't close her

mouth. Tears blurred her vision, and she squeezed Asa's hand. It was always a forever thing.

Before she could shout "Yes," Jacob slid into a kneel beside his dad and said, "And me too!"

The room rumbled with laughter as Asa and Jacob each pulled out a ring. Was she laughing or crying? Either way, she couldn't see the rings through her tears.

"Yes, and yes!" she shouted.

Her friends and family cheered as Asa and Jacob wrapped her in a hug. Lyric clung to them and drank in the comfort of the two people who would soon be hers in every way.

Asa whispered in her ear, loud enough to be heard over the cheers, "When do you want to get married?"

She looked up at him and wiped the back of her hand over her eyes. "How soon do you think we can get all these people together again?"

Asa whispered, "Next week?"

Lyric laughed. She'd laughed so much since the snow storm that brought them back together, and she had a feeling there was more to come. "You think Brenda would let us book the cabin for a honeymoon?"

Asa's eyes widened, and he scanned the cheering crowd. "I'll go ask her now."

Lyric tugged him closer. "Don't you dare. I'm not letting you go for the rest of the day."

Asa smiled down at her with that determined look she loved. "I'm never letting you go."

BONUS EPILOGUE
DAWSON

Dawson rested his elbow on the open window and stared out the windshield of his cruiser into the parking lot. Vehicles were parked in perfect rows in front of the high school. Every once in a while, someone would open the doors to the gym, and the cheers and whistles burst into the parking lot.

Highway patrol was boring, and security for a volleyball game was even boringer.

Was boringer even a word?

Great. He'd resorted to questioning his own grammar. There wasn't even anyone around to ask. Now he'd have to wait until he got back to the station to ask Asa. Maybe he'd ask Jennifer. She was smart.

Dawson's phone dinged in the cup holder, and he lifted it to read the text message.

Asa: Can you be at Oscar's on Thursday for a suit fitting?

Dawson: A suit? I don't get to wear a tux?

Asa's reply was almost immediate.

Asa: No.

Asa: I told you it's casual. Lyric doesn't want anything over the top.

Dawson sighed. He looked great in a tux. At least he had at his senior prom. How long ago was that? Twelve years?

Wow. Where had the time gone? He'd always thought he'd be married with kids by thirty.

Seriously, where had the time gone?

A charcoal-gray Mazda 6 zoomed down the straight road in front of the school, humming along like the thirty-five mile per hour speed limit was little more than a suggestion.

Officer Jason Guthrie shifted his cruiser into drive beside Dawson.

No way on God's green earth was Jason taking this one. Dawson shouted out the window. "Hey!"

Jason looked over. His determined expression could take a chill pill.

Dawson pointed north where Olivia's car was disappearing from view. "She's mine."

Jason shook his head and shifted back into park. "Don't let her get away."

Dawson grinned. "Not on my watch."

He pulled out of the parking lot and started after Olivia. Wasn't that his lot in life? He'd been chasing Olivia for years. Maybe one day, she'd let him catch her.

Today, he'd settle for saving her from a speeding ticket.

Thank you for reading Love in the Storm.
Are you ready for Dawson and Olivia's story? Check out *Love for a Lifetime*, the second book in the Love in Blackwater series.

LOVE FOR A LIFETIME
LOVE IN BLACKWATER BOOK 2

They'll always be friends, but they can never be more.

Dawson Keller has held a torch for his best friend's little sister for as long as he can remember. He might be a flirt, but his heart will always belong to Olivia.

Olivia Lawrence lives to serve others and work on the family farm. Helping people and tending animals keep her mind off the one thing she wants but can't have—a family.

Her brother's best friend might joke that they're meant to be, but he doesn't know how little she has to offer a husband. Especially a man like Dawson who loves kids and makes everyone laugh.

On top of that, Olivia's best friend is head over heels for Dawson, and hurting her friend is out of the question.

Dawson keeps showing up to save her at all the wrong times. From a disastrous wedding date to an unfortunate camping incident, Dawson is always there when Olivia needs him.

When Dawson finds out her secret, and her friend feels betrayed, Olivia is at risk of losing them both.

If you loved the Blackwater Ranch series and the Wolf Creek Ranch series, get ready to fall in love all over again in Blackwater, Wyoming.

WANT MORE FROM MANDI BLAKE?

<u>Blackwater Ranch Series</u>

The Harding brothers are tough as nails, but they fall hard for the strong women who wrangle their hearts. Through heartbreaks, reunions, and celebrations, the Hardings will fight for love and the future of the ranch.

<u>Wolf Creek Ranch Series</u>

These cowboys know how to treat a lady and never back down when things get tough. Through secrets, revenge, forgiveness, and redemption, the men of Wolf Creek Ranch will have to fight for love, and they'll do anything to protect the women who steal their hearts.

<u>Love in Blackwater Series</u>

If you loved the Blackwater Ranch Series and the Wolf Creek Ranch Series, get ready to fall in love all over again as more of your friends fall in love.

<u>Unfailing Love Series</u>

Visit Carson, Georgia and fall in love with the swoonworthy friends who will give you all the feels as they fall for the women who steal their hearts.

<u>The Heroes of Freedom Ridge Series</u>

Visit Freedom and enjoy the faith, friendships, and

forever-afters in this Christmas town nestled in the
Colorado Rockies.

The Christmas in Redemption Ridge Series

If you loved the best-selling Heroes of Freedom Ridge
Series, you'll love this spin-off series with all new
characters and traditions, but the same magic of
community and romance readers love.

Mandi Blake was born and raised in Alabama where she lives with her husband and daughter, but her southern heart loves to travel. Reading has been her favorite hobby for as long as she can remember, but writing is her passion. She loves a good happily ever after in her sweet Christian romance books and loves to see her characters' relationships grow closer to God and each other.

Made in United States
Troutdale, OR
06/19/2025

32252885R00225